George Warrington Steevens

In India

George Warrington Steevens

In India

ISBN/EAN: 9783337062361

Printed in Europe, USA, Canada, Australia, Japan

Cover: Foto ©Andreas Hilbeck / pixelio.de

More available books at **www.hansebooks.com**

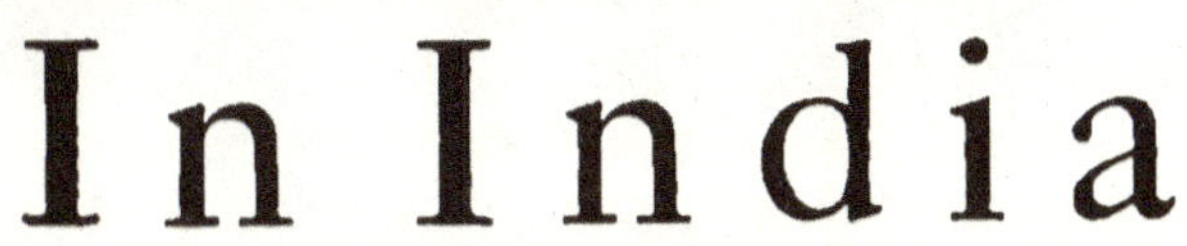

In India

By

G. W. Steevens

Author of "The Land of the Dollar," "Egypt in 1898," "With Kitchener to Khartum," etc.

New York

Dodd, Mead and Company

1899

CONTENTS

Contents

vii

IN INDIA

I

A VICEROY'S WELCOME

The thud of three guns, dull in the lazy air, told the passengers of the P. and O. Company's "Arabia" that they were at the door of India.

From the steamer the sights of the shore were muffled, like its sounds, in the breathless haze that expects the sun. We lay on still, colourless water in a channel. To port were shadows of ships, and presently, behind them, a thicker bank of grey wherefrom white faces of ghostly buildings shone without lustre. But to starboard the mainland of India raised itself on its elbow against a horizon that every minute grew rosier. Broad belts of black and pink fired and fused into liquid carmine; the elbows turned from grey to black, and the water began to stir and laugh over a mile of shining dimples. India was awake.

A glance back from the launch showed the "Arabia" at the very moment of awakening. Along the dark hull three tiers of sleepy yellow port-holes blinked at the shadowed water; above, every point and spar and rope were picked out in the intensest black against the crimson sky. The flags, with which she was dressed from prow to rail, hung solemnly motionless. Hugely graceful, the union of power and fineness, revealing unsuspected curves and angles, she had kept the fulness of her beauties, coquettishly, until the moment of good-bye.

The other ships, as we stole past them, turned in like manner from film to the clearest silhouette—the heavy-hulled trooper, the low turret-guardship with awnings from stem to stern like turtle-decks, the slim cruiser, and the slips of torpedo-boats. Higher up lay black and red cargo-boats; lower down, white-winged yachts. On the nearing shore the dim shapes of buildings cleared, separated, and combined into a tall, white-limbed city, warming and blushing like a bride. The launch stopped at a pier beneath a white and amber pavilion. Then suddenly the sun shot up behind the mainland; welcoming reflections sprang everywhere to meet him; the world pulsed with colour. And I was standing in India.

It was good luck for the prying stranger to land at Bombay off the same boat as a new Viceroy. The splendours which otherwise must have been sought out with diligence and found in detail came there to meet the landing and combined themselves. The vestibule of India was swept and garnished. The pavilion that ushered us in was spread partly on Venetian masts, partly on living trees; but their trunks were wrapped round with white and amber also, lest anything dirty should smirch the new Viceroy's gaze. Down the middle ran a broad aisle; on each side of it a battalion of chairs; at the top, above the water, was a clear space for the most notable people, and a triumphal arch in the shape of a tower. A hedge of shrubs round the whole lent it the air of a flower-show. Outside these again was a hedge of native police—little, sturdy, brown men in navy blue, with bare legs, and sandals, and bright yellow caps. At the entrance on the inland side were British military police in white, regulating the traffic.

I looked down the broad avenue that led into Bombay—a vista of white, shining palaces set in green, tier and gable and turret climbing skywards out of massed trees. But before there was time to do more than look, a couple of companies of British infantry, cool to the eye in their white uniforms, marched up, stiffened into line, and grounded arms with a rattle along one side of the pavilion. Directly on that arrived the rulers of Bombay.

They made a strange blending of splendour and shabbiness. Clear-skinned men and bright-eyed women drove up in victorias that showed more dust than paint; a servant in gorgeous livery was on the box, and the stuffing was coming out of the horse's collar. The white men and women wore white, as befitted the freshness of the golden morning; even generals and colonels showed no other colour than the ribbons on their breasts. The dark blue and gold of naval uniforms and court dress, the epaulettes of the very consuls, looked dull in the shimmer of the sun. But the rich natives paid for all. They shone in the gathering crowd like rainbows. There were women in purple and yellow-green draperies, servants in flaming scarlet, masters ablaze with bullion and jewels. Nothing was too resplendent for their modesty or too incongruous for their taste. A black gown like a clergyman's, a spectacled face under a black oilcloth cap—its shape like two hats, one balanced upside down on top of the other—only threw up the neighbouring butterfly in a peaked turban of vermilion and gold, a ring in his ear with a bloated bunch of pearls and emeralds, strings of pearls round his neck, and a gold-embroidered muslin blouse which died away—alas!—below the waist into shrunken pyjamas, no socks, and broken elastic-sided boots, with frayed tabs flapping moodily behind him. Beside this vision of radiance you could hardly see the puff-cheeked, moist-eyed gentleman in a frock-coat and a deerstalker; and the eagle-nosed yellow youth in reach-me-down blue-striped flannels was barely saved from extinction by the green and crimson embroidery on his purple velvet smoking-cap. Every race, every creed, every colour, every style— the rajah with his diamonds and the thin-legged

A Viceroy's Welcome

sweeper outside in the street—they grouped themselves to present on the threshold of India a living
epitome of the hundred-headed incongruities that
swarm within.

Boom! came the first gun from the white warship,
the first of thirty-one.   A launch flickered across the
dazzling water.   Along the parapet glided a funnel
and the point of a flagstaff.   The uniforms and court
suits and academic gowns clustered at the head of the
steps.   They stood for a minute, two, three, in the
bunched but shifting group that means greeting and
introduction, then broke.   " God Save the Queen ! "
crashed the band ; all stood uncovered ; and the new
Viceroy stepped serenely into his government.   A
slow procession along the aisle ; a pause and a silence
which hinted that the Corporation of Bombay was
delivering an address ; a few clear-cut sentences of
reply ; clapping ; a grey hat bowing from a carriage ;
the scrunch of wheels ; red-and-white lance-pennons
whirling into column—and the first glimpse of India
shifts and breaks like a kaleidoscope and leaves its
first city naked to curiosity.

BOMBAY

THE first sight of India is amazing, entrancing, stupefying. Of other countries you become aware gradually: Italy leads up to the Levant, and Egypt passes you on insensibly to the desert. Landed in Bombay, you have strayed into a most elaborate dream, infinite in variety, spinning with complexity, a gallery of strange faces, a buzz of strange voices, a rainbow of strange colours, a garden of strange growths, a book of strange questions, a pantheon of strange gods. Different beasts and birds in the street, different clothes to wear, different meal-times, and different food—the very commonest things are altered. You begin a new life in a new world.

It takes time to come to yourself. At first everything is so noticeable that you notice nothing. You pin your eyes to the little fawn-coloured, satin-skinned, humped oxen in the carts, to the blue crows that dance and spar in the gutters. They are the very commonest things in India, but just because they are common bullocks—yet with humps!—common crows—yet blue!—their fascination is enthralling. The white ducks you wear all day are like a girl's first court dress, and you sit down to breakfast at eleven off a fish called pomphlet with the sensations of a Gulliver.

When things begin to come sorted and sifted, Bombay reveals itself as a city of monstrous contrasts. Along the sea-front one splendid public building follows another—variegated stone façades with arch and colonnade, cupola and pinnacle and statuary. At their feet huddle flimsy huts of matting, thatched with leaves, which a day's rain would reduce to mud and pulp. You sit in a marble-paved club, vast and airy as a Roman atrium, and look out over gardens of heavy red and violet flowers towards choking alleys where half-naked idolaters herd by families together in open-fronted rooms, and filth runs down gullies to fester in the sunken street. In this quarter you may see the weaver twirling his green and amber wool on a hand-loom—a skeleton so simple and fragile that a kick would make sticks of it; go to the street corner, and you see black smoke belch from a hundred roaring mills, whose competition cuts the throat of all the world. In the large open spaces Parsis bowl each other under-hand full-pitches and cry, " Tank you, tank you," after the ball; by the rail squats a Hindu, who would like, if only the law would let him, to marry babies and burn widows.

Yet, for all its incongruities, Bombay never will have you forget that it is a great city. If it had no mills it would be renowned for its port; if it had neither it would be famous for its beauty. Its physical configuration is something like that of New York. Bombay lies at the southern end of a long narrow island; its oldest part, the Fort, is toward the southernmost extremity. Here are the landing-piers, the public buildings, the newspapers, the principal business centres. Next comes the native city; and the fashionable quarter for residence once lay northward where the Byculla Club, the best in Bombay, still marks its site. But flowing business, as in New York, has risen and surged over the city; it has washed the native quarter northward, and the Club now stands an almost solitary land-mark among cotton-mill chimneys and teeming native tenements. The Europeans, with the ever-multiplying class of rich natives, now live further westward on the Ridge or on Malabar Hill, which, turning south to face the old town, forms the western horn of Back Bay. From the narrowness of the original city, and the four-miles' drive between it and the Ridge, it follows that rents are high and land continually more valuable; and from that follows that the native town is not one- or two-storeyed as elsewhere in India, but laid out in great tenement blocks, which lend themselves to picturesqueness and to plague.

So that in the drive from the Apollo Bunder to Malabar Point, all India is unfolded in one panorama. First the business houses and the great buildings—

those the richest, these the stateliest in India, and challenging comparison with almost any city in the world. Every variation of design is theirs, but they find a link of uniformity in the red-brown colours common to most, and in the oriental profusion of ornament. First comes the Venetian Secretariat, then the Gothic University Library and the French University Hall; between them the great Clock Tower, which peals forth hymn-tunes on Sunday, and on week-days " God Save the Queen ! " and " Home, Sweet Home." The white-pinnacled Law Courts follow in Early English, then the Post and Telegraph Offices in Miscellaneous Gothic. But the jewel of Bombay is the Victoria Railway Station, a vast domed mass of stone fretted with point and column and statuary. Between them all you catch vistas of green mead and shrubbery, purple-belled creepers, scarlet-starred shrubs. The whole has its feet in bowers of succulent green and its elbows on shining-leaved banyan-trees. A proud and comely city, you say, the Briton feels himself a greater man for his first sight of Bombay.

Then suddenly the magician turns his ring and new has become old, plain is coloured, solid is tumbled down, the West has been swallowed up utterly by the East. Cross but one street and you are plunged in the native town. In your nostrils is the smell of the East, dear and never to be forgotten : rapturously you snuff that blending of incense and spices and garlic, and sugar and goats and dung. The jutting houses close in over you. The decoration of Bombay henceforth is its people. The windows are frames for women, the streets become wedges of men. Under the quaint wooden sun-hoods that push out over the serried windows of the lodging-houses, along the rickety paintless balconies and verandahs, all over the tottering roofs—only the shabbiness of the dust and dirty plaster relieves the gorgeousness of one of the most astounding collections of human animals in the world. Forty languages, it is said, are habitually spoken in its bazaars. That, to him who understands no word of any of them, is more curious than interesting. But then every race has its own costume; so that the streets of Bombay are a tulip-garden of vermilion turbans and crimson, orange and flame colour, of men in blue and brown and emerald waistcoats, women in cherry-coloured satin drawers, or mantles, drawn from the head across the bosom to the hip, of blazing purple or green that shines like a grasshopper. You must go to India to see such dyes. They are the very children of the sun, and seem to shine with an unreflected radiance of their own. If you check your eye and ask your mind for the master-colour in the crowd, it is white—white bordered with brown or fawn or amber legs. But when you forget that and let the eye go again, the scarlets and yellows and shining greens—each hue alive and quivering passionately like the tropical sun at midday—fill and dazzle it anew: in the gilding light the very arms and legs show like bronze or amber or the bloom on ripe damsons. You are walking in a flaring sunset, and come out of it blinking.

Look under the turbans. At first all natives look alike, but soon you begin to mark distinctions of dress and even of type. The first you will pick out is the Arab horse-dealer. His long robe and hood, bound round with cords and tufts of camel's hair, mark him off from the wisp-clothed native of India. The Arab gives you the others in focus. He is not much accounted by those who know him; yet, compared with the Indian, his mien is high, his movements free and dignified, his features strongly cut and resolute. The Bagdad Jew is hardly a type of lofty manhood, but under his figured turban and full-tasselled fez his face looks gravely wise. The blue-bloused Afghan is a savage frankly, but a strong man also. By the side of any one of them the down-country native of Bombay is poor and weak and insignificant. He looks as if you could break him across your knee. His formless features express nothing; his eyes have the shining meekness, but not the benevolence, of the cow's; he moves slowly and without snap, like a sick man. He seldom speaks, and when he does his voice is small. Sometimes he smiles faintly—laughs never.

To the nervelessness of the Bombay natives one race furnishes an exception—the Parsi. The Parsi, as his name tells you, comes from Persia, whence he was persecuted for worshipping fire. Persecuted races develop their own virtues and their own aptitudes; and now, under the British peace, the Parsi flourishes exceedingly. He is the Jew of the East—leaves other people to make things while he makes money. Banking, agency, commission, brokerage, middleman's profits are the Parsi's Golconda. He has perceived the advantages wherewith a European education equips him for these pursuits, and has sedulously educated himself into the most European of all Asiatics. He walks out with his wife—a refined-looking creature in a pale pink or lemon-yellow gown, with a pea-green, crimson-edged shawl passed over her head—to hear the band at sunset, and talks to her as a man might talk to his friend. He takes a holiday at Darjiling in the starving frost, and professes himself much braced by it. And when the young Parsi speaks of "going home," he means not Persia —where he would not be received with enthusiasm— but England.

You can see the change in the dress of two generations. The elderly Parsi wears his shirt outside his cerise trousers, and on his head a weird plum-colour structure, like a Siamese-twin of a hat that you can put on either way up. The young Parsi wears, as a rule, a short frock-coat buttoned over white duck trousers, and on his head a linoleum helmet, something between a Prussian grenadier's and a fly-paper man's. He is shocked at our denial of representative institutions to India, conceiving that if they were granted he would be a representative, and forgetting that, we once gone, the Mussulmans would straightway push him into the sea and take his rupees unto themselves.

For the Parsi's rupees are very many. Sir Jamshidji Jijibhoy, the richest, is worth about five millions sterling. Many others hasten in his footsteps. So greenly flourish the Parsis that they have nearly filled up all the eligible sites on the Ridge, the best part of Bombay, and soon there will be no place for the Briton. While the rich Parsi lives in an airy bungalow, English ladies have to hire land and live thereon in tents.

Bombay is the extremest case of a commonplace but irritating evil which is felt in Calcutta also, and will in time be felt, unless it be provided against, in all the great Indian cities. The British residents, supposed to be lords of the city, have no place to live in. Our rule has enriched the natives till they outbid us for the luxuries and even the necessities of life. The pinch has come first in Bombay, partly because the Parsis have been quicker and abler than other races in taking advantage of the peace and industrial facilities we have afforded, partly because the city, lying on a narrow island, can only extend in one direction. Nobody grudges the Parsi the fruits of his level-headed enterprise. But he is not always a pleasant neighbour to the fastidious eyes and ears and nose of the European—though, indeed, things have now gone so far that the European would put up with that in return for a possible bungalow, and cannot get it. The best part of Bombay is the Ridge and Malabar Hill, and here house after house is passing into native occupancy. The result is that young and slenderly paid Europeans—and even many married men—have literally nowhere to live. The chambers in the clubs are all full, and so, in the season, are the comfortless hotels. At an exorbitant rate they hire land to pitch tents on; and even from this they may be driven at the will of the native owner. The remedy for this state of things is to mark off reservations in all large cities to be occupied by Europeans alone. It should be done at once, for every year makes it more difficult and expensive.

It must be said that if the Parsi knows how to get, he knows also how to give. Every Parsi educational institution or charity, for men or women, is endowed beyond the dreams of London hospitals. One cotton-spinner is said to have given £200,000 to the University of Bombay; many others are hardly less munificent. To them, to the Bagdad-Jewish Sassons and—last, but after all essential to the prosperity of the others—to the British Government, Bombay owes the stately public buildings, the spacious open places that give her the grand air above almost every city of the West.

For Bombay is indeed a queen among cities. Drive

Bombay

down from the Ridge by the white, flooding moon-
light, beneath fleshy green leaves as huge and flowers
as languorously gorgeous as in any fairy tale,—beneath hundred-fingered fronds of palm and wax-
foliaged banyans that feel for earth with roots hanging from their branches; past tall, broad-shouldered
architecture rising above these, Western in its design,
Eastern in the profusion of its embellishment; looking always out to the blue-veiled bay with the golden
lights on its horns.   Then think of the factory smoke,
the numberless bales of cotton, the hives of coolies,
the panting steamers in the harbour, the grim-eyed
batteries, and the white warships.   Bombay is a
beautiful queen in silver armour and a girdle of gold.

III

LORD, HAVE MERCY ON US!

" HERE-we-have-some-ve-ry-char-act-er-is-tic-and-typ-i-cal-tem-per-a-ture-charts," said the doctor. A Parsi speaks English with a staccato that accents every syllable alike. But for that you would hardly have distinguished the doctor, in his gold-rimmed spectacles, well-cut flannel suit, and grey pith helmet, from a swarthy European. The truth is that he has never been in Europe at all; yet he is one of the best-known authorities on bubonic plague in the world.

Down the long, light, and airy ward—plague and light and air cannot live together—was a double row of some thirty beds, covered with violet blankets. From under each protruded a dark, small, close-cropped head. Some lay quite still with eyes tight shut; some stared up at the pointed roof with eyes moist and shining; one boy grinned almost merrily. All were sick of the plague; on statistics it was to be expected that three out of every four would die in the next few hours.

At its first onset, two years ago, plague killed its two hundred and forty a-day; now it has sunk to fifty a-day, but it goes on steadily. Bombay has resigned herself to another four or five years of it—which means, at the present rate, that one-tenth of her population will die of it between now and 1904.

Then what is to be done? asks the practical Englishman. Ask the uneducated native, and he will say that the white Empress is angry because some blackguards defaced her statue two years ago; now that it is restored again things may be expected to go better. Ask the educated native, and he will placidly reply, "Nothing." Let it spend itself, let it become endemic, says he, finding much consolation in the Greek word. Human life has always been abundant and cheap in India. Here is the spectacle of a great city where one disease has killed its thousands in two years, and is killing its hundreds now every week; and nobody cares. White man and brown alike accept it as a new circumstance of their existence, and that is all.

Yet not quite all, nor is it quite just to say that nobody cares. It seemed that at present all that can be done, short of pulling down Bombay, was being done, and—it seemed for the moment—not wholly in vain. The municipality had partly recovered from the paralysis which overtook it at the enemy's first attack; it had come back to Bombay again, even the most enlightened native no longer feeling his life in danger. The military visitations had ceased. They frightened the natives. In one case, I was told, when a couple of naval officers, with bluejackets and native infantry, arrived to inspect a large tenement house, they found that every one of the three hundred tenants had bolted in the night—leaving only two men to die alone of plague—and had spread themselves to sow contagion all over the quarter. Now the municipality does what is to be done, especially the few British members of it.

I had the luck to fall in with men who could show me the whole process, from cause to cure—or death. The cause was simple enough : two minutes in the native quarter, and you saw and smelt and tasted it. The cause is sheer piggery, dirt and darkness, foul air and rabbit-warren overcrowding. The huge houses, with their ranks of windows, their worn plaster and scratched, rickety shutters, have slum written all over them in a universal language; but for wooden hoods projecting like gargoyles to shade some of the windows, they might be in Edinburgh or Naples.

But walk in, and what you see surpasses everything European. On stamped earth floors, between bare walls, by the dimness of one tiny window, you see shapes squatting like monkeys. They stir, lithe but always languid, and presently you see that they are human. Babies, naked children, young women and youths, mothers and fathers, shrivelled grandsires and grand-dams—whole families stifle together in the thick darkness, breed, and take in lodgers. In the room, where there is hardly space to move, they sleep and work at trades, and cook their food with pungent cakes of cow-dung. Because January is cold to their bare limbs, they shut doors and windows, to fug and fester worse. The lower rooms are worn down beneath the level of the street and of the drains; the upper are holes beneath the sloping roof, where a man cannot stand upright. On the storeys between these are dens lighted only from the dark corridor. You look into them, and at first see no more than a feeble wick fluttering in a night-glass; then moist eyes shine at you out of the darkness, and again two, four, six, ten men and women are sitting motionless against the wall. They neither speak nor stir—just sit and ripen for pestilence.

On the door-jamb of this house are a dozen red marks—dates with a line round them, in some semi-circular, in others a complete circle. Each means a case of plague—the full circles a death, the halves a removal to hospital. For your own part you wonder that anybody in the poisonous lair is left alive.

Improvement is coming—tardy and partial, still an improvement on the worst. At this house we fell in with an English gentleman, a man of business and a member of the municipality, who was devoting his money and time and life to saving these wretches. Equipped with large powers of compulsion, he was forcing the landlord to pierce shafts through the whole height of the house, to replace small windows by big, to do away with the garrets. The landlord, a Hindu, had all the native's terror of spending a farthing: he had argued and pleaded and dallied, but this morning he was at last beginning. We came across him—a fat, yellow toad in spotless white turban, shirt, and drawers, with a red kummerbund—half-sulky, half-fawning, trembling to the naked eye. For most of his rooms he will be getting two rupees (2s. 8d.) a-week. A native docker's pay is only seven; but a native can easily live on two rupees a-week, and afford the rent out of the five. There are perhaps fifty rooms in the house, so that it is not wonderful that the yellow toad grows fat.

The English councillor had persuaded some of the worst-lodged to run up shelters of bamboo and matting and live in the yard outside. It was light and airy at least, though foul, whereas the rooms indoors were mostly clean. Here, little isles of brown skin and scarlet, white and yellow cotton, sat families amid the carts and humped oxen, the goats and the fowls. In the house the goat and kid lived upstairs with the people; at one door a cooped duck was quacking mournfully. In the yard the oxen lived in the open, for the councillor had converted the byre with bamboo and limewash into an emergency hospital.

Going out—it was good to open your mouth and nostrils again—we passed blocks of the new buildings the municipality has provided,—hideous, like all works of corporations, but solidly built of stone and brick, with at least a chance of seeing and breathing. We came next to a segregation camp, where they isolate and watch people who have been in contact or under suspicion of contact with the plague-stricken. It was a little village of white bamboo-matting, with an open compartment in a big shed for each family. As it was already eight o'clock, most of the inhabitants were out; here and there sat a nose-ringed woman among the few brass cooking-pans which made up the family furniture. The inmates of these camps may go to work, but they must be back by six; meanwhile, the spectacled, unshaven native apothecary in charge strolls up and down chambers as soundless as if they were already graves.

For the climax of the dismal story we come to the hospital and the Parsi physician—one native, at least, who knows his duty and does it. As he walked from bed to bed there stepped in from the sun-steeped garden a golden-haired English girl in a white-and-red uniform—a nurse who had volunteered to come out for plague duty, and has lived with death for two years. As they passed, one skeleton raised brilliant eyes and cried out thickly. "It-is-the-ty-pi-cal-voice-of-plague-as-in-in-tox-i-ca-tion," remarked the doctor. The next was a boy with facial bubo—a hideous enlargement of one cheek and jaw to double the size of the other. The next lay and panted; the next—his wrists tied firmly to the bed—muttered and struggled in delirium. The next was recovering, but had lost his reason. On the breast of the last of the row was

Lord, Have Mercy on Us!

a great stain of treacly gangrene with a yellow border round it.

Outside there was a clash of cymbals, and raucous voices seemed to be singing a round. A dozen men strode briskly up the street carrying a bier and a shape under a pall strewn with flowers.

NOTE.

The foregoing description was written in the first week of January 1899. In the first week of March I was again in Bombay and found a very different state of things. Plague had increased fearfully, and the natives were once more in full flight. In the first week of February the deaths that admittedly resulted from plague were five hundred and eighty-eight. The next week they rose to a hundred a-day. By the end of the third week in February they were over one hundred and twenty a-day; and in the first week of March it was admitted that over one hundred and fifty cases were dying daily of plague, while every unofficial person you met insisted that the official estimates were designedly optimistic, and put the daily mortality between two hundred and fifty and three hundred. Thousands of natives fled daily; and though, to my eye, the city seemed as full as ever, I was assured by residents who knew it well that I was mistaken. In addition to this, plague was reappearing at Poona, was very severe at Bangalore, while on the Kolar gold-fields, in Hyderabad territory, at least one European had been infected, and the flight of the coolies had thrown all work into disorder. About the same time plague made its reappearance in Calcutta; it was asserted—of course unofficially—that several Europeans died of it. With the advent of the hot weather, which in these parts of the country begins at mid-March, plague has hitherto always declined.

It is difficult to be certain of statistics in a country like India, where a constitutionally nervous government withholds all the information it can; but even the few figures quoted disclose a situa-

22

tion which in Great Britain would be thought appalling. In India nobody cares. Yet it is easy to see that if plague is to recur every cold weather in Bombay with added severity—and there is apparently no scientific certainty in the pious hope that it will exhaust itself in seven years or so—the only possible end will be ruin to the city. Suppose an average mortality of one hundred a-day spread over one hundred days in the early part of the year. Even this moderate estimate comes to ten thousand a-year, and for one that dies you may assume that at least ten bolt till hot weather returns. In a year or two business will be paralysed by quarantine and segregation and by the lack of labour, and Bombay, at the present rate, will sooner or later cease to exist as a great city.

Of course this is not to be taken as a prophecy. The one certain thing about plague—and it is the only excuse for the apathy of the Indian Government in presence of it—is that nobody knows anything certain about it. Conferences and commissions dot the country, and medical Lieutenant-Colonels give evidence before them; but nothing coherent emerges from the mass of detail and opinion. Nobody seems quite certain whether inoculation will keep off, much less cure, the disease. Nobody would be surprised if it were to become endemic in India—a second cholera, only far worse; on the other hand, nobody would be surprised if it disappeared as suddenly as it came.

In this uncertainty most of the provincial governments prefer to sit still and hope, rather than irritate native opinion by taking strong measures of local segregation. Most Europeans in high office applaud this policy; most others despise it. Some say that it would have paid better to burn Bombay to the ground as soon as plague broke out; others, more moderate, deplore the abandonment, in deference to native prejudice, of the strict measures of visitation and segregation which were at first enforced in Bombay. There are three methods of dealing with plague. The first is that attributed—let us hope mistakenly—to the Lieutenant-Governor of Bengal. Being pressed by the Viceroy, who was in turn pressed by the Home Government, to take strong measures to enforce sanitation, observation of suspects, and segregation, in Calcutta, the

Lord, Have Mercy on Us!

Lieutenant-Governor—so the tale goes—refused, and threatened to resign if he were pressed further. The only possible reason for such a refusal would be sheer cowardice—the fear of an agitation in the native press and possible riots in the native quarters; its only possible result would be contempt of government among the governed, and, sooner or later, thousands dead of plague. The second method was pursued with great success in a large village in the Punjab. Plague had broken out, and the infected persons were to be taken away. The civil servant and police-officer went into the village to fetch them, whereon the inhabitants collected on the roofs and pelted them with tiles. As long as only the white men were hit, this was very entertaining sport; only by bad luck a few ill-aimed tiles fell among the Pathan policemen who were following. These at once opened fire and killed eight of the villagers. The infected persons were then peacefully taken away, the village isolated, and the attack of plague nipped in the bud. The third method, employed with great success at Poona by (I think) Colonel Creagh, V.C., is a combination of the other two. He employed soldiers to visit suspected houses, and Brahmans to go with them to explain the necessity of the measures taken. This is probably the best method of the three. The fatalistic attitude hitherto adopted by the provincial governments—with the meritorious exception of Madras—seems explicable only as a convenient means for keeping down the overgrowth of Indian populations.

IV

THE MOST SPORTING COUNTRY IN THE WORLD

IN the ignorant West we think of India as a land of giant palms shooting from matted undergrowth of languorous scents and steaming heat. The India you run through between Bombay and Jodhpur is mere prairie—coarse grass, scanty trees here and there, thin goats and cattle, sand, and shivering villagers. As for steaming heat—w-w-w-wr!—bloodless fingers trembled helplessly round buttons as I tried to dress in the railway carriage. Tropical India! W-w-w-w-wr!

The kindness of the superintendent of the railway had postponed the agony from three till seven in the morning by uncoupling my carriage at Jodhpur. I blessed his name, and the easy, unbuttoned habits of native States, as I stepped out on to the empty, spotless platform and found the sun just rising. Half-a-dozen bare-legged natives cowered under the well-built offices—shaking violently, shrunken, miserable, half-dead, waiting for the sun to kindle them back to life. For luckier me came a carriage with three footmen, and a cart drawn by a couple of towering camels—their noses thrust heavenwards in vain, indignant protest—to take the baggage. We rolled forth into the independent Rajput State of Jodhpur.

Its inhabitants seemed different from the flabby creatures I had left in Bombay. They were taller, held themselves straight, and looked before them; most grew strong, black, bushy beards, self-respectingly oiled, parted in the middle, and brushed stiffly upward and towards the ears. Many of them were on horseback, sitting upright, with a firm and easy seat, controlling spirited ponies with a touch on a single snaffle. There seemed, indeed, an extraordinary number of horses out that morning about Jodhpur. Sandy rides bordered the well-metalled road on both sides, and almost a continuous string of horses stood tied up to the regularly planted trees. As I reached my host's gate, a man holding a chestnut Arab stood up on the wall and salaamed.

An hour later I was privileged to meet the Prime Minister. He wore a pith topi—which means sun-helmet—a padded and quilted box-coat, and beneath it strange breeches of drab cloth, of which the continuations came down, without gaiters, over his boots. His conversation was of pig-sticking and the mouthing of young horses. Presently, riding out, we came to the cupolas of the Maharajah's suburban palace. A dozen saddle-horses stood outside it, and a string of sheeted thoroughbreds was being taken out to exercise. The living part of the palace is neither large nor luxurious as maharajahs' dwellings go; but the stables are vast beyond the dreams of Tattersall. Every more than usually palatial building in the environs of Jodhpur turns out to be a stable. The palace establishment is a great quadrangle of loose boxes about the size of Russell Square. Saddles and sets of carriage harness, new and old, frayed and glorious, Wilkinson and Ram Singh, line the walls in battalions. His Highness was unhappily not out this morning; a week before, schooling a two-year-old on the racecourse, he had been carried into a post and had hurt his arm. It was still in a sling, and the Maharajah—a handsome but languid lad of eighteen or so—was deeply depressed. "I am feeling a bit chippy this morning," he explained: carriage exercise was no use to him; he wanted to be on horseback or with his dogs and gun.

We trotted on with the Prime Minister for the further inspection of Jodhpur. Beyond the palace— his Excellency larking over a couple of fences on the way—we came to a spacious polo-ground laid down with faultlessly rolled grit: to this is attributed the fact that they had never had anybody killed at this game. Past the polo-ground was a racecourse; on it more horses were being exercised; and when you raised your eyes to the sandy horizon, behold! it was thick with horses on every side—young horses and old, Walers and Arabs and country-breds, racers and pig-stickers and polo-ponies, hackneys and even a pair of Shetlands, greys, chestnuts, and blacks,—the whole country was a whirl of horses wherever the eye could see and as far as the eye could reach.

The Jodhpur riding-breeches—breeches and gaiters all in one piece, as full as you like above the knee, fitting tight below it, without a single button or strap —have been taken up, as I am told, by a London artist, and are on the way to be world-famous. The Jodhpur standing martingale is as yet less known: it is thought that leather chafes a horse in the hot weather, so a long band of soft cloth is used instead. The State polo team has beaten most in India, and no cavalry regiment thinks itself quite ready for a big tournament till it has put in a fortnight's practice at Jodhpur. It is many years now since the Jodhpur-owned Selwood, the Prime Minister up—"I riding niny-seven, English jockey-boy riding sixy stone, I beating him"—won the Calcutta Derby. The present chief, himself the most beautiful horseman among all the hard-riding princes of India, entered into his inheritance a year or so ago. He instantly started a racing stable in Calcutta, a stable at New-market, stud-farm in Australia, and, of course, every-thing conceivable at Jodhpur. As for the Jodhpur pig-sticking, is it not famous over the length and breadth of India? The Jodhpur Imperial Service Lancers are as smart a tent-pegging corps as exists in the world. A member of the Royal Family, re-turning from the Jubilee of '87, brought with him, as the best of our contributions to human wellbeing, a hansom cab, which he personally drove across country. Briefly, Jodhpur spells horse. The small-talk of a hunting county is varied and cosmopolitan beside that of Jodhpur. Even in Newmarket there are some half-a-dozen people who have no visible connection with racing. Altogether Jodhpur can probably claim without arrogance to be the most sporting country in the whole world.

The territory of the State of Marwar, whereof it is the capital, lies in the western part of Rajputana. Fringing the great Indian desert, it is itself half-desert, with a scanty rainfall and a sandy soil. An ideal rain first breaks up the hard ground in early June, then falls lightly till September, when, the sort of millet on which the Marwaris live being husbanded, another heavy fall is desirable to fill the tanks for the cold weather. But ideal rains are rare, and Marwar is a relatively sterile country—level and soft-going for horses, though perhaps a little heavy for training racers—but none too rich even in grass, and niggardly of food to men.

So that a generation ago the natural disadvantages of the country having been sedulously supplemented by mismanagement, the State was bankrupt, the people were crushed by taxation, the Government was a mass of corrupt inepitude, a Government only in name. Then came a man, an English resident, who knew how to work on the pride of the Rajput, the son of fifty generations of kings: he made men of them and a State of Marwar. To this day they quote his admonitions with a simple adoration, half-childish, half-manly. "This sahib very fine rider, good for polo-play, good for pig-shtickin'. This sahib telling me, you gentleman *hai*, do gentleman things, work like gentleman."

They did work like gentlemen. They did not build a museum and a school of art, as did the neighbouring State, where a Bengali babu is Prime Minister; but they put the taxation and law courts on a footing of rough-and-ready justice, they ventilated the jail, and especially made a branch line to connect with the Rajputana railway. At the urgent instance of the superintendent of their railway, they made a great reservoir to hold the summer rain and an aqueduct to bring it to the city. In dry seasons the people used to have to migrate elsewhere; now they get sufficiency, if not abundance, of water throughout the worst of years. They have instituted a little Decauville railway to carry the sewage out of the city; they have made roads all round their city and planted trees —you may see the young ones, each in a cup of carefully moistened mud and fenced with a wall of mimosa thorn—where before was nothing but desert.

Conceiving the British to be the only true sportsmen in the world besides themselves, the men of Marwar are loyal beyond suspicion to their suzerain. They look on their Resident not as a spy or a taskmaster, but as a friend. "You thinking, sahib, being

more war soon ? " they will ask him anxiously, for
they ask no better than to have a chance of showing
what their cavalry can do for the Empress.

But with all the modern improvements and the
British sympathy, Marwar is not over-governed. Its
political life is simple like itself. State affairs are not
neglected, but the cavalry and the polo, the racing and
the pig-sticking, remain the serious business of life.
The horse, who abases the base, is to these simple
aristocrats the salt that keeps their life sweet and
clean. He keeps them in a happy mean between the
half-baked civilisation of the babu and the besotted
sensuality of the old Asiatic rulers. He solves for
them the great problem of the ruling races of India
—how to employ themselves innocuously now that in
India there is no more war.

How simple and manly they remain you may easily
gather from half an hour with such of them as have
been to England. Petted in London drawing-rooms,
pampered at Ascot, admitted to easy intercourse with
Royalty, they remain unaffected, modest, sincere, now
exploding in boyish laughter, now gravely respectful
to the sahib as to a father. The babu, you see, feeling himself inferior at heart, is jerkily familiar ; the
Jodhpur Rajput, knowing himself your equal, can
afford to call you Sahib and salaam. The intimacy
of princes cannot raise him ; the friendship of the
plainest cannot lower him. He is a Rathore Rajput ;
he can never be more, and he can never be less.

V

A RAJPUT CITY

THE Rathores, the ruling family of Jodhpur, are probably—bracketed with one or two other Rajput stocks—the most noble house in the world. Their pedigree begins with the beginning of time, but for practical purposes it need not be followed back beyond 470 A. D. At that time they are certainly known to have been kings; and kings they have been ever since—at first in Kanauj, in the Ganges Valley, and afterwards, driven thence, in Rajputana. In the undesirable scrub and desert they cut out their kingdom, and perched their fort on the rock; seven centuries of unequal war with Afghan and Mogul emperors, with Maratha rievers and with their brother States of Rajputana, had left them faint but surviving, when the British Peace came to give them rest.

As the Rajputs are the purest blood of India, so their social structure is the oldest—a mixture of feudalism and clanship, where the nobles hold the lands their ancestors won in war or received from kings as younger sons' portions. Elsewhere in India the Maharajah is the State and his subjects nothing; in Rajputana he is the head of the family, first among his

peers. The lower castes, descendants of the conquered aborigines, are nothing; but the poorest Rajput is kin to the king.

The cenotaphs of the Rathore rulers are at Mandor,
three miles out. There they had their capital before,
in 1459, Jodha built his castle above the city that
bears his name; and here their ashes were buried.
Through a gate of carved stone, you come into a
garden cool with green leaves, starred with ruddy-
purple bougainvillea, blooming richly under the brow
of bare precipices. Beyond are the tombs—tapering
masses of dark, red-brown stone, as proud as pyra-
mids, as graceful as spires. Terrace rises from
square arch, pillar and capital climb above terrace;
over all towers a cone-shaped dome—not the plain
dome we know, but the union of a multitude of tiny
ones running one into the other, till the whole is
ribbed and fluted and looks like a pine-apple. From
a coping-stone here, from a seam in the pine-apple
there, looks out the sculptured head of the royal elephant. At one tomb, says the custodian with a tear
for the past and a sigh for the degenerate present, no
less than eighty-four widows were burned.

But before you come to the cenotaphs of the kings,
—and this is the point, as illustrating Rajput society,
—you will have passed a gallery something between
statuary and fresco. Under a colonnade is a huge
procession of coloured figures in relief—colossal and
crude, with faces like the necklaced cats you buy in

china shops, and horses less horse-like than the toys of our childhood. They are so naïvely hideous, the contrast between the babyish statuary and the effortless, masterly architecture is so astounding, that you ask the Vakil whether these are not gods. The Vakil is officially a sort of agent between the Marwar Government and the Resident, and personally a pleasant, dark-faced, black-moustached young man in a sweater and tunic and the celebrated Jodhpur riding-breeches. " No, sir, not god," he replies. " Kings, then?" " No, sir, not king—gentleman—like me." These are heroes who have distinguished themselves in war—not monarchs, not necessarily of the immediate Royal Family; simply Rajputs, "gentleman, like me," and as such fitted for any gallery of glories.

In the city that nestles under the sheer scarped rock you will see those who are not Rajputs—the subjects. Driving in through the gate, under the battlements of the broad, crumbling wall, you are instantly in complete India, unspoiled and unimproved. Jodhpur has its Decauville railway, you are aware; it also has its froward camels, who lie down across the High Street and refuse to move for royal carriages. Over any booth in the bazaar, on any poor man's house, you will see stonework—latticed windows, mouldings, traceries, cornices overhanging the street—so exquisite that they seem wafted out of a fairy tale. Yet, when it wanted but another foot of stone, another week of work, to be perfect, the artist broke off, and the delicate masterpiece is finished by a few rough-hewn slabs piled on anyhow, a mat or a heap of sods, a paintless broken shutter framed in a jewel of carving. It is the East, you murmur, enraptured—the undiluted East at last, opulent, shiftless, grotesque, magical. There is a temple—pure Orient. The central shrine rises in tiers of jutting eaves like a pagoda; the front is an embroidery of stone screens; down over the windows droop long crescent-shaped cornices like a gull's wings; at each side of the entrance-steps stands a marble-elephant, all straight lines and square corners, as if it had just stepped out of a Noah's ark. Passing on, you catch a glimpse of another façade of tracery, lavished on a street a yard wide where nobody could ever see it; on the other side, over a bunch of wood-and-straw hovels on a rock, soars another pine-apple dome. There is another marvel of stonework, arches and window-frames finished with the finger-nail but blending into one long harmonious front; the thousand points of its cornice overhang a row of shabby shops, whose fires have blackened the fretwork with generations of smoke.

This is surely pure East. Your eye has strung itself to the high tones of colour by now, and what at first only dazzled now shows you shades and symphonies. The people group themselves for you: every window-space and roof is full of their radiance. Blues soften from cobalt through peacock to indigo; turbans are no longer merely flaring red or yellow, but magenta, crimson, flame-colour, salmon-colour, gold, orange, lemon. The group of women bunched in the street in worn garments is a study in brick-red and old gold. Every shop in the bazaar—an old man squatting among metal pots, a boy with liquid eyes dilating at the unknown sahib, both in a bare cube of dirty plaster four steps above the street—becomes a picture in its frame. Here is the Royal Mint, and they bring you a chair to see the fashioning of gold mohurs and silver rupees. One man weighs out the metal, another fuses it in a blow-pipe flame to a fat disc, another holds it on a die, and yet another smites it with a die-hammer. The coin jumps out jingling, and they will sell it you warm; only the mauve-clad master of the mint forgets how much it is worth, and will send you your change to-morrow. Next, jingling bells and flinging abroad their harlequin rags of yellow, dull red and citron, come a group of fakirs; round the next corner is a yet holier man, flowing grey-bearded, his face white with ashes; turn again and a votary is sitting cross-legged on an empty petroleum-box with his nose against a six-armed, three-headed, monkey-grinned god. Then you pass through a wide market, floored with sacks of corn and roofed with clouds of blue pigeons, to the tank—a sheet of green-gold water walled with stone, with parapets and broad staircases, and at the foot of each, purple- or brown- or carnation-clad women dipping with shining brass.

Oh yes, pure East—and here vaguely sways an ele-

phant up the street; and there—there—O disillusion!
—a little shabby box on wheels switchbacks along
little rails, bumps into camels, jaggernauts over lop-
eared goats, and bears the inscription, " Jodhpur
Tramways." And now I see, amid strange vegetables
and fruits, amid loin-clothed bakers kneading strange
dough into strange confectionery, cheap, gaudy Ger-
man pictures, illuminated for the export market, daub-
ing native gods even more brutally hideous than the
reality.

Alas! there seems no East without its smudge of
West. Come up to the fort on the rock; perhaps we
shall find an untainted sanctuary there. The rock
springs sheer up from the nestling town, every face
scarped into smooth precipice; the ancient palace of
the Rathores lifts its diadem from the summit. To
reach the zigzags that climb to it you must sweep all
round the city, up rock-fringed serpentines; and when
you have climbed to the gate the palace seems more
inaccessibly lofty than before.

Look up. White walls, half bastion, half Titanic
pillar, mount up and up; small over your head, up in
the very sky, leaning over dizzy nothing, hang blush-
red fairy houses with pin-point windows. Under a
frowning gateway, past the trapping-houses of the
royal elephants, turn, and up another steep-walled
slope, another—there are the rough heaps of stone
still in place to hurl down on to a storming party—till
you come to another tall, grim gateway. Here on

slabs on either side you see the rough prints of hands
—five on the right, some thirty on the left—each the
mark of a queen as she came down from the fort for
the last time to be burned with her dead lord.

You still feel like a beetle as you look up at the
brows of the palace, but there is only one long ramp
to pull up.   And then you stand in front of buildings
laced all over with carving, rigid as the stone it is,
light as the air it breathes.   You pass from arch to
arch, to court within court, till you are mazed with
gull-wing window-shades, lattice-windows, fretted
screens, thousand-pointed pendent cornices, the epitome of all the beauties below.   Description melts
away powerless before the myriad touches, the
majestic whole: you can only murmur, a fairy tale
charmed into stone.

And then when you go into the royal saloons
you find them illuminated like an old missal with
labyrinths of gold and azure and scarlet, lustrous
with gold and rose-coloured silks, and furnished with
the crudest, ugliest, gaudiest, vulgarest drawing-room
suites and ottomans and occasional tables.   You look
for the ticket on the back : " In this style, complete,
one million rupees."   And the richest apartment of
all is bile and jaundice with cheap green and yellow
panes from the window of a suburban lavatory !

Yet it is very good.   They can turn splendour into
grotesqueness, but after all they will hardly face the
stone poetry with red brick and stucco.   And there

always remains the fort. The rows of guns on the terrace—from the little dragon-mouthed, dragon-tailed one, almost scraping ground with its fat belly, to the black four-wheeled leviathan that must have used up elephants on elephants to mount here—the antique guns will always look out to the white and green checker-board of Jodhpur. At sundown, when the mile-long columns of cattle trail in from pasture, and the golden clouds rise up from the Prime Minister's polo-ground, the naked rock and hard-browed walls stand up, steadfast, indestructible, proud, above the dust-veil and the city sheltering at their feet. At sundown they are lambent in every seam and wrinkle with cold violet-blue; at dawn they will glow with hot carmine; but always they will be there. The city may change, the cattle and the very polo may pass away; but, night and morning, the fastness of the Rathores will endure for ever.

VI

THE CAMP OF EXERCISE

THE Inspector-General of Cavalry had his camp under the further side of the Ridge. Its flawless order was a joy to see—the unswerving straight lines of the roads, the exact set of the tents, with the occupant's name on each and his servants' tent behind, the abundance of fodder in the horse-lines, the spreading office- and mess-tents. These were floored with matting and furnished with desks and easy-chairs. In the smaller officers' tents you saw writing-tables and dressing-tables perfectly set out. In India your tent is more than half a home, and what India does not know of camping is misleading heresy.

A mile beyond was encamped the Southern Division, five miles beyond that the Northern. In this winter weather—and, oh, how wintry it is, once you get out of the sun!—English hours rule: we get up comfortably at daybreak, eat a lordly breakfast at nine, and jog off in the dust at ten to see the day's fight. The Inspector-General rides off with about a dozen of a staff: such luxuries as D.A.Q.M.G.'s are never stinted in India. With them rides a young maharajah in khaki, very frank and manly, carrying good-comradeship to the point of larking with British officers, but eating his sandwich and plain soda alone like a self-respecting Hindu—not at all your idea of the oriental potentate. The leaf-fringed road is lively with horsemen and horsewomen, dogcarts, and the miraculous native cabs of Delhi. They look half jaunting-car, half ice-cream barrow—a gay-painted box, on whose lid two or four people squat cross-legged, back to back, under a shabby canvas awning. Also any number of natives on foot pad out to see the sahibs play at war.

Just past the Northern camp we came to the line of the East Indian Railway, at a point where its embankment was pierced by a bridge. Roughly parallel to the line was the road; between, the ground was level, but for two or three hillocks to the left of the bridge, and covered with rough grass. The other side of the line was similar ground for the best part of a mile, only broken by a mass of tumble-down walls just opposite the debouch from the bridge, and finally ringed in by a semicircle of thick trees. This was the scene of the day's work. The bridge represented a defile, and was the only way from one side of the line to the other; the rule was that, though dismounted men might line the railway bank, nobody was to cross it.

Beyond the line we saw the black ranks of nine squadrons of cavalry and a horse-battery. It was just eleven o'clock, and as we saw, they formed into column and started to pass through to our side of the bridge. They were going to look for the enemy, who was advancing from somewhere the other side of the road. When they found him, they would reconnoitre him; and if he proved too strong to be fought in the open, would retire and attack him as he passed the defile. As it happened, everybody knew he would be too strong; he had thirteen squadrons of the twenty-two—six regiments, two British and four native— which made up the whole division. Then the weaker commander, knowing the ground on his side of the bridge, might attack the stronger force as they came in column through the defile, and roll them up before they had time to deploy and make their numbers tell. It was a very pretty problem.

Out came the weaker force from the railway bridge. "Hang the men!" muttered the Inspector-General. "Why don't they come faster? They'll get jammed under the bridge." The general is a great race-rider and pig-sticker, and a very hot man all round, and especially he realises the vital value of pace in war as in sport. Next instant they quickened to a trot; a scrunching roar showed that the guns were coming through, and the long columns were half-way to the road.

It was my first sight of Indian cavalry, and I looked curiously. Bigger than the down-country natives I had seen hitherto, they were very light men compared with Europeans—small-boned and spare. That was the first idea; the second was that they would be bad men to pursue and worse still to run from. Dark-skinned, black-bearded, keen-eyed, swinging easily in the body and gripping the horse hermetically with the legs, they looked born troopers all over—swift and fierce and tireless. Their uniform was in their character—huge turbans, blue, blue and white, blue and red or crimson, lowering over bushy brows and wild eyes, and dancing in the breeze behind long tunics of dark blue or khaki, relieved by brilliant kummerbunds, breeches like divided skirts, and tight putties below. It was almost startling to see white officers in such a kit—a brick-burned face with yellow eyebrows and moustache looking out from under a peaked cap of scarlet velvet with a vast blue turban wound round it; a huge chest under a khaki tunic, whose long tails proclaim it first cousin of the oriental shirt; a broad scarlet kummerbund under the regulation belt; orange breeches, and long black boots. It was one more revelation of the wonderful Englishman who can make himself into half a savage to make savages into half-civilised men.

By this time the force was across the road, and before it stretched miles and miles of yellow grass, sparsely tufted with a few bushes—the ideal of cavalry ground. Already, far ahead of the long lines that walked warily forward, groups of little ant-like creatures trailed swiftly over this plain: they were officers' patrols, an officer and a man or two going forward to feel for the enemy. They went on, till from ants they became black dots, then stopped. On the bushy horizon appeared other dots—the enemy's patrols. Then all the dots moved again,—going on ? —coming back ?—yes, coming back at a racing gallop. The dot came back to an ant, and the ant suddenly leaped into a tearing horse and man, bringing the kind of news which in the real thing may mean life or death to regiments or armies or nations. The hindmost were dodging pursuers ; one or two were taken ; but before there was time to watch the last, the first had reported : the lines of riders and the guns whipped round and moved briskly back towards the road and the defile.

A belch of smoke from the plain and a muffled thud, another, another : the superior force's guns had seen the retreating masses and opened fire. Then a grating bang close by : the opposing battery had unlimbered and was replying. But that will not do for long when you are retreating with calvary at your heels : after two or three rounds the teams clattered up, the guns swung round, and were off again ; and the next thing was that the plain was black with the advancing squadrons of the stronger side, and the weaker had disappeared off the earth.

Slowly, cautiously, the attackers crept up, straining their eyes, moving behind huts or hillocks, edging off flankwards among trees. They had need of all their caution: a squadron was moving across the front along the road when—crack, crack, crack-k-kle—dismounted squadrons were firing at it from the embankment on both sides of the bridge. The guns opened, too, from beyond the line. The weaker force was there, prepared to show his teeth. The thing to do was to contain his fire with artillery and dismounted men, and then slam in the rest of cavalry through the defile. In the mouth of the bridge we waited and waited; but for the carbine-fire on the line the place seemed empty. Then suddenly on the attacking side guns appeared behind the mounds, separated into teams and pieces, and fired. Khaki figures were kneeling under cover on either side the guns, firing. The whole place was a roar and a rattle— till dashed out a cloud of wild horsemen, tossing lance-points, flying puggaris, steaming towards the bridge.

Now! Beyond the bridge the dismounted squadrons of the defenders were hurrying down the bank to their horses. For the rest, the plain seemed empty. The head of the on-coming lancers thrust through the bridge, and swung rightward in a lengthening column. But all in an instant a squadron in line burst from behind the ruined walls, then another, and bore down at a thundering gallop. The first met the first squadron of the assailants, which had wheeled into line; the second caught the second squadron still in column, and would have crumpled it up. Now more and more riders were pouring through the defile, more pouring down to meet them.

Cease fire! It is the annoying thing about manœuvres that they have to stop just at the exciting point. All you could say of this fight was that in real life the best men would probably have won. So now back to lunch in the sumptuous mess-tent of a hussar regiment. Think of it! War till lunch-time —then pâté-de-foie-gras, champagne, and ladies. In the afternoon the Southern Division went through the same exercise, only this time it was the superior force dismounted men on the bank, and hammered away with carbines and with guns—at nothing. Of the defenders, not one sign! The assailants came through and deployed—one squadron straight forward, one half-right, one half-left. Still nothing; till, all at once—bang, bang, bang!—three guns, wide apart, fired full into the centre squadron, and the plain came to life. At each squadron that had come through galloped a squadron from out of the trees. The arena was a thunder of hoofs, a criss-cross of rigid lines—khaki, blue, crimson, steel—hurling themselves straight at each other from every point; then —cease fire!

Again the best men would have won, though the first squadron through would have been knocked to pieces. But the next day we won—we all won—for we were the British-India army fighting an imaginary enemy. On each flank of a ridge one division formed up. Guns opened from our ridge and from the enemy's opposite; in the dip between our infantry and theirs were seen mutually advancing with a splutter of fire. The idea was that the Russians—I mean the enemy—were too strong for our infantry and guns, and that the cavalry was to retrieve the day: what more congenial? The left flank division was to get behind the enemy's right rear, take his guns, crumple up his reserves, and then come on to support the right division, which was meanwhile to crumple up his cavalry and then pursue. A few minutes we watched the skeleton infantry blaze away; then the cavalry went. Going forward to the enemy's left, we saw the troopers of our leftward division galloping up behind his right flank—single riders, groups, lines black and fast and terrible filling up the ground. Then came our right division at the charge against the flags that marked the imaginary squadrons—officers well ahead, dark masses behind them extending and quickening, extending and quickening, over rock and furrow and fissure. Then a furious thudding—and they were on us, manes flying, horse-heads tossing, knife-edged shrieks from the sowars and breathless "Damns!" from the British—a thunder, a whirl, a cloud of dust—and they were tearing up the earth a quarter of a mile beyond. It was as thick and yellow with dust as a London fog: you were lost in it—and then, before you could see ten yards, another thunder. The other division whirlwinded past in support and

pursuit—an overtaking blur in the dust-fog, a rushing
phantom of manes and leaping puggaris and gleaming
white eyeballs, and then a diminishing thunder in the
dust again.

In the pursuit I should prefer to be on the side of
the British-India cavalry.

That was the last day of active operations. For
the wind-up there was a grand open-air Military
Tournament between the camps, with jumps, and
tent-pegging, and guns minuetting at the gallop,
and all the other joys; also—lest they forget—native
women peeping through the closed shutters of carriages, and native men standing on their horses to
see over the crowd. It was all very fine and enjoy-
able—only to read it now you naturally think it a
little dull. Perhaps; but still you may be glad to
know what the British army—the real British army
—looks like and does and is in the country where it
exists for business. For to find the real British army
you must go to India. Thousands of our people at
home pass their lives without ever seeing a soldier,
millions without ever seeing a brigade. Perhaps one
in ten thousand of home-keeping Britons has seen
more than one regiment of cavalry together. India is
otherwise. Here also, it is true, there are broad
countries—Bengal, for instance, with three-fourths of
the area of France, and nearly twice the population
of the British Isles—which hardly ever see a bayonet
or a lance. But to other districts—the great canton-

ments and the garrisons of the North-West Frontier —the sight of regiments and brigades is as familiar as that of policemen to you.

So that it was nothing for India to have twelve regiments of cavalry, with four batteries of horse artillery, assembled for the camp of exercise. It would be difficult to assemble this force in England— there only are fourteen regiments in Great Britain— and when it was assembled it would have no room to move; even Salisbury Plain hardly supplies reconnoitring ground for a single day. But the whole of Northern India consists of one single alluvial plain, nearly as large as France, Germany, and Austria put together, with hardly a hill and hardly a stone throughout the length and breadth of it. You can find tracts as large as English countries with scarcely a crop to ride over. Not that crops would stop the manœuvres, or anything else; for in India the army is taken seriously.

If you do not find good cavalry and lifelike cavalry manœuvres in India, therefore, you may despair of British military organisation at once. But you do find them. Every year the Inspector-General of Cavalry fixes the time when regiments are marching across country changing stations, selects his force, and then sets them to march at each other. This year part of the force took the field at Umballa and part at Aligarh—two hundred miles apart. By easy marches, but making up good days' work with manœuvres by the way, they converged on Delhi. When the Southern Division was within a dozen miles or so of the city, it was met by a skeleton force holding a village and railway junction, which it had to dislodge. Next day the Northern regiments were reconnoitred by a similar skeleton force, which it was their business to push back without revealing their strength. The day after that the two divisions came into collision and fought, after which each went into standing camp. Next came another couple of engagements between them; then the two fights at the defile you have just heard of; then the combined attack on the skeleton enemy. Upon each day's operations the Inspector-General delivered brief but complete criticisms. Everything was business-like, thorough; in India—except perhaps in the Government offices—they realise that the army exists to fight, and give their minds to fit it for fighting.

You would be surprised to find how much thinking out, and what lightning-rapid thinking out, a cavalry action requires. It is not at all just a matter of slamming your men at the enemy, and hoping they will be too good for him. For instance, if your cavalry is masking your own guns while your enemy's are knocking holes out of your line just before the moment of collision, the best men in the world will be hardly good enough for the worst. Points like this will take a deal of study, and it seems that even now there is room for new ideas. The Inspector-General's is that cavalry advancing in three lines ought to throw their guns right forward. It sounds almost blasphemous to put precious, tender guns in the forefront of everything. But then you must remember that horse artillery can move quickly, if necessary, and especially that cavalry can move quickly enough to come up in effective support at the shortest notice of danger; and the forward position of the guns may give vast advantages. The guns that are up in front are likely to come first into action, and may cripple, sometimes actually defeat, the enemy before he can retaliate. They are more likely to have him in effective range at the moment when the cavalry shock comes. Especially this formation may often give the leader who adopts it the choice of ground. Suppose your enemy gets into attack formation on the left of his guns, you will probably move forward your cavalry to the left of your own guns. Then the enemy can only get at you either by moving across behind his guns under fire of yours, or else in front of them, and masking them while you pound him. On the other hand, if the ground suits you better on the right of the guns, you move to that side: in any case you dictate the ground.

That is the theory; it must take a quick eye and a quick hand to bring it successfully into practice. With the view of giving officers the best chance of bringing off such rapid movements, the new idea in India is that the commander should ride well to the front of his main body, and with him the leaders of his three lines of cavalry and of his artillery. When the enemy's strength, formation, and line of advance are observed, there is still time for these leaders to gallop back to their men with verbal orders from the commander; which, having seen the enemy at his side, they are certain to understand. The commander remains in front to see whether the enemy changes his tactics at the last moment; if he does, the subordinate leaders, having seen, are still in a better position to understand their final orders.

Another point insisted on is the importance of sending forward selected officers on selected horses to observe the enemy at the earliest possible moment. Your ordinary eye might not take in the situation instantly; your ordinary horse might be caught by the enemy. As the advanced patrols are the eyes of the cavalry, and the cavalry is the eye of the whole army, you cannot have men or beasts too good for such work.

For example, they must usually be British officers. The native officer, with all his many fine qualities, has not, as a rule, the trained intelligence, observation, and self-control necessary for such work. It has been urged by a few good judges, and many bad ones, that the present status of the native officers is unsatisfactory, because they have no opportunities of rising to the highest commissioned ranks. At the time of the camp of exercise we were hearing a good deal of this from London and Calcutta, but not, curiously, from the native regiments at Delhi. The complaint is loudest—need it be said?—among Bengalis, who do not, and never will, furnish a single native officer or sepoy to the whole Indian army. The manlier races make no such claim for themselves: the native officer is content with his present position, and finds his present duties sufficiently honourable and responsible. Three distinctions the native officer receives, and dearly prizes, from his white superior. The Briton shakes hands with him—it breaks a Hindu's caste, but still he likes it—calls him Sahib, and acknowledges his right to sit on a chair. He can rise to resaldar- or subadar-major, which is a grade between captain and major. In the cavalry—where prompt and unswerving decision is especially required—the squadrons are led by Europeans; the company commanders of the infantry are native subadars. With these privileges and duties, the fighting races—being simple-minded, and conceiving the British to be in most points a superior race—are well satisfied. The Prime Minister of Nepal has actually made it a condition of the supply of Ghurka recruits that they must always be led by Englishmen.

It is true that the limited field of ambition may disincline some of the best elements among the ruling classes from the military career, which would be their natural vocation. But the general view appears to be that this is inevitable. In the first place, it is none so certain that the ruling classes want commissions. The flower of Indian chivalry, the Rajputs, certainly prefer the soldiering they get in their own Imperial Service Corps to a life which, after all, whatever prospects might be opened to native officers, must always bring them into direct subordination to a British officer of one rank or another. A maharajah will usually be loath to obey even a major-general. The practical difficulties, too, would be great, not to say insuperable. It would be difficult to mix British and native officers in one regiment; when a man's religion forbids him to eat with you or touch your hand, it must needs militate against corporate spirit in a mess. To officer battalions and regiments wholly with natives would be equally difficult : the more warlike races have not as yet made much progress in education, and they are apt to lose their heads in action through untempered gallantry. Left to himself, the native officer will sometimes forget to give his men the range, or charge at large on sight. With British officers he remains cool, having no more responsibility than he is equal to, and plays an invaluable part. You must remember that fighting in these latter days is becoming as complex as quadratic equations, with a good deal more to flurry the operator. When a Sikh or a Pathan or a Ghurka passes into Sandhurst it will be time to consider the question further.

Certainly the native officers did not look a discontented class. As they marched past Sir George Luck at the end of the manœuvres, stiff yet easy in ·the saddle, and flashed their tulwars in the salute, they bristled with pride in their position—behind the sahibs, ahead of the men.

VII

DELHI

DELHI is the most historic city in all historic India. It may not be the oldest—who shall say which is the oldest among rivals all coeval with time ?—though it puts in a claim for a respectable middle-age, dating from 1000 B. C. or so. It has at least one authentic monument which is certainly fourteen or fifteen hundred years old. At that time Delhi's master called himself Emperor of the World, and emperors, at least of India, have ruled there almost ever since. Mohammed, an Afghan of Ghor, took it in 1193; Tamerlane, the Mogul, sacked it two hundred years later; Nadir Shah, the Persian, in 1739; Ahmed Shah Durani, another Afghan, in 1756; the Marathas took it three years later. Half a century on, in 1803, General Lake took the capital of India for Britain. And British it has been ever since—except for those few months in 1857, when the Mutiny brought the ghost of the Mogul empire into the semblance of life again; till Nicholson stormed the breach in the Kashmir Bastion, and dyed Delhi British for ever with his blood.

Look from the Ridge, whence the columns marched

out to that last capture : the battered trophy of so many conquerors remains wonderfully fresh and fair. It seems more like a wood than a city. The rolls of green are only spangled with white, as if it were a suburb of villas standing in orchards. Only the snowy domes and tall minarets, the cupolas and gilded pinnacles, betray the still great and populous city that nestles below you and takes breath after her thousand troubles.

Yet Delhi is still seamed with the scars of her spoilers, and still jewelled with remnants of the gems they fought for. If you take them in order, you will go first, not into the city, but eleven miles south, to the tower Kutb Minar. Through the dust of the road, rising out of the springing wheat, among the mud-and-mat huts before which squat the brown-limbed peasants, you see the country a litter of broken walls, tumbling towers, rent domes. There are fragments of seven cities built by seven kings before the present Delhi was. Eleven miles of them bring you to the tower and mosque of Kutb.

Kutb-ed-Din was a slave who raised himself to Viceroy of Delhi when the Mussulmans took it, then to Emperor of Hindustan and founder of a dynasty. Whether he or his son or the last of the Hindu kings built the tower, antiquaries are undecided and others careless. It is enough that here is one landmark in Delhi's history, one splendid monument reared for a symbol of triumph by a victor whom now nobody can certainly identify. It is a colossal, five-storeyed tower, two hundred and forty feet high, of nearly fifty feet diameter at the base, and tapering to nine feet at the top. Tiny balconies with balustrades mark the junctions of the storeys: the three lower are red stone, the two upper—dwarfed just under the sky—faced with white marble. All the red part is fluted into alternate semicircles and right angles, netted all over with tracery, and belted with inscriptions under the balconies. But the details strike you little: the vertical lines of the fluting only give the impression that this is one huge pillar with a red shaft and a white capital—a pillar that might form part of the most tremendous temple in the world, yet stands quite seemly alone by reason of its surpassing bigness.

Pant to the top. It will do you good, though the view is nothing. The country is an infinite green-and-brown chess-board of young corn and fallow, dead-flat on every side, ugly with the complacent plainness of all very rich country. Beyond the sheeny ribbon of the Jumna, north, south, east, west, into the blurred horizon, you can see only land and land and land—a million acres with nothing on them to see—except the wealth of India and the secret of the greatness of Delhi.

Then look down past your toes and you will see the evidence of some of Delhi's falls. From the ground you will have noticed ruins about you; but there the Kutb Minar dwarfs everything. Now .you see that you stand above a field of broken arches, solitary pillars, stumps of towers, and in the middle of what must once have been a town of mosques and tombs. Before it was that, it was a town of Hindu temples and palaces. In the court of the ruined mosque stands a solid wrought-iron pillar—little enough to look at, but curious, because it is at least fifteen hundred years old, and there is nothing else quite like it in the world. It bears a Sanskrit inscription to the effect that this is "the Arm of Fame of Raja Dhava, who conquered his neighbours and won the undivided sovereignty of the earth."

Poor Raja Dhava! The temples of generations that had already forgotten him are swept utterly away; the mosque of their conquerors stands now only as a few shattered red arches and pillars with defaced flowers wilting on them. Beyond that is the base of what was once to be a tower more than twice as high as the Kutb Minar, but was never even finished. The very tower you stand on has been buffeted by earthquake, and great part of it is mere restoration. And Delhi, which in the year One stood here, has drifted away almost out of sight from the summit and left these forlorn fragments to decay without even the consolation of neighbourhood.

Poets and preachers have already pointed the necessary moral: let us go back to the city. Here at least is the Jumma Musjid, the great mosque, saved complete out of the storms—a baby of little more than two hundred years, to be sure, but still something. It is said to be the largest mosque in the world— a vast stretch of red sandstone and white marble and gold upstanding from a platform reached on three sides by flights of steps so tall, so majestically wide, that they are like a stone mountain tamed into order and proportion at an emperor's will. Above the brass-mounted doors rise red portals so huge that they almost dwarf the whole—red galleries above them, white marble domes above them, white marble min- arets rising higher yet, with pillars and cupolas and gilded pinnacles above all. Beside the gateways the walls of the quadrangle seem to creep along the ground; then, at the corners, rise towers with more open chambers, more cupolas and gilded pinnacles. Within, above the cloistered quadrangle, bulge three pure white domes—not hemispheres, like Western domes, but complete globes, only sliced away at the base and tapering to a spike at the top—and a slender minaret flanks each side.

The whole, to Western eyes, has a strange effect. Our own buildings are tighter together, gripped and focused more in one glance; over the Jumma Musjid your eye must wander, and then the mind must connect the views of the different parts. If you look at it near you cannot see it all; if far, it is low and seems to straggle. The West could hardly call it beautiful: it has proportion, but not compass. Therefore it does not abase you, as other great buildings do: somehow you have a feeling of patronage towards it. Yet it is most light and graceful with all its bulk: it seems to suit India, thus spread out to get its fill of the warm sun. It looks rich and lavish, as if space were of no account to it.

Between this mosque and the Jumna river stands the fort—the ancient stronghold and palace of the Mogul emperors. A towering wall encloses it, Titanic slabs, always of the same red sandstones, moated and battlemented. You go in under the great Lahore Gate—its massiveness is lightened by more domes and arches, more gilt and marble on top of it, —you come in—alas and alas!—to barracks and married quarters and commissariat stores. You look for turquoised hubble-bubbles, and you find the clay of Private Atkins. It is disillusion, and yet it is very Delhi. The remains of Aurungzebe's palaces are lost among the imperial plant of Aurungzebe's inheritors.

Yet search diligently for the remains; since, except in Agra, you will never find anything like it in the world. You come first to the Hall of Audience, an open redstone portico with a wall at its back, and are about to pass it. The gleam of marble arrests you. Within, against the wall, is a slab of white marble; above it a throne of the same with pillars and canopy. But it is not the marble you look at— it is the wonderful work that veins it; the throne is embroidered with mosaic. And the wall behind is a sheet of miniature pictures—birds and flowers and fruit—all picked out in paint and precious stones. You marvel, but pass on to the Hall of Private Audience. Then, indeed, your breath catches with amazement.

It is an open, oblong portico or pavilion on columns, with an arched and domed squarer pavilion beside it, whence a bay-window steps out of the wall to look over the swamps and the river below. The whole is all white marble asheen in the sun, but that is the least part of the wonder. Walls and ceilings, pillars and many-pointed arches, are all inlaid with richest, yet most delicate, colour. Gold cornices and scrolls and lattices frame traceries of mauve and pale green and soft azure. What must it have been, you ask yourself, when the peacock throne blazed with emerald and sapphire, ruby and diamond, from the now empty pedestal, and the plates of burnished silver reflected its glories from the roof? The Marathas melted down the ceiling, and Nadir Shah took away the throne to Persia; yet, even as it is, the opulence of it leaves you gasping. It is not gaudy, does not even astonish you with its costliness: it is simply sumptuous and luxurious, surpassing all your dreams.

After this chaste magnificence you may refresh your eye with the yet purer beauty of the Moti Musjid, the Pearl Mosque—a fabric smaller than a racquet-court, walled with cool grey-veined marble, blotched here and there blood-red. Just a court of walls moulded in a low relief, with a double row of three arches supporting a triple-domed roof at its end —simple, spotless, exquisite.

You have passed below the cloud-capped towers, out of the gorgeous palaces—and here is Silver Street, Delhi's main thoroughfare. The pageant fades, and you plunge into the dense squalor which is also India. Along the houses run balconies and colonnades; here also you see vistas of pillars and lattice-work, but the stone is dirty, the stucco peels, the wood lacks paint. The houses totter and lean together. The street is a mass of squatting, variegated people; bulls, in necklaces of white and yellow flowers, sleep across the pavements, donkeys stroll into the shops, goats nibble at the vegetables piled for sale down the centre of the street, a squirrel is fighting with a caged parrot. Here is a jeweller's booth, gay with tawdry paint; next, a baker's, with the shopkeeper snoring on his low counter, and everything an inch thick with dust. At one step you smell incense; at the next, garbage.

Inimitable, incongruous India! And coming out of the walls, still crumbling from Nicholson's cannon, you see mill-chimneys blackening the sky. Delhi, with local cotton, they tell you, can spin as fine as Manchester. One more incongruity! The iron pillar, the ruined mosque, the jewelled halls, the shabby street, and now the clacking mill. That is the last of Delhi's myriad reincarnations.

VIII

CALCUTTA

THERE are three Calcuttas—the winter capital of India, the metropolis of the largest white population in the country, and the tightest-packed human sardine-tin known outside China.

As you see it first, it is the only British town in India. Both as seat of Government and centre of European population it has taken on an English aspect, which you do not find elsewhere. Not only are buildings English, but they are English buildings of good standing. The prevalent style is eighteenth-century classical; the colour is the buff-white of Regent Street. As a matter of history, the houses are adaptations of Italian and Sicilian models; but they look Greek. Almost every one has its portico, its Doric or Ionic pillars, its balustraded roof. In the filthiest native quarters you will come on such houses, grimy, peeling, tumbling to pieces—the homes of forgotten sahibs, now forlorn islands in a lapping sea of bamboo shanties. Calcutta, you can see, has not merely a history—every town in India has that—but a British history.

Its history, indeed, and its greatness are all British,

wherein it is unique among Indian cities. It is not the cradle of British India: the cradle was Surat, which was opened to British trade in 1612, and in the Imperial Library at Calcutta you reverence, as the oldest archives of British India, the letters of the Surat factors. To the profane mind the most natural touch is found in the list of them, wherein an unfortunate, otherwise obscure, Val Hearst, is branded to eternity as " drinking sott."

It was in 1687 that the Company came to Calcutta, and named Fort William after the Dutch king who came two years later. In those days, and long after, distinction between the imperial and commercial was not : despatches then were letters from " the gentlemen at Fort St. David's," and the administrator who now becomes an Honourable Member of Council then aspired to the office of Export Warehouse-keeper. Only in 1774, when Warren Hastings became first Governor-General of Bengal, with a vague superintendence over Madras and Bombay, did Calcutta begin to be imperial.

The year before Fort William had been finished, and still remains—a ludicrous anachronism now, for what need could there be of a fort in Bengal ?—but an imposing document of Anglo-Indian history. An octagon of fosse and grass-grown rampart, bastion and curtain and sally-port, with the Governor's buff-white Georgian house standing up out of it—it remains to remind you of what nowadays you might easily forget: there lived strong men before the North-West Frontier.

The other later public buildings of Calcutta are neither few nor mean, but they hardly do themselves justice. They either hide behind trees or else they step forward on to your toes, so that you must rick your neck to look at them. Government House is in the fashion. From the high rails and sentries you infer that something important is within; but unless you chance to turn your head in the right direction from the Maidan—Calcutta's park—you might live in the place for weeks and never see what it was. But when you see it, it is plainly a king's palace. Designed, as everybody now knows, after Kedleston Hall, which Adams built, the imitation was begun by Lord Wellesley exactly a hundred years ago: at the time the Directors of the East India Company were painfully shocked at his extravagance. Government House stands in a garden full of lawns and tall trees. From the central building, which is crowned by a truncated dome, radiate galleries connecting with four wings; so that the impression of the house from either side is of a light buff semicircle with Ionic columns and a porch in the centre, and similar columns outlining the wings. To the porch of the main entrance you go, a couchant sphinx on either side, up a double flight of steps, imperially wide; the impression of solidity combined with lightness is distantly suggestive of the Capitol at Washington. Left and right of this staircase shoot two tufted palms with ivy clinging round their trunks—England and India intertwining. Left and right and in front are antique cannon on pale blue carriages; that in the middle rests between the wings of a dragon.

South of the proconsulate spreads the Maidan, which is Arabic and Persian and Hindustani for a flat open space. To the profane mind the broad expanses of burnt grass—about a mile and a half square—suggest Clapham Common in August; but the Maidan is much more. At one corner is a racecourse, elsewhere tennis-courts, golf-links, bicycle-tracks, cricket-pitches, riding-roads. It is an exercise-ground for horses and dogs, a playground for children, and a fashionable promenade for all Calcutta. In the evening, when the sky is red over the bank of factory-smoke beyond the Hughli, and the spars and tackle of the ships and barks are silhouetted on it like diagrams, the unending file of carriages rolls up and down the balustraded Red Road, or lingers over the river to watch the cool sunset. Then the band plays in the Eden Gardens, and Calcutta promenades at ease till it is time to dress for dinner. The Maidan is very English —Clapham Common, Hyde Park, and Sandown Park all in one—a necessity of English life. And the statues with which it is starred everywhere—Hardinge, Lawrence, Mayo, Outram, Dufferin Roberts—are also part of the life, the imperial life of British India.

Part of the life also is on the river, for the Hughli

is as essential a limb of Calcutta as the Thames is of
London.   In the days when Simla was not, Viceroy
and merchants alike retreated out of the city stenches
to Barrackpur and other spots on the riverside.   For
two hours you steam, first past the black-funnelled
liners and the black-smoked chimneys, then through
fleets of country boats and bathing natives, then between low banks punctuated with red and grey temples,
bordered with an unbroken fringe of trees, out of
which palms lift their heads daintily.   Reach after
reach, till the thickets part and you see long stretches
of grass; you pull up at a stage wherefrom leads a
path that is a tunnel of green.   At the end you are in
an English garden and park translated into India.
Broad drives cleave through undulating lawns.   The
undulations are artificial, for drainage; but at this
rainless season the grass is grey.   Yet the bushes and
creepers blossom opulently into blue and purple and
scarlet.   This is a botanical garden in itself, with
banyan and dusty-seeded teak and pipul spreading like
a pyramid.   There are scores of other trees with
botanical names, bright green and black, brown and
red—trees swayed by the wind into bows, trees shooting bolt upright or drooping to earth, symmetrical or
gadding in feathery tumult.   Between them you catch
vistas of the blue-bosomed Hughli, dotted with bamboo boat-cottages, embroidered with palms and pagodas.   This is Barrackpur; but besides Barrackpur
there are half-a-dozen suburbs, and the merchant keeps

his steam-launch as in Finchley or Merton he used to keep his carriage.

Yet the life of Calcutta, the thirty-five-years' resident will tell you, is not what it was. In the old pictures you see Chowringhee, the great street along the Maidan, a range of pillared bungalows; now much of it is red brick, stores, hotels, boarding-houses. In the pictures the sahib drives in a chariot, often with four horses; now he uses a victoria or a dogcart. Comfort, groan the elder men, is dying out of Calcutta. In the sixties, when it took four months to come out, men found it worth while to settle down in India and make it their home. Now it is very rare to find a man who has been ten years on end in the country; though in Calcutta and among the planters of Behar and Assam you will still find some who have not seen home for fifteen and twenty years. But now, as a rule, a man goes home after five years and marries; after ten years his children go home; his wife goes to see them every other year or so. Life is dislocated. Nobody is quite sure whether he lives in India or Europe, and is at home in neither. Among the merchants—the legitimate, if not the lineal, heirs of the "gentlemen at Fort William," and still the backbone of Calcutta—there will be, say, three partners, of whom one is always spending a year at home. Or else the senior members live at home altogether and send junior assistants to India, to the detriment of British trade.

And yet, though croakers croak, trade in Calcutta is still a great and imposing business. If in cotton its ten mills cannot compare with Bombay's hundred and more, it has a monopoly of jute-spinning, and over a score of tall chimneys smirch the lucid Indian air. For every kind of retail trade it is the finest centre in India: it has the largest white population among the cities, and it is the emporium for the largest white country populations—the indigo and tea planters of Behar and Darjiling and Assam. And of late years Calcutta's trade has received a powerful impulse from the development of the Bengal coal-fields. The mines are mostly within a hundred and fifty miles west and north-west of Calcutta; the production has leaped in twenty years from 957,000 tons to 3,142,000; the exportation in ten years from 300 tons to 136,000. As steam coal it may not be so good as the Cardiff stuff: nothing is. It makes much more ash; but then, east of Suez, it is very much cheaper. When you can buy it in Colombo at 22s. a ton, and have to pay 29s. for Cardiff coal, the expense of an extra hand or two in a stoke-hold is a small matter.

If you want to be convinced that Calcutta is first of all a city of business, you need only look at its river and docks. On any day, at any hour, the Hughli carries a traffic that would not disgrace the Pool of London. Here is the British India Company, with a fleet of over a hundred steamers, alongside of the boat with which every Bengal peasant goes to market as the London tradesman goes with his cart. Up and down they ply—narrow open canoes with a tiny deck-house, Indian gondolas; or fat barges, as broad as they are long, built all over with bamboo into floating cottages, a platform above the roof for the captain, and a post and rail to fence the cargo.

The bigger ships lie three and four deep along the shore, liners and tramps, and especially sailing-ships. You wondered why you never see the big, full-rigged ships and four-masted barks about the sea or in ports of call; the reason seems to be that they are all in the Hughli. Here is the "Somali" of Liverpool, the biggest British sailing-ship, and here is the broadest-beamed boat in the world, who twice tore her own masts out by the weight of her cargo. By the side of the new boats with their high freeboard, the long, low-waisted ships of older date look like toys—but toys of what beauty! Their spars and tackle are like a web of gossamer, and their hulls, black and white, grey or green, sit down to the caressing water as a swan sits.

You can travel ten or twelve miles on a trolley round the wharfs and docks of Calcutta. Here are ships coaling or loading by basket, which is cheaper than machinery; here a steamer coming into dry dock to be cleaned; a dumpy-masted Dutch boat, her decks mere mounds of coal, filling up for Sumatra; a tank-ship waiting for a job; a British India boat tied up by the cat's cradle of railway siding, discharging a cargo from Mombasa. And among them all crawl dredgers and barges of grey mud, and the docks are checkered with brick-fields, for the port is ever increasing.

Labour is not extraordinarily cheap—a good coal-coolie makes a rupee a-day, or eight shillings a-week; which is only a couple of shillings less than some English country labourers—but it is abundant. For Calcutta is stuffed with people as a pod with peas.

You have only to look at the map. In most maps of cities the ground represents open space and the blots on it houses; in Calcutta the ground is all dwellings with little squares of open space dotted over it. You can twist and turn for hours in passages that rub each elbow as you walk through them. In some places you have to go sidewise and edge along thoroughfares like a crab, so narrow are they. The rest is dwelling-place, pigsty, cesspool, or whatever you like to call it.

The workshops are smoke-black sheds, and the workers sit with just room between them to half-use their arms. Other shops are all counter; the keeper squats on his heels among his groceries, and sleeps among them at night. Many huts are built of bamboo-matting stretched on poles, or of transparent wattle-work; but these are clean and wholesome compared with festering lanes in which people sleep and breed and sicken, because there is no room in the dens.

These people are of a new type to the stranger coming in from the North-West. The Bengali is of a yellow-brown complexion ; his face shows quick intelligence, but his eye is shifty. He goes, as a rule, bare-headed, his black hair carefully parted and oiled down. His dress is a white calico garment looped into loose drawers ; above it, in the cold weather, he wears a woollen plaid, generally brown, draped round his shoulders, or drawn over his head and mouth. Also, if he is any way prosperous, he wears ribbed woollen stockings or socks fastened up with garters or suspenders. Black is the usual colour, but I have seen sky-blue gartered with sea-green ; with a glimpse of fat brown thigh between the stocking and the drawers, it is, on the whole, the most indecent dress I know.

But by his legs you shall know the Bengali. The leg of a free man is straight or a little bandy, so that he can stand on it solidly : his calf is taper and his thigh flat. The Bengali's leg is either skin and bone, the same size all the way down, with knocking knobs for knees, or else it is very fat and globular, also turning in at the knees, with round thighs like a woman's. The Bengali's leg is the leg of a slave.

Except by grace of his natural masters, a slave he always has been and always must be. He has the virtues of the slave and his vices,—strong family affections, industry, frugality, a trick of sticking to what he wants until he wears you down, a quick imitative intelligence and amazing verbal cleverness; dishonesty, suspiciousness, lack of initiative, cowardice, ingratitude, utter incapacity for any sort of chivalry.

But his chief and marvellous trait is his abundance. Calcutta and Bengal breed, and breed, and breed. Stand on the Hughli bridge at sunset—on the east side, the factory-smoke lying in a sullen bank under the glowing scarlet; on the west, the cornfield of masts, and the funnel-smoke and the city-smoke fouling the ineffable stillness of Indian evening; a free space of blue overhead, so clear and soft and pure that it seems no longer the canopy of the world, but the embosoming infinity it really is; and the Bengalis crossing the bridge. On one side going in to Calcutta, on the other coming out, an endless drove of moving, white-clothed people, never varying in thickness, never varying in pace, never stopping, no interval, just moving, moving, like an endless belt running on a wheel. Just population : that is Bengal. Food for census, food for census!

IX

ON NATIVE SELF-GOVERNMENT

IT is generally supposed in Great Britain that India is governed wholly by our countrymen. Of the few people at home who profess to know anything about India, most encourage this delusion. The native, they will tell you, has no word in any affair of government—unless you count the annual shriek set up by a collection of half-Europeanised lawyers which, belonging to a dozen different breeds and representing none, calls itself the National Congress. The truth, as you might expect in this land of ironies, is widely different. In practice, as we shall see presently, the actual work of government is almost entirely in native hands, and largely conducted according to native methods; and in theory the government of almost every considerable town in India is in the hands of a municipal council, the majority of whose members are inevitably native. There are about seven hundred and fifty municipalities in India, which is more than twice as many as there are in England and Wales. There is also a district board—a kind of rural County Council—in each administrative district in India.

It was a generous ideal, the qualification of India

by Britain for self-government; but unluckily, like other ideals, it has not yet achieved itself. The machinery of self-government is there, but the capacity has not kept up with it. In the smaller town councils and the district councils self-government is no more than a name. The civil servant is chairman: he announces the business in hand—the repairing of a road, the imposition of an octroi on goods brought into the town—and makes a suggestion. The honourable members fold their hands before their faces and murmur, " As my lord says, so let it be." The native members feel it a vague compliment to be allowed to sit with the sahibs, but yet understand nothing at all of the business. The official sahibs are obliged by the law to keep up the farce of constitutional discussion and voting, though they well know that the council is only a more cumbrous way of doing work that they would have to do in any case.

The larger municipalities are different. There may be an official white chairman, but the councils are large, and they deal with large revenues and important business. By them you may fairly test the aptitude of the more intelligent, though less manly, races of India for self-government. It so happened, at the time of my visit, that two of these were prominently in the public eye—if you can talk of a public eye in India—as the objects of reformatory measures. These were Calcutta and Agra. Of Agra there is no need to say much: the council, to put it brutally, had been stealing the octroi duties, and it was temporarily disestablished by the Lieutenant-Governor of the North-West Provinces. On the Calcutta question there was more to be said—it even enjoyed a listless afternoon in the House of Commons; and it may fairly be taken as a convenient object-lesson in the aptitudes and tendencies of legislation by babu.

The history of municipal self-government in Calcutta is impartially discreditable to everybody concerned in it. Up to 1876 it had passed through some half-dozen incarnations, which need not trouble us; none worked well, and some did not work at all. In that year an elective municipality was created, and its constitution was modified in 1888. On the universal admission of all authorities, the two Acts creating this municipality are badly drawn, vague, and inevitably productive of bad administration; but for twenty years neither the Bengal Government nor the elective corporation took the least trouble to improve them. Neglect finally issued, as might have been predicted, in violent corrective action on the part of the Government, and in factious and hysterical opposition from the native municipality.

The Corporation of Calcutta consists of seventy-five members, called Commissioners. Fifty are elected, fifteen nominated by Government, and ten by the various commercial bodies. The franchise is confined to ratepayers, who total just two per cent. of the whole population of Calcutta. The Chair-

man is a member of the Indian Civil Service, nominated by Government. He is supposed to be the
head of the executive, but, as a matter of fact, is
liable to the control of a general committee, of eight
standing committees, and of the general meeting of all
the Commissioners, who can upset any of his actions
with retrospective effect: consequently the executive
power is in the hands of the whole body of seventy-
five Commissioners. Of these, fifty-two per cent.
are Hindus, nearly eighteen per cent. Mussulmans,
and the remaining thirty per cent. of other sections.
Less than twenty-seven per cent. are Europeans or
Eurasians. Of the fifty elected Commissioners,
twenty-three are lawyers. The municipality, therefore, deliberative and executive together, is wholly in
the hands of a working majority of Bengali Hindus.

It was duly set up, however, amid the plaudits of
the friends of progress, and all went ill till November
26, 1896. On that day the municipality was in-
augurating new drainage works, and asked the Lieutenant-Governor of Bengal, Sir Alexander Mackenzie,
to lay the foundation-stone. He complied; but when
it came to his speech, instead of the oily platitudes
awaited on such occasions, the horrified Commissioners found themselves listening to a round denuncia-
tion of themselves and all their works—or want of
them. They were an impracticable organisation from
the first, said his Honour; they talked too much;
their executive was too weak; the sanitary condition

of Calcutta was a scandal; and if they did not mend their ways there would come radical changes.

They gasped; but they did not mend their ways. On March 19, 1898, when a new Calcutta Municipal Bill was introduced into the Lieutenant-Governor's Council, they gasped yet more. As a leading organ of babu opinion puts it, " Nobody could ever dream that the citizens of the first city in India could be sought to be punished in this cruel manner by a ruler whom they had in no way offended, and whom they had given such a hearty welcome." You will note the delicious blend of Western citizenship with the oriental assumption that unpopular action on a ruler's part might naturally be due to a defect of enthusiasm in his reception. But in truth the self-governing babu had grounds for his consternation.

The Bill, after the kind of Indian official documents, is a volume of the size of a small ledger, and contains—again I quote the babu contemporary—" seven hundred sections, many of them one cubit long." Briefly, it remodelled the whole constitution of the Corporation. The Chairman was to have full power over the executive officers; and the conduct of all important business except the Budget—which was left to the whole body of Commissioners—was transferred to a general committee of twelve members; of these the Government, the commercial bodies, and the elected Commissioners were each to choose four.

" Could a greater calamity than this be conceived?" cries the native newspaper. "Now, at last, we shall have a city it will be possible to live in," said the European men of business. The controversy went fiercely on, and so did the Bill. Pamphlets, leaflets, refutations, counter-accusations, speeches, and rejoinders hurtled through Calcutta.

The first reflection that occurs to the impartial mind, on the Calcutta Bill in particular and native self-government in general, is that it was a colossal and unpardonable blunder to introduce an elective municipality at all. Representative government, a Western invention, has failed in most nations of the West: was it likely to succeed in India? India may be barbarous or civilised,—that is a question of words; but, for all the veneer of education, it is changelessly, whole-heartedly oriental. When you find a Master of Arts gravely dissertating on "a pure and noble character gradually degraded by an unhealthy passion for a beautiful young widow," what is the use of talking to him about sanitation or a General Purposes Committee? He catches up his phrases readily enough, and talks rapidly about the "slight measure of self-government," and of "strengthening the executive at the expense of the rights of the people." But, of course, the people has no right to self-government, and never has had; and the huge mass of it does not want any, and the Indian and Home Governments were incredibly weak and foolish to give any. They should have known, what the babu cannot be expected to understand, that the right to govern yourself should be exactly proportioned to your ability to govern yourself well.

Moreover, " the rights of the people " in this case means next to nothing—merely the rights of the one man out of fifty in Calcutta who has a vote. In seventy-three cases out of a hundred this voter is a Hindu. What Government really did then, in making two-thirds of the Commissioners elective, was to hand over the city to the Hindus. Numerically these form the vast majority of the population of Calcutta, but they have not the same vast preponderance of interest. It is the commercial community—European, Eurasian, Jew, Parsi, but not Bengali; for the Bengali will never trust his money in another man's hands—which has made Calcutta a great city, and maintains it such. The trade of Calcutta is responsible for three-fourths of its land value and two-thirds of its population. If it were not the centre of the largest European population in India, it would cease to be the winter capital to-morrow. For above all—why not speak plainly ?—the principal interest in Calcutta is the interest of British rule. The present municipal administration sacrifices the interests of trade and government, with others, to a single important, but far from all-important, section. On the balance of factors in the city's wellbeing, the Hindu is vastly over-represented.

On Native Self-Government

But let us get out of the bog of theory. What is the Corporation's record, and how is the new scheme likely to better it? These are the only relevant questions; and the answer to the first is that the Corporation's record is exactly what you would have expected of it. It is absurd to expect the native to be born administrator, but it is equally absurd to blame him for not being one. How should he be? In the course of struggles towards the native point of view, I interviewed one of the Commissioners—a plump, round-faced, gold-spectacled gentleman in a clerical coat, waistcoat, and trousers of dove-colour. He led off briskly with facts and figures, until he found I knew something of the Bill. The initial form of the dialogue, which it would be unprofitable to report in full, was something like this :—

Babu. " And-now-the-pro-pos-al-is-that-we-should-meet-only-once-a-year-which-re-du-ces-us-to——"

I. " How often ? "

Babu. " Four-times-but-I-was-con-sid-er-ing-it-from-the-bud-get-point-of-view-and——"

I. " How often do you have budgets now, then ? "

Babu. " Well-on-ly-once-an-nu-al-ly-of-course-but-our-re-ve-nue-is-on-ly-from-land-and-house-tax-where-as-in-Bombay——"

I. " Only land and house tax ? "

Babu. " Well-of-course-there-is-al-so-the-car-riage-tax-and-the-an-i-mal-tax-and-the-li-cence-tax-but——"

However, my friend's chief point, when he came to it, was one in which many good white authorities agree with him. How could you expect us to do perfectly, he said, when we entered on municipal life utterly without training or experience, when Government let us severely alone and did nothing to help and instruct us? How, indeed? Only what the Commissioner did not see was that his argument could be used as a condemnation of the elective system altogether; for why elect Commissioners if Government still has to do their work for them?

But the Government, whether of Britain, of India, or of Bengal, cannot use that argument ; for it created representative government and then wholly neglected to use its power to direct it in the right way. In England corporations have the Local Government Board to keep them straight, and need it. In Calcutta Government could have made by-laws, amended the law where it was defective, instituted inquiries into abuses, suggested reforms, rewarded good Commissioners with titles or decorations, and especially set up proper judicial establishments to enforce the sanitary laws. Instead, it left the Commissioners to stew in their own juice—and they left the slums of Calcutta to stew in theirs.

If you care to go a little into the details of the case for and against the present Corporation of Calcutta, there is no need to enlarge except on two principal points. The question whether the Commissioners talk too much came much into the discussion, but after all it is a minor one. They say they do not; others say that if you are outside the door during one of their meetings you would think they were tearing the Chairman to pieces. Britons and Bengalis have different standards of the necessity for talk. " You have drunk too much fire-water," said the missionary to the Indian chief. " I have drunk enough," he replied. " You have drunk too much." " Well, too much is enough," said the chief: and it is so with the Bengali and talking.

My babu's contention seems reasonable enough. People think the Commissioners are always talking, said he, only because the long debates are reported, while the undiscussed business is not; the same misapprehension exists about our own L.C.C. The relevant question is, Talk or not, do they do the work ?

On the whole, with every effort to be fair, I should say that they do not. It is partly their own fault, but more the Act's, and most of all native self-government's at large. If you take a number of superficially educated Bengalis of the middle class, dignify them with the title of Commissioners, and give them the control of a vast city, it is certain that they will grow a little above themselves. They will want to have their fingers in every pie, and the Calcutta Act makes this particularly easy. In Bombay the executive, under the official Chairman, is almost independent of the deliberative body; in Calcutta it is wholly subordinate.

This is a risky arrangement, even in London; in India it is foredoomed to disaster. The Corporation has grown much too strong for its Chairman. Of late the Chairmen have been frequently changed, often before they had settled into their work. To match your wits for four hours on end, in the hot weather, at the end of a long day's work, against anything from a dozen to half a hundred fluent and verbally ingenious Bengalis, is trying to the hardest man: some were ripe for furlough when they began it—all became over-ripe after a season of it. It has been comparatively easy, therefore, for the Commissioners to concentrate all power in their own hands. To make it easier yet they hit on an ingenious device, called the Complaints Committee. It was customary two years ago to have enormous standing committees; one had forty-eight members out of the seventy-five, and this Complaints Committee had thirty-three. It was formed to receive complaints against the executive officers of the Corporation. The native is always burning to petition somebody about something, and complaints came in a turbid spate. They arrived at the rate of twenty a-day, and a single one took a fortnight to dispose of. By the end of a year, at this rate, there would be 7274 of them awaiting attention. So it was settled that the Committee should only consider complaints referred to it by the Chairman or a

Commissioner. Who now so important as the Commissioner? Who so prosperous as the half-dozen or so dishonest men among them? The native they quarrelled with had to wait eighteen months for permission to put up a latrine; the relative or the friend or the man with a little money to lay out in the right quarter was able to evade the building acts and increase his rent-rolls.

With a system like this it would be folly to look for good executive administration. The constitution, it has been said, is all brake-power and no engine. There is no motive power. The Chairman can be overruled and his action annulled. The committees are jealously watching, checking, economising. As for the subordinate officials—the engineer, surveyor, health officer, down to the very inspector of nuisances —they hold their offices at the pleasure of the Commissioners at large, and owe their appointments to them. A Hindu lives with all his relations under one roof, and nepotism with him is almost a religious duty; hence unblushing solicitation, touting, and occasionally bribery. A bad officer can get his post if .he is agreeable to the Commissioners; a good one can lose it if he offends them or any of their relations.

Considering all this, it is wonderful that the municipality has done even as much as it has. It is not denied that the Commissioners have made some halting progress. Their credit is good, and they have reduced their rate of interest in seven years from five to three and one-half per cent.; loans have been tendered for five and six times over. They have cut Harrison Road from the Hughli Bridge eastward through some of the worst slums of Calcutta—a broad avenue nearly five miles long, garnished with trees, established with tall, well-built, and airy houses, —here the long wooden verandahs of tenement-houses rising over lines of shops, there brick or stone places of business. It is a street to which any city might point proudly. But it is an isolated case, and my babu Commissioner's own figures condemn him. He produced tables which showed—deducting suburban expenditure, which only came into the municipality's functions in 1889—that his council had spent proportionately less in the improvement and sanitation of Calcutta than did the Justices of the Peace who administered it before their time. He excused this by explaining that the resources of the Corporation were very limited; but the damning fact remains that it has not raised as much revenue as it is entitled to do. Its Act allows a rate of twenty-three per cent., which is very low compared with our rates at home; for the last seven years it has only raised nineteen and one-half per cent.—and that although the value of land in Calcutta is very high and the profits of owners prodigious. In some parts of the city land is worth £40,000 an acre, and the most valuable plots are precisely those which are covered with flimsy hovels crawling with naked humanity.

For, after all, in sanitary matters, you must judge authority not by what it has done, but by what it has left undone; and on this showing the verdict must be black against native self-government. Calcutta is a shame even to the East. In its slums dock-coolies and mill-hands do not live: they pig. Houses choke with unwholesome breath; drains and compounds fester in filth. Wheels compress decaying refuse into roads. Cows drink from wells soaked with sewage, and the flour of bakeries is washed in the same pollution.

What wonder that the death-rate of the whole city is thirty-six in the thousand—in one ward, forty-eight in the thousand? The deaths that might be prevented by decent cleanliness are reckoned at more than one in every three. It is a miracle that plague struck Calcutta as lightly as it did; for its state is an invitation to pestilence and a menace to the world. So far it has escaped by sheer luck; next year or the next we may hear of thousands on thousands of victims. You cannot be astonished at anything when the Commissioners—who had known of all these things for twenty years—though they formed committees and established hospitals with exemplary zeal, formed vigilance committees to notify cases of disease which did nothing at all.

Why? Because the B. A. is still an Oriental: either in his heart he hates sanitary regulations as fervently as the sweeper, or he is afraid of the sweeper's anger if he enforces them. He wants to combine Western representative government with Eastern dirt, Herbert Spencer with the laws of Manu—to eat his cake and have it. "My nephew," lamented a native lady, "will be the ruin of us all. I am a widow with young children, yet he must needs join a vigilance committee. He will be knocked on the head and we shall all come to ruin; why must he interfere with other people's business?"

The truth is that we have made a capital error with the Bengali—capital in any case, fatal with him. We have instructed, but not educated, him. We have taught him from books instead of facts, taught him the words of civilisation and not the things. We have therefore failed with him, as we deserved.

X

THE HIGHER EDUCATION

It is hard to determine who is the more unfortunate man here—a man who has a marriageable daughter, but cannot provide for her marriage, or a man who has a son who has failed to pass an examination. Take the case of the latter first. He starves himself to provide for the education of his son. The son, let us suppose, does his best to pass an examination—most boys do so in this country. But it happens that he falls ill on the first day of his examination. He must thus wait another year. The subjects of his study disgust him, for he had once gone through them. He appears at another examination, but unluckily a sudden dizziness seizes him one day while writing his answers; he fails to recollect something with which he was quite familiar, and again fails in the examination. When the news is brought to him that he has failed, he falls down in a swoon—or something worse happens to him. The blow makes him something like an idiot for life. If his unthinking parent chastises him after this, he purchases four pice worth of opium and kills himself. What is a failed candidate? He is a doomed man! He is as doomed as a life-convict. Night-keeping and hard study had destroyed his health. Luckily he does not live long. A failed candidate, generally speaking, does not survive his disgrace. He dies either of consumption or of indigestion. He knows he is not wanted in society. If he has evil propensities, he becomes a dangerous member of society. But, luckily, youths belonging to those classes who compete for university honours seldom carry with them any criminal proclivities.

No; you are not dreaming. This is an exact transcript of a leading article which lately appeared in one of the most influential of the native newspapers in Calcutta. I give you my word it did.

Having read it, you can begin to form some idea of that wonder of nature, the babu; or, at least, you can begin to perceive how impossible it is to form any sane idea of a wonder so unnatural. This extract is the babu displayed, complete and essential. I suppose there is nothing like it in the world—thousands of people, speaking and writing an alien tongue almost as if it were their own, yet thinking and feeling a whole world apart from the spirit of it. This grotesque prodigy is the fine flower of the system of education which we, with infinite care, have grafted on to the Indian intelligence.

When we began to organise the higher education of India, it was decided, mainly on the impulse of Macaulay, that it should be founded on an English basis. The ancient languages and the ancient philosophies of India were depressed into a secondary place: in the five universities we have set up in Bombay, Calcutta, Madras, Allahabad, and Lahore, Sanskrit or Pali stands on much the same footing as Latin or Greek, with which India has plainly but the remotest concern. Examinations, whether in high schools or in universities, are conducted in English: English literature, English mental and moral philosophy, English systems of mathematics, English methods of science, are the highroads to a degree. The educated native is to be intellectually indistinguishable from the educated Briton.

On the surface this experiment has been astonishingly successful. In Bengal, and to a great extent in Madras and Bombay, the native took to European education as a duck to water. It is true that he never learned to talk or write exactly like an Englishman—his speech and style have always an exotic flavour; yet the numbers who learned to speak, read, and write fluently, and who passed fairly difficult examinations in a foreign tongue, testify to an application and an elastic intelligence which you will hardly parallel elsewhere in the world. Thousands matriculate in the universities yearly; more than a thousand take degrees. The experiment seems triumphant; and none, naturally, triumph louder than the natives themselves. "We fully admit," writes the organ I have quoted above, "that the Englishman is very intelligent and shrewd; but we also contend that the Indian"—meaning the Bengali—"is fully his peer." Or, another day, "It must be borne in mind that the Indian populace are more intelligent than a London populace." Ten minutes in a native village are enough to establish the imbecility of this last proposition; yet on paper it would seem to be true.

Unfortunately the whole system of higher education in India is radically vicious in plan, and, if not actually disastrous, at least almost profitless in effect. It is organised solely with a view to results on paper.

The Higher Education

The universities have been modelled on that of London, which is probably the worst in the world. They do not teach, but only examine. Not merely that; they only examine on set subjects and on set books. The candidate must not be expected to know anything outside his cram-books. Such an examination can never be any real test of capacity or even of knowledge, but only of memory—a useful gift, but no more: of real education it furnishes no criterion whatever. The consequence is that, in Calcutta at least, a man of fair but not extraordinary intelligence, but of powerful memory, can attain to his B.A. degree by simple, ignoble learning by rote. An analysis of the examination papers shows that a native, if he will take the trouble to learn by heart the introductions and notes to his books of English literature, the texts of his books on psychology and ethics, the introductions to his Latin books and Bohn's translation of the same, can write himself B.A. without the feeblest approach to anything that could be called a thought of his own.

That, you say, must be a very bad examination; but you can hardly believe that anybody would have the memory or the application to perform such a feat. You are wrong: it is actually done, or as near as makes no difference. A few years ago, at Calcutta, a candidate for the degree of M.A. took up Latin. His translations were literally flawless. Only the examiner noticed that in every case he began his rendering a few lines before the passage which was printed on the paper given him and finished a few lines later.   He had learned the crib by heart, fixing his places by proper names, or, when these were scarce, by some mnemonic arrangement of his own —and there he was!   After all, the same thing has been done at Oxford and Cambridge.   Many of us used to know whole books of Virgil and Horace by heart in Latin; why should not a Bengali, speaking English and with a direct pecuniary interest in the business, be able to learn them in English ?

The examiner in this case reported that his man had failed, whereon the candidate appealed to the governing body.   This was mainly composed of natives, who, having the interests of education—that is, of getting degrees—at heart, insisted on the man being allowed to pass in Latin, though, on his own admission, he hardly knew a word of the language.   For the bad system is made worse by the fact that the universities have been allowed to come under native management, which means laxity and utter carelessness about true education.   There used to be a *viva voce* examination at Bombay, and, as I learn from a gentleman who had much experience of it, its disclosures were sufficiently amusing.   " You say in your papers here," he would say to the examinee, " that Sir Walter Scott is a most beautiful writer. Now here are his works: pick out your favourite." Whereon the examinee would turn green, for this was the first time he had ever set eyes on so much as the covers of the works of that beautiful writer Scott. But the natives abolish this part of the examination; and in general they are always tending to lower the standard.

It is true that the standard, especially of Bombay, is still fairly high—about that of London, and considerably above that of the pass-man at Oxford or Cambridge. But as it is all a matter of rote, it matters little what the theoretical standard may be. The candidate has a direct pecuniary interest in passing, and no labour will stop him. In the first place, there is Government service. The various Secretariats absorb a vast number of graduates as clerks, and though the general influence of the clerk on Government is here, as everywhere, most pernicious, they make very good clerks indeed. But then, there are not nearly enough clerkships to go round. The calendar of the University of Calcutta shows over five thousand of B.A.'s alone—a couple of batches of three to four hundred apiece, by the way, named Bandyopadhyay and Mukhopadhyay respectively. Those who get into the public service are established for life; but the others feel that they have been ill-used. They have not yet got clear of the idea—so skin-deep is their Europeanising—that to have a degree is in itself a passport to public employment. How should they, when even to have failed in an examination is regarded as giving a claim to a salary? It sounds like comic opera; but I· know many men who have had natives again and again appeal for posts with the sole qualification that they have failed in a university examination. Consumption and indigestion spare them somehow, and now failure is almost a degree in itself. " F. M., Calcutta "—Failed in Matriculation —may shortly be expected to appear on the babu's card.

The surplus Bandyopadhyays, for whom Government finds no room, go to reinforce the native press. They are discontented; they have their grievance,—though, mark you, they have been educated at the public expense—at the expense, that is, of the ryot,—and consequently the native press is steadily disaffected. Most of it professes loyalty, but it never misses a chance of carping at the Government, or at white men in general. So far, then, as the native press is a danger, it is one which, by the usual irony of India, we have created for ourselves in a sincere attempt to benefit the native. I fancy, for myself, that the Anglo-Indian official is apt to be a little nervous about the native press, and by taking notice of it to feed the vanity on which it lives. It is impertinent, certainly, often wilfully inaccurate, and sometimes, in the vernacular, filthily scurrilous; but the best way to deal with it is probably to do nothing. Let disloyalty talk and write as it will; after all, why should a native of India be loyal to Britain? But the moment it begins to act, shoot and spare not.

The Higher Education

Much better to enjoy quietly the unfailing deliciousness of the native press. There is, for instance, a monthly review called " The National Magazine," which never fails to please. Its tone is consistently moral, sensible, and dignified, but occasionally its English flowers a little luxuriantly. " It was some time before I could extricate him," writes an expert bicycle-rider of a pupil, " when, lo! a very much bruised and sprained-ankle man was he." Or here is a description of a young man's first step in vice. " He heard the soft, delicious, soul-abandoning sounds of music, and saw the youthful nautch-girls, robed in voluptuous dress, come and seat before him, while the distribution of garlands of jasmine and sprinkling of rose-water lent what is generally termed a double arrow to the Cupid's bow." A local correspondent of a daily paper is happily inspired when he says that some of the officials " are in the jungle with gun in the jolly time of Xmas joy." But perhaps obituaries offer most facility for elegance of composition. One organ says of a pleader—and remember that nearly all the prominent babus follow this trade—" his child-like simplicity fascinated all, and was proof against the demoralising influences of his honourable profession." Another gentleman " was a man of uncommon sense, devoted to God all along his life." By the death of a patron he " was compelled to live in his nativity at Somsa. . . . The deceased was the gem hidden at Somsa, quite unknown to many, but known to almost all the Pundits of Bengal. His death has made this part of the country dark as it were." Finally, lest you think there may be exaggeration in stories of babu English, take this extract from an appreciation of certain orators of the native Congress. The subject is a gentleman called Pundit Madan Mohan Malavayya.

His speech is as mellifluous as his name. He has a sweet voice, and is one of the most enthusiastically welcomed of men on the Congress platform. Neither tall nor short, not stout but thin, not dark, dressed in pure white, with a white robe which goes round his shoulders and ends down below the knees, Mr. Madan Mohan stands like Eiffel's Tower when he addresses his fellow-Congressmen. He stands slanting forward, admirably preserving his centre of gravity. His speeches are full of pellucid and sparkling statements, and his rolling and interminable sentences travel out of his mouth in quick succession, producing a thrilling impression on the audience. There is music in his voice; there is magic in his eye; and he is one of the sweet charmers of the Congress company.

And now, do you know one more reason why the native seeks university distinctions? The gentleman who learned the Bohn by heart was asked why he put himself to so much trouble. To raise his price in the marriage market, he serenely replied. He would get a wife with a larger dowry as M.A. than as B.A.; how much larger than as F.M. or nothing? If you do not believe me, listen to a writer in my " National Magazine," who himself deprecates the practice. " Let alone the boy," he says; " his father of maturer years will not be ashamed to demand from you cash to the tune of not less than 2000 rupees, if you will only ask him to marry your daughter to his son. And why so? Only because the boy has obtained a certificate of matriculation from the university." It is sober truth: the fathers of daughters will pay heavily—and do—to purchase sons-in-law who have passed examinations.

Did I say comic opera? It is beyond farce; it is beyond the games of the nursery. We have given India the treasures of our Shakespeare, our Bacon, our Huxley; and India uses them as convenient pegs wherefrom to hang quotations on the husband market!

O India, India! What jests are perpetrated in thy name!

THE MAHARAJAH BAHADUR

THE first time I met my friend the Maharajah, he was wearing his blue and green. An ultramarine satin tunic over grass-green silk trousers is a combination which arrests the European eye at any time. In this case it enclosed a little wizen-faced man, with eyes now tending together, then flitting here and there with an abundance of white eyeball. Add a little jewelled satin cap, a drooping black moustache, and pointed yellow-leather shoes: with joyful recognition—Heaven forgive me—I cried, " An illustration of Aladdin ! "

I repented of my irreverence later, for he is one of the greatest men in Bengal, which is little, and deserves to be, which is much. He is the largest landowner in the province, and his tax-free rent-roll comes to about a quarter of a million a-year. Elsewhere in India, you must understand, the State is usually the landlord, according to the immemorial custom of the land. But in Bengal, a hundred and six years ago, the Government made what is called the Permanent Settlement—giving over the land to zemindars, who, under the Mogul rule, had been hereditary land-agents and tax-collectors. Finding the zemindars collecting rent from the cultivators, it is possible that the Indian Government mistook them for landlords in the European sense ; at any rate, they were declared proprietors of the land, subject to a fixed yearly tax, which was never to vary. It never has varied ; in the meantime, the population of cultivators has increased vastly, and their industry has reclaimed vast tracts of waste land. All this increment has been swallowed by the zemindars, who have repaid the ryot in many cases by raising his rent and confiscating his land. The average zemindar does no public service in return for the vastly enhanced income which he owes to the security of our rule : he does not even pay income-tax, since in India income-tax and land-tax are never paid together : thus the Bengal zemindar escapes on both counts. On the other side the Government loses revenue which it would otherwise reasonably exact, and the ryot loses everything he has. It is encouraging, in the face of accusations of perfidy, that our Government in India prefers to struggle against deficits when it could easily put its Budget straight by breaking the promise of a century back—an expedient that any other Government there ever was or could be in India would have flown to long ago.

The Maharajah is a zemindar among zemindars— the richest of them all—yet no true zemindar at heart. The ryots of his estate—until a few months back his brother's—instead of having the records of their rights suppressed and destroyed and their fields then let to a higher bidder, have found their landlord always munificent in every public enterprise. The new Maharajah, to complete the inventory of him, has spent a couple of years in the Civil Service for the benefit of his mind, and a couple as a half-naked fakir for that of his soul, is a member of the Viceroy's Legislative Council, and a constant reader of the London newspapers. I mentioned this to a friend as almost incredible. "If he told you so," was the reply, "he does. He always tells the truth, and so did his brother. It's unusual in this country."

To-day he was to be formally invested with the title of Maharajah Bahadur—which means "Lord-Great-King"—by the Lieutenant-Governor of Bengal. His village is comparatively near Calcutta, so that I only had to start the night before. I changed carriages, half-asleep, and the next thing I knew— the Ganges.

The holy Ganges floated great and grey at my feet. Out of the blackness of the west it came naked into the muffled grey of dawn. Except the bare train that had brought me to the ghat and the bare steamer that was to carry me across, I could see nothing but chill yellow shore and sandbank and chill white water. A pilgrim issuing from some little shrine, where he had slept, shivered and shook knee-deep in the stream, and his soaked white drawers clung to him dankly.

The Maharajah Bahadur

When you travel in small countries you generally find
that you start and arrive at convenient hours—catch
your train after a comfortable breakfast, and get to
your destination in easy time for dinner. In a country
of the size of India you must take your arrivals and
changes as you find them. So that I found the palm-
fringed, basking Ganges of my dreams to be a broad,
noiseless, colourless flood, which the red ball of the
sun hardly awoke to more than the clammy lustre of
a dead fish's eye. The seams of sandbank were pale
with cold; the shores were only sandbank prolonged
to a greater capacity for numb desolation.

But the sun climbed undiscouraged, rent the mists,
and began to warm India into life again. The cease-
less caw of crows began to half-soothe, half-madden
for another day; the keen smell of dung-fires rose
into the lighter air. By the time the melancholy
Ganges had sunk into its desert behind us the land
was possible for life, and we were puffing briskly
through the brilliant tobacco, dark indigo, and pale
opium-poppies of Behar. We puffed and puffed,
halting or changing now and again, till the astounding
sight of five white men in a carriage together hinted
that something unusual was afoot. A station or two
later, sure enough, appeared arches shouting "Welcome!" and "Long live the Empress!" There was
a concourse of servants in maroon and gold liveries,
and a great array of dust-clothed natives. From the
station the road was marked by green and red flags

every ten yards or so, with half-uniformed native policemen standing at attention to guard them. We were plainly there.

As we drove from the station, the crowd became every moment thicker. By the time we swung in under the last of the arches there was a wall of them—a purple or yellow turban here and there, but for the most part an unaffected peasant crowd in the labour-stained white calico of their working days. Their demeanour was respectful but confident, they came very near the apogee of looking glad. And it was evident in a minute that we were on a model estate. The garden we were rolling through was without reproach for order and neatness—perhaps the only native's garden in India that is. Presently we came to the stables: I rubbed my eyes, and asked if this were really untidy India. Solid buildings, speckless cleanness, sound drainage, air everywhere—it was no wonder that coats were like satin, eyes bright, and action free. Here was a scion of the house of Danegelt, English coachers, Arabs, Walers, country-breds, and scientific crosses—well over a hundred in all. Not that either the late or the present Maharajah is a great sportsman; they are simply needed to do the work of the enormous estate and household.

While we looked, the team was put into the coach and off we went, four-in-hand, to see the grounds. It was not easy to tell their size, for the drives wound in and out, twisting till you could hardly tell whether you had gone a couple of miles or had circled back to your starting-point. In this season they were parched; leaves were pale, and grass almost white. But even so they were cooled to the eye with blue lakes and the shade of swishing trees. They were tufted with every variety of palm, pillars of grey stem with capitals of green sheath, or the dwarf crowns of fronds that till lately it cost a man's life to smuggle out of Japan. Below them sloped tiers of bushes, green, red, and yellow; below these nestled flowers. It was the East for profusion, the West for trimness.

So we came to a denser crowd before a walled court, and entered; and then looked and blinked. There was a guard of honour of police and half-a-dozen finely mounted sowars in the Maharajah's maroon and gold. There was a Eurasian band in short jackets, white-braided trousers, and little round braided caps stuck on one side—the band from a South Coast pier slightly soiled. But that was nothing. Besides them, standing vacuously or lolling on the grass, were wondrous creatures in the most flaring raiment eyes ever ached to contemplate. Their tunics were of such a green as cold words can never hint at—the colour of green baize fired with a tinge of the hottest yellow. Below they wore orange trousers, and vermilion decorated and inflamed the whole. They bore great fans on long silver poles—fans of yellow and crimson satin, with suns and stars embroidered on them with gold thread and pearls.

The Maharajah Bahadur

Suddenly the Maharajah bounded on to the scene, again in his ultramarine and grass-colour, dashed into the durbar tent, rushed at his guests, his English tumbling over itself in all the excitement of a child on his birthday.   Then he sprang into his state carriage, amid a boom of blessing from selected priests, and was away to meet his Honour.   I went inside the durbar tent, and gasped again.   On a dais stood the Lieutenant-Governor's chair—green velvet back, rose velvet seat, silver frame, gold borders, promiscuous pearls. Before the dais, on the right, was a similar chair for the Maharajah.   Behind was another group of baize-and-fire green, orange and vermilion; more fans; also an old gentleman in silver-flowered crimson silk with a bossy silver trumpet-shaped mace as long as himself: he smiled with concentration at nothing, and appeared to have been drinking his new lordship's health.   And to round off the silver and gold and pearls, there depended from the roof about forty chandeliers and lamps, cheap green, cheap blue, cheap purple, their wire skeletons askew, short of a drop here and a drop there, insulting the daylight, reminiscent partly of seaside lodgings, partly of the morning after an Oxford wine-party.   O India!

The pavilion was already full.   There were the European managers of the estate—something like a dozen of them—and the babus of the estate also. Portly gentlemen in spectacles and weak beards, in black or fawn garments, half coats, half shirts, but with clear skins, twinkling eyes, and smiles neither fawning nor patronising—these Behari babus were by far the cleanest men of this class I had seen. And there, especially, were all the Maharajah's rich relations to support him—and his poor relations also, to be supported. They are all Brahmans of the most exclusive sanctity: all wore white turbans of a peculiar shape, with a low peak over the forehead, and all had elaborate designs in white and red paint on their foreheads. All dripped with attar of roses. One tiny, liquid-eyed, small-boned nephew wore Prussian-blue velvet and lemon yellow; his brother at his side, droop-headed like a flower, and dissolving in smiles like a woman, was content with black and a faded Kashmir shawl—again that seaside landlady!—worn something like a bath-towel. Others wore flowered silk—lilac shirt and carmine trousers, both rippling with silver. Behind you could see the headpieces—half crowns, half pastrycooks' caps—of solemn-faced babies. And most gorgeous of all was a very important relation from off the railway line, a big man, speaking nothing but a kind of jungly Hindustani, with a caste-mark as elaborate as a cobweb on a forehead the colour of a pickled walnut, attired in a gown all of white satin and gold and pearls, twitching his leg incessantly on the pivot of a yellow-leather toe, massive, grim, and gorgeous—Mr. Rutland Barrington as Pooh-Bah.

The scrunch of wheels outside, the splutter of the

everlasting salute, "God Save the Queen," from the Eurasian band, with one flute playing like a dentist's file! Then the Maharajah for a moment: but he must not be seen at the beginning. Then another carriage, and a rosy, rather chubby, British gentleman in a plain frock-coat with the Star of India. The Lieutenant-Governor bowed his way through bows and salaams to the dais. Then two of his staff walked to the farther door and led back the Maharajah. The little Maharajah—but how resplendent! His rose-silk turban sparkled with bullion and diamonds, and three jewelled aigrettes stood up from it. Over the blue and green he had a mantle of black velvet, richly broidered with white: the white was all pearls. Round his neck was a heavy necklace, with sapphires and topazes and diamonds and emeralds as large as your finger-tip.

He crept rather than walked forward to the dais. The fresh-coloured, bright-eyed Lieutenant-Governor stood up; the Viceroy's patent was read, and then his Honour addressed his Highness in a speech. The Maharajah, so radiant and so tiny, crouched before him; he crushed his handkerchief in his damp hand, and the caste-mark was sweating off his forehead. He looked again like a little boy, not quite sure whether his schoolmaster would call him good or naughty.

It was all over in ten minutes: a shining attendant brought forward attar of roses and beetle-nut in gold vessels, the Governor dispensed a little of each, and the Maharajah was now Maharajah indeed. Then, as all filed out, he slipped off his velvet mantle, for the pearls shower from it so peltingly that he has to be followed by a man with a bag. After that, it was just like a coming-of-age—lunch, which the orthodox Brahman host did not attend, speeches, sports in a meadow so thronged that you could have walked on brown heads. But you seldom see a coming-of-age at home with forty-five elephants in line, swaying their great foreheads under pink and scarlet silk, and flashing back the sun from howdahs of silver and carved ivory.

Yet the sight of all that stuck was the little scented, jewel-crusted atomy perspiring before the gentleman in the plain frock-coat. If the Maharajah came to England he would have all our greatest men and fairest women in a ring round him; St. James's and the Mansion House would compete for his smiles, and Windsor would delight to honour him. When the Lieutenant-Governor comes home, the odds are he will take a little place in the country, and be very poor and not over-healthy; and his neighbours, who will find him rather dull, will say that they have heard he was something in India. The man that was as God to seventy-five million people! And the other that cowered at his feet! Good Lord! what do we know?

XII

DARJILING

In Calcutta they grumbled that the hot weather was beginning already. Mornings were steamy, days sticky, and the municipal impurities rose rankly. The carter squatted over his bullocks with his shining body stark naked but for a loin-cloth.

At Siliguri, the bottom of the ascent to Darjiling, the rough grass and the tea-gardens were sheeted at sunrise in a silver frost. What few natives appeared happed their heads in shawls as if they had toothache.

It takes you an afternoon and a night to get as far as Siliguri. What you principally notice on the way is the dulness of the flat, moist richness of Bengal, and the extraordinary fulness of the first-class carriages. Even at this winter season the residents of Calcutta snatch at the chance of being cold for twenty-four hours. When you get out of your carriage at the junction station, you see on the other side of the platform a dumpy little toy train—a train at the wrong end of a telescope with its wheels cut from beneath it. Engines and trucks and carriages seem to be crawling like snakes on their bellies. Six miniature easy-chairs, three facing three, on an open truck with an awning, make a first-class carriage.

Darjiling

This is the Darjiling-Himalaya Railway—two-foot gauge, climbing four feet to the hundred for fifty miles up the foothills of the greatest mountains in the world. It is extraordinary as the only line in India that has been built with Indian capital. But you will find that the least of its wonders. A flat-faced hill-man bangs with a hammer twice three times on a spare bit of railway metal hung up by way of a gong, the whistle screams, and you pant away on surely the most entrancing railway journey in the world. Nothing very much to make your heart jump in the first seven miles. You bowl along the surface of a slightly ascending cart-road, and your view is mostly bamboo and tea. Graceful enough, and cool to the eye—the bamboos, hedges or clumps of slender stem with plumes of pale leaf swinging and nodding above them ; the tea, trim ranks and files of short, well-furnished bushes with lustrous, dark-green leaves, not unlike evergreens or myrtle in a nursery at home,—but you soon feel that you have known bamboo and tea all your life. Then suddenly you begin to climb, and all at once you are in a new world—a world of plants.

A new world is easy to say, but this is new indeed and a very world—such a primeval vegetable world as you have read of in books and eked out with dreams. It has everything you know in your world, only everything expressed in vegetation. It is a world in its variety alone. Trees of every kind rise up round you at every angle—unfamiliar, most of them, and exaggerations of forms you know, as if they were seen through a microscope. You might come on such broad fleshy leaves by way of Jack's giant beanstalk. Other growths take the form of bushes as high as our trees; but beside them are skinny, stunted starvelings, such as the most niggardly country might show. Then there are grasses—tufted, ruddy bamboo grass, and huge yellow straws with giant bents leaning insolently over to flick your face as you go by. Smaller still grow the ferns, lurking shyly in the crevices of the banks. And over everything, most luxuriant of everything, crawl hundred-armed creepers, knitting and knotting the whole jungle into one mellay of struggling life.

The varieties—the trees and shrubs and grasses and ferns and creepers—you would see in any tropical garden; but you could not see them at home. You could not see them in their unpruned native intercourse one with the other. The rise and fall of the ground, the whims of light and air, coax them into shapes that answer to the most fantastic imagination. Now you are going through the solemn aisles of a great cathedral—grey trunks for columns, with arches and vaulted roofs of green, with dark, retreating chapels and altar-trappings of mingled flowers. Now it is a king's banqueting-hall, tapestried with white-flowering creeper and crimson and purple bougain-villea; overhead the scarlet-mahogany blossoms of a sparse-leaved tulip-tree might be butterflies frescoed on a ceiling.

Fancy can compel the wilderness into moments of order, but wild it remains. The growths are not generally buildings, but animate beings in a real world. You see no perfectly shaped tree, as in a park or garden; one is warped, another stunted, another bare below—each formed, like men, by the pressure of a thousand fellows. Here is a corpse spreading white, stark arms abroad. Here are half-a-dozen young creatures rolling over each other like puppies at play. And there is a creeper flinging tumultuous, enraptured arms round a stately tree; presently it is gripping it in thick bands like Laocöon's serpent, then choking it mercilessly to death, then dead itself, its bleached, bare streamers dangling limply in the wind. It is life, indeed, this forest—plants fighting, victorious and vanquished; loving and getting children; springing and waxing and decaying and dying—our own world of men translated into plants.

While I am spinning similitudes, the Darjiling-Himalaya Railway is panting always upwards, boring through the thick world of trees like a mole. Now it sways round a curve so short that you can almost look back into the next carriage, and you understand why the wheels are so low. Now it stops dead, and almost before it stops starts backwards up a zigzag, then forwards up another, and on again. In a moment it is skating on the brink of a slide of shale that trembles to come down and overwhelm it; next it is rumbling across a bridge above the point it passed ten minutes ago, and below that which it will reach ten minutes hence. Twisting, backing, circling, dodging, but always rising, it unthreads the skein whose end is in the clouds and the snows.

Presently the little engine draws quite clear of the jungle. You skirt opener slopes, and the blue plain below is no longer a fleeting vista, but a broad prospect. You see how the forest spills itself on to the fields and spreads into a dark puddle over their lightness. You see a great river overlaying the dimness with a ribbon of steel. The ferns grow thicker about you; gigantic fronds bow at you from gullies overhead, and you see the tree-fern—a great crown of drooping green on a trunk of a man's height—standing superbly alone, knowing its supreme gracefulness. Next, as you rise and rise, the air gets sharp; through a gauzy veil of mist appear again huge forests, but dark and gloomy with brown moss dripping dankly from every branch. Rising, rising, and you have now come to Ghoom, the highest point. Amid the cold fog appears the witch of Ghoom—a hundred years old, with a pointed chin and mop of grizzled hair all witch-fashion, but beaming genially and requesting backsheesh.

Then round a corner—and here is Darjiling. A scattered settlement on a lofty ridge, facing a great cup enclosed by other ridges—mountains elsewhere,

here hills. Long spurs run down into the hollow, half black with forest, half pale and veined with many paths. At the bottom is a little chequer of fresh green millet; the rim at the top seems to line the sky.

And the Himalayas and the eternal snows? The devil a Himalaya in sight. Thick vapours dip down and over the very rim of the cup; beyond Darjiling is a tumult of peaked creamy cloud. You need not be told it,—clouds that hide mountains always ape their shapes,—the majestic Himalayas are behind that screen, and you will not see them to-day, nor perhaps to-morrow, nor yet for a fortnight of to-morrows.

You must console yourself with Darjiling and the hillmen. And Darjiling is pleasant to the eye as you look down on it, a huddle of grey corrugated-iron roofs, one stepping over the other, hugging the hillside with one or two red ones to break the monotone. There is no continuous line of them: each stands by itself in a ring of deep green first. The place is cool and grateful after an Indian town—clean and roomy, a place of homes and not of pens.

In the middle of it is the bazaar, and my day, by luck, was market-day. Here, again, you could never fancy yourself in India. A few Hindus there are, but beside the dumpy hillmen their thin limbs, tiny features, and melting eyes seem hardly human. More like the men you know is the Tibetan, with a long profile and long, sharp nose, though his hat has the turned-up brim of the Chinee, though he wears a long bottle-green dressing-gown open to the girdle, and his pigtail knocks at the back of his knees. But the prevailing type, though as Mongolian, is far more genial than the Tibetan. Squat little men, for the most part, fill the bazaar, with broad faces that give room for the features, with button noses, and slits for eyes. They wear boots and putties, or gaiters made of many-coloured carpet-bagging; and their women are like them—with shawls over their heads, and broad sashes swathing them from bosom to below the waist, with babies slung behind their backs, not astride on the hip as are the spawn of India. Their eyes are black as sloes—puckered, too, but seeming puckered with laughter; and their clear yellow skins are actually rosy on the cheeks, like a ripe apricot. Square-faced, long-pigtailed, plump, cheery, open of gaze, and easy of carriage, rolling cigarettes, and offering them to soothe babies—they might not be beautiful in Europe; here they are ravishing.

But you come to Darjiling to see the snows. So on a night of agonising cold—feet and hands a block of ice the moment you cease to move them—must follow a rise before it is light. Maybe the clouds will be kinder this morning. No; the same stingy, clammy mist,—only there, breaking through it, high up in the sky—yes, there are a few faint streaks of white. Just a few marks of snow scored on the softer white of the cloud, chill with the utterly disconsolate cold of ice through a window of fog. Still, there are certainly Himalayas there.

Up and up I toiled; the sun was plainly rising behind the ridge of Darjiling. In the cup below the sunlight was drawing down the hillsides and peeling off the twilight. Then, at a sudden turn of the winding ascent, I saw the summit of Kinchinjunga. Just the summit, poised in the blue, shining and rejoicing in the sunrise. And as I climbed and climbed, other peaks rose into sight below and beside him, all dazzling white, mounting and mounting the higher I mounted, every instant more huge and towering and stately, boring into the sky.

Up—till I came to the summit, and the sun appeared—a golden ball swimming in a sea of silver. He was sending the clouds away curling before him; they drifted across the mountains, but he pursued and smote and dissolved them. And ever the mountains rose and rose, huger and huger; as they swelled up they heaved the clouds away in rolls off their shoulders. Now their waists were free, and all but their feet. Only a chasm of fog still hid their lower slopes. Fifty miles away, they looked as if I could toss a stone across to them; only you could never hope to hit their heads, they towered so gigantically. Now the clouds, clearing to right and left, laid bare a battlemented range of snow-white wall barring the whole horizon. Behind these appeared other peaks : it was not a range, but a country of mountains, not now a wall, but a four-square castle carved by giants out of eternal ice. It was the end of the world—a sheer rampart, which forbade the fancy of anything beyond.

And in the centre, by peak and col and precipice, the prodigy reared itself up to Kinchinjunga. Bare rock below, then blinding snow seamed with ridges and chimneys, and then, above, the mighty summit—a tremendous three-cornered slab of grey granite between two resplendent faces of snow. Other mountains tiptoe at the sky snatch at it with a peak like a needle. Kinchinjunga heaves himself up into it, broadly, massively, and makes his summit a diadem. He towers without effort, knowing his majesty. Sublime and inviolable, he lifts his grey nakedness and his mail of burnished snow, and turns his forehead serenely to sun and storm. Only their touch, of all things created, has perturbed his solitude since the birth of time.

XIII

THE VILLAGERS

THE tents of my host, the landlord of fifty villages, were pitched under a black-green mango-grove. The headman of the next village but one had come into camp to conduct the Presence to see his property—a tall, thin-legged old man with white hair and moustache, wearing only a dust-white shirt and drawers and a little linen band round the middle of his right calf. When he came up he salaamed and salaamed, and then held out a rupee in the palm of his hand. The landlord touched it and salaamed,—the one signifying thereby that all that was his was his lord's, the other that of his bounty he remitted the same.

We plodded off in the happy sunshine, over a switchback track of caked mud and powdered dust, through cornfields pancake-flat for as far as a man could see. With the barley they had sown rape, now in tall, yellow bloom or just making seed. Here and there a grove of trees; now and again a brown-legged, bowing cultivator; all the rest was a canopy of pale-blue sunlight spread over a carpet of full-blooded green shot with gold.

119

The Villagers

When we came to the tumble of mud-wall and grass thatch, peasants streamed out from every hole! All bore rupees, and hurried, salaaming, to have them touched and remitted: such is the use of India. But as rupees have ever been scarcer than men, you saw one furtively pass the wherewithal for the necessary salutation behind his back to another. They led us with ceremony to the village meeting-place—a fair-sized open portico of sun-dried mud brick, with a yard before it under trees. There two old wicker chairs were set for the sahibs, and the village stared in a semicircle before us. A few white-bearded elders —the ryot does not often live to fifty—many young men, more children, they stood or squatted on their heels after the native mode; not on the ground, understand, but literally on the tendons of their heels. As it was midday, most of them were naked but for a loin-cloth. There was little enough of the rainbow brightness of city costume; a shawl or two had once been red, but most had never been more than white, and were now but a shade whiter than their owners' fields. As the landlord discoursed of crops and rain and canals, fathers held their babies on their hips— the women, of course, were hidden indoors—and it was a little pathetic to contrast the pot-bellies of the children with the skin-and-bone of the men. It is scarce exaggerating to say that every rich native in India is fat: watch him shovelling rice into himself by the handful, and you will agree that it would be a miracle if he were not. Wherefrom you infer that the hundreds of millions of skeletons are lean because they must—because they live from harvest to seed-time and through to harvest again with bellies half empty.

But they are a patient people, the villagers of India; they have been hungry these thirty centuries or so, and it has never occurred to them that they have any claim to be filled. They grumbled a little, to be sure: what tiller of the soil ever did else? They could not get enough water from the Government canal, and the Christmas rains had not fallen; and they were poor men. When, in due course, we went out to inspect everything—from the fields to the cakes of cow-dung fuel that were being stacked and covered up against the rainy season—the landlord observed a broken well, and offered to pay one-half of its repairing if the village would pay the other. They responded with effusion that if the sahib would find bricks and mortar and labour they would do the rest. Yet, though not self-helpful, they remained polite, and desired that their lords would honour them by drinking a cup of milk. So two little earthen cups were brought, of the material of flower-pots, and into them was poured milk still hot from the udder. Their lords drank; and then the cups were smashed to earth. They were useless now: the man of meanest caste would never drink out of a cup that had been polluted by white lips. Water was brought, and the man who had poured out the milk washed his hands thoroughly. The landlord asked his manager if he would take milk too: he shook his head, with a smile; for he is a Brahman, and is as much above drinking from a vessel that a lower caste has touched as the lower caste is above drinking after a sahib.

Now, as the bits of potsherd were still trembling on the ground, there struck up a loud, half-rollicking, half-wailing chorus behind the corner of the wall. There appeared a little group of women in very faded garments, half-veiling their faces carefully, half-turning their backs. These were low-caste women, and they were singing a hymn expressive of the virtues of the landlord. That also is use and wont. The subject of their praise called up one grand-dam and gave her silver, and the chorus stopped, amid the approving salaams of the village. They will call you "Lord" and "Protector of the Poor"; they will sing hymns to you; but they smash the bowl you drank from. What could be more eloquent of the land of contradictions?

The cultivator, to whom both these formalities are religion, is not, you will have concluded, a being of developed intelligence. He is neither beautiful nor rich, gifted nor industrious, nor especially virtuous, nor even amiable. He loves and cherishes his children with a solicitude that is truly beautiful: for that, and because he is a simple creature, you love him. Yet he is as malignant as he is simple, always has an enemy, and sticks at nothing in the world to ruin him. The cultivator presents only one point of interest, which is that there are two hundred and forty millions of him. He is clothed in calico and fed on unleavened dough, called chaputties, and on pulse. He has two distractions—marriages and funerals. At these he feasts all his neighbours, and spends all he has and more. To make up, he borrows from the village bunnia, who is shopkeeper and Shylock in one. The bunnia charges thirty-seven and a-half per cent. as a minimum. When harvest comes, he takes over the ryot's corn and credits him for it, not at market price, but on a scale of his own. The ryot keeps back enough, perhaps, for a few weeks' food: after that he must come to the bunnia for seed at sowing-time, and weekly through the year for his children's food. The bunnia lends him back his own corn at thirty-seven and a-half to seventy-five per cent. Presently, it may be, the bunnia takes one of the ryot's bullocks in part-payment, and the man makes shift to plough with one. He does it very badly, though not much worse than he would have done with the two. Then, perhaps, the bunnia takes the other bullock, and then—but rarely, for this is killing the goose—the land. Or it may be the ryot has the luck to live all his life without paying his creditor anything beyond his whole income, less his bare livelihood. Then he dies happy, and bequeathes the remainder of his debt to his son. On that capital the son cheerfully starts upon life, and never dreams of repudiating.

Nevertheless, when the landlord offers to buy crops at market rate and to advance seed-corn at market rate, charging only six per cent. interest, the cultivator smiles cunningly and declines. He knows that the landlord will not lend him for weddings and funerals, and if he borrows seed from the landlord neither will the bunnia; so he goes back to his thirty-seven and a-half. He has only his own ignorance, indolence, and thriftlessness to thank for his wretchedness. He is miserable, and he is content. Everybody else in India has a grievance: the cultivator, the backbone of the country and the worst-used man in it, has none.

That his situation really is his fault, you may convince yourself by going on ten miles or so to a Jat village. The Jats are a not very illustrious tribe, whose centre a hundred years ago was Bhurtpur: at that period they rose to military eminence, and whenever they were short of cash looted Agra; also they inflicted on our arms one of the severest defeats we ever got in India. As cultivators, the Jats are excellently good, being both expert and of an unwearied industry.

Even before their village peeps from behind its thickets, you notice that the road is exceptional—not metalled, of course, but still flat and fairly level. The bullocks you meet in the heavy-wheeled carts are

big and well-thriven.   In the village itself, the houses
are mostly of sun-dried mud, it is true, but they are
stable and lofty; moreover, before several of the best
lay piles of fire-burnt brick.   One Crœsus actually
had a tall burnt-brick gateway with a many-pointed
arch.   There were more brass vessels to be seen than
earthern, which is a sure sign of prosperity.   Then
there was a little hole in the corner wall for a lamp at
night, which reeked of public spirit; and in one rich
man's court were no less than two horses.   His house
was well-built; its sole furniture was six wood-framed
cord-strung bedsteads and some brazen pots.   But
that is all he and his family want, and his two-
year-old filly will bring him a little fortune at the
horse-fair next month.

Even in the excitement of the landlord's visit, the
secret of Jat prosperity was plain enough—simply
work.   At the entrance to the village the sugar-mill
was going—three dumpy, upright rollers revolved by
a lever, which two oxen pulled round and round; as
a boy thrust in the cane, the squeezed fragments of
stalk fell out on one side to be used for fuel, and the
juice ran into a tank on the other.   It was boiling in
vats under a roof hard by, and the yellow result—
pease-pudding you would have called it at ten yards
—was already being made into cakes of the finished
product.   The man who invented the machine gets
back its cost in two years' hire of it, and has made
a fortune.   But the Jats do well with their sugar,

despite the rent of the machine.   They work day and night at it, yoke relieving yoke of oxen ; and they toil thus at everything.

But in this world even Jats are not always happy. When, at the village meeting-place, after the milk-bowls were duly smashed, the landlord asked if all was well, a mean-looking young man, holding the manager's horse, cried aloud that it was not.   He was of a low caste, which in towns usually works in leather, in villages does any menial labour it can. Now, in this village were sixteen families of the caste, and the manager had promised them the lease of certain land then held by the headman of the village. But Hukm Singh had not given it up, cried the shabby youth, and, moreover, had oppressed their people and got a decree from the law-court by fraud and attached their standing crops.   " Is it even so ? " said the landlord.   " Come then to my tents in the afternoon, and let Hukm Singh come also."   For the headman, at the moment, was discreetly absent. " Will I come ? " cried the young man of low caste. " I will run ; I will follow my lord now."

Every afternoon the sahib sits in his office-tent and his tenants squat before him and cry aloud their plaints, and he does justice between them, as it was in the age of gold.   First comes, out of politeness, the owner of the mango-grove we are camped in.   " You see, I am again camping on your land," says the sahib. " I am my lord's," replies the owner, radiant in gold-braided cap, dove-coloured cloth coat, and clean white drawers that cling like a skin, " and all that is mine is my lord's." Then he goes on to complain that he has lost three thousand rupees by a speculation in corn, and more besides by hoar-frost and the want of the Christmas rain. He recalls with a sigh the golden day when a cavalry regiment, marching from Aligarh, camped in the middle of his wheat-field; whereafter the native officials did indeed intercept his compensation on its way to him, but by reason of the manure he got the best crop ever seen in any country. " If the merciful God will send us rain," he sighs, rising, " it may yet be well"; and goes out, knowing himself none the less to be a rich man and the best-reputed in all the country-side. For when his father died he feasted sixteen villages!

Next the complaints. The manager sits on the floor at the landlord's feet, and the clerk, sitting beside him, reads out Hindustani documents in a decorous official drone. While he still reads, the plaintiff, squatting on his heels in the dust-clothed, pucker-faced, starveling ring outside the tent, breaks in; before he is well started the defendant adds a third voice to the chorus. Each slaps his palm and waves his arms with conviction. All the complaints are of robbery, of fraud upon the poor by the not-quite-so-poor. An official of the estate has taken five shillings of rent and given no receipt; a man was granted a plot for his house, but his brother, who already had enough, has seized it, and will not let him build thereon.

Then come the low-caste people and the headman. The case, which the courts only made worse, now takes what you call a sensational development. " My lord," says the defendant, " it is even so. I lied before the court, but before the Presence I cannot lie. It was thus. When I told the manager I would quit the land, I believed it was to be let to men of my own caste. But when I found it was to these, what could I do? So I told the manager I would give up the land and did not." It should be explained that a landlord can only evict a tenant during three months of the year, when the fields are presumably bare of tillage; and by his promise to the manager the wily headman had staved over this period. " Then, when these people trouble me," he adds, entirely unashamed, though his victims and half his acquaintance are squatting by, " I went to the village accountant, and since three families of them owed me money and I had no bond, I induced him to write in his register that this was not a loan but rent. So I went to the court and we swore, and attached their crops." Again, it must be explained that there is a summary process to recover rent, but not to recover other debts : the headman had bribed the accountant to falsify his register by way of putting on the screw; and the court had believed the headman and the registrar.

The Villagers

The rich man told his story without a blush, and none of his countrymen condemned him. But the Presence ordered that the attachment should be taken off and the land leased to the poor families; at the same time the debtors must give a bond and repay by easy instalments at six per cent. From all of which proceedings you will perceive that the ryot's foes are of his own household.

So, having protected the poor, the landlord strolls forth into the divine Indian evening. The pungent peat-smelling smoke from the fires lies in low grey stripes in the breathless silence. From a tower in the village floats the voice of the muezzin as he calls the believers to prayer. At the well mild-eyed bullocks draw a rope down an incline; a huge leather bucket comes up, and is emptied into the stone cisterns and conduits about the base. Men are washing their clothes, women their cooking-pots; the water-seller fills his skin and carries it away, dripping, on his brown back. Through the conduits the water sluices out among the barley; in the fields men with big-bladed hoes break down or build up the little earthen embankments that guide the blessed water this way and that. The canal the Government made is full to-day, so water is plentiful; it runs even into the waste pool whence the Government made a drain and siphoned it under the canal to carry off the water-logging of the wet season. At the pool the washer-men are beating clothes clean against large stones.

The Villagers

In a field embanked into little chequers an old man is pricking out onions. "I am planting them for my lord," says he with politeness, "since frost killed the potatoes that were here." "Did the frost then go so deep down into the ground as to kill the potato roots?" asks the landlord, incredulous. "If you cut off a man's head," responds the sage, "how shall he walk upon his feet?"

XIV

THE CITY OF SHAH JEHAN

THE north-eastern approach to Agra is through a waste of land at the same time flat and broken. Formless hillocks and ditches, colourless sand and dead turf, the whole scene was mean and depressing. I raised my eyes, and there, on the edge of the ugly prairie, sat a fair white palace with domes and minarets. So exquisite in symmetry, so softly lustrous in tint, it could hardly be substantial, and I all but cried, " Mirage ! " It was the Taj Mahal.

And now we were clanking over an iron bridge above a dark-green river that filled barely a quarter of its sandy bed ; deep, broad staircases stepped down to its further bank with pillared pleasure-houses overlooking them. Now on the right rose a great mosque, its bellying domes zigzagged with red and white ; dawn from the left frowned the weather-worn battlements of a great red fortress. This was the city of Shah Jehan, emperor and devotee, artist and lover.

And this, in a few words, is the passionate story of Shah Jehan. He was the grandson of Akbar the Great, the first Mogul Emperor of Hindustan. While yet Prince Royal, conquering India for the Moguls, he married the beautiful Persian, Arjmand

The City of Shah Jehan

Banu, called Mumtaz-i-Mahal, the chosen of the palace, and loved her tenderly beyond all his wives for fourteen years.   But only a year after he became Sultan she died in travail of her eighth child.   Shah Jehan in his grief swore that she should have the loveliest tomb the world ever beheld, and for seventeen years he built the Taj Mahal.   Also he built the palace of Agra, the fort and palace of Delhi, and the great mosque of Agra; he took to wife many fair ladies, and lived in all luxuriousness, ministering abundantly to every sense, till he had reigned thirty years.   Then his son Aurungzebe rose up and dethroned him, and kept him a close prisoner in his own private mosque, which he had built within the palace of Agra.   There he lived seven years more, attended by his daughter Jehanara, who would not leave him, till at last, in 1645, being grown very feeble, he begged to be laid in a chamber of the palace wherefrom he could see the Taj Mahal. This was granted him, so that he died with his eyes upon the tomb of the love of his youth.   There they buried him beside her.   And his daughter, when her time came, wrote a Persian stanza begging that no monument should be set up to " the humble transitory Jehanara," and praying only for her father's soul.

Agra is the mirror of Shah Jehan.   In the fort and palace you can read all the story of the warrior and the lover—in the fort so nakedly grim without and the palace so richly voluptuous within.   Under the brow of the sheer sandstone walls you are dwarfed to

a pigmy. Before and beneath the great gateway
stands a double curtain of loophole and machicolation
and tower : you go in through cavernous guard-houses,
up a ramp between sky-closing walls. Only thus do
you reach the real entrance—the great Elephant
Gate—two jutting octagon towers supporting spacious
chambers thrown across the passage. On the lower
storey all is closed, and only white plaster designs re-
lieve the savage masses of the sandstone ; in the upper
balconies are windows and recesses, all decked with
white, and above all runs a gallery crowned with cupolas.

Under this arch you go, a dome above, deep and
lofty recesses on either hand ; now you are past the
sternness. Shah Jehan is soldier no longer but artist
and amorist at large. You come to the Pearl Mosque.
There is a Pearl Mosque at Delhi, sandstone slabs
without, marble within, as this is ; but the Delhi
mosque is a bauble to this. This is a broad court,
paved with slabs of marble, veined with white and
blue, grey and yellow. This is all marble—marble
walls with moulded panels, marble cloisters of multi-
foliate arches, marble gateways breaking three walls
of the square, marble columns supporting bell-cupolas
above them and at each corner, a marble basin in the
centre of the court, a marble sundial beside it. Along
the west side of the court shines the glorious face of
the mosque itself—only a roofed quarter of the whole
space, a mere portico, but colonnaded with three rows
of seven pillars apiece, each branching to right and

left, to front and back, with eight-pointed, nine-leaved arches. Along the entablature above runs a Persian inscription in mosaic of black marble; on the roof, over each pillar of the front row, is a cupola with four columns, and at each corner a cupola with eight columns. Three domes fold their broad white wings behind and above all.

Three steps for the mullah to preach from, and that is all the catalogue. No altar or shrine or image: there is no god but God. No carving or lattice-work: but the simple pillars and arches, the few cupolas and domes, are yet the richest of ornamentation. No paint or gems—only the clear harmonious veining of the marble. Only space and proportion, form and whispers of colour—and it is so beautiful that you can hardly breathe for rapture. The radiant marble ripples from shade to shade—snow-white, pearl-white, ivory-white—till it seems half alive. The bells and pinnacles are so light that they seem to float in the air. It cannot be a building, you whisper: it is enchantment.

But now go on to the palace. It has been battered and sacked—the Jats of Bhurtpur carried away the precious stones from the walls; but through the restorations you can dream of some of its delights when it held the houris of Shah Jehan. Dream this and it is all enchantment; you have arrived at last—at last, after so many years, after so many leagues—in the dear country of your earliest dreams, and the Arabian

Nights are come to life. Under this pillared hall the ambassadors of Shiraz and Samarkand are making their obeisance and displaying rich gifts. Above, in the marble alcove festooned with flowers and tendrils in pietra dura, reclines the Sultan of the Indies on a couch of white marble. Up the stairs—and here, enclosed by a colonnade of two storeys, is the fish-pond; on the upper terrace under that canopy, which is one block of creamy marble embossed with flowers, sits the lovely favourite Schemselnihar, and makes believe to angle. She rises and follows the other lights of the harem into the little square court and portico that miniature the great Pearl Mosque without. But some of the beauties turn aside to the gallery, where, below, is an enclosed bazaar; handsome young merchants of Baghdad tempt them with silks and brocades —and with looks that sigh and languish. They had best be prudent: eyes as fathomless as theirs have grown dim in the dungeons under the terraces, below the water. From lust to cruelty is only a step; and when the Sultan raised the marble and the gems he sank the dungeon, remote in a labyrinth of tunnels. Across it is a beam with a noose for soft necks and a shoot for frail bodies that tumbles them into the Jumna.

The Sultan has risen from his audience: he walks round the terrace, through the delicious Hall of Private Audience, whose walls are marble, whose pillars are festooned with creepers in agate and jasper, jade and cornelian, whose ends are profound and graceful recesses, half-arch, half-dome. He passes to the heavy slab of the black marble throne on the riverside brink of the quadrangle; in the pit below they let out buffaloes and tigers to fight before him; on the white seat behind him sits the court jester to make him merry.

And now—it is the full moon that rises from an arch of the pavilion to the right—the full moon, though it is still broad day ? It is the Sultaness-in-Chief looking out at the fight from her abode in the Jasmine Tower. She has grown tired of throwing the dice, while her handmaidens stand for pieces on the pachisi-board that is let into her marble pavement—there, behind those duenna screens, the gauze of lattice-work that encloses her courtyard. She has grown tired of dabbling in the fountain that tinkles on the shallow basin of figured marble, weary of her bower of marble inlaid with gems. The Sultan rises, and it is the signal for the bath—the bath in the dark Mirror Palace, lighted with a score of flambeaux and walled with a million tiny mirrors, that reflect . . . No; we must not think of it—nor of the feast in the Private Palace, under the ceiling emblazoned with blue and crimson and gold—nor yet of the disrobing in the Golden Pavilion, where the ladies thrust their jewels into holes in the wall too narrow for a man's arm to follow them. . . . No; you should not listen to what the Jester is saying now.

But if you envy Shah Jehan, look again later into

the tiny Gem Mosque and the cupboard at the side, too small to turn in, where he is the uncrowned prisoner of his son. No Mirror Palace now: the ceiling is black where they heat the water for his bath, in a hole of a cistern where he cannot stretch out his limbs. Look again into the little gilt-domed cupola, where he lies dying, and Jehanara's voice sounds suddenly far away; and the very Taj, though he knows every angle and curve of it, swims in a grey-white blur; and nothing is left clear save the voice and face of the beautiful Persian, Arjmand Banu, whose palankeen followed all his campaigns in the days when empire was still a-winning, whose children called him father—Arjmand Banu, silent and unseen now for four-and-thirty years, the wife of his youth.

Now follow him to the Taj. Under the great gateway of strong sandstone ribbed with delicate marble, its vaulted red arch cobwebbed with white threads, and then before you—then the miracle of miracles, the final wonder of the world. In chaste majesty it stands suddenly before you, as if the magical word had called it this moment out of the earth. On a white marble platform it stands exactly four-square, but that the angles are cut off; nothing so rude as a corner could find place in its soft harmonies. Seen through the avenue, it looks high rather than broad; seen from the pavement below it, it looks broad rather than high; you doubt, then conclude that its pro-

portions are perfect. Above its centre rises a full
white dome, at each corner of whose base nestles a
smaller dome, upheld on eight arches. The centre of
each face is a lofty-headed gateway rising above the
line of the roof; within it is again a pointed caving
recess, half arch, half dome; within this, again, a
screen of latticed marble. On each flank of these,
and on the facets of the cut-off angles, are pairs of
smaller, blind recesses of the same design, one above
the other. From each junction of facets rises a slim
pinnacle. Everywhere it is embellished with elaborate profusion. Moulding, sculpture, inlaid frets and
scrolls of coloured marbles, twining branches and garlands of jade and agate and cornelian—here is every
point of lavish splendour you saw in the palace combined in one supreme embodiment—superb dignity
matched with graceful richness.

But it is vain to flounder amid epithets; the man
who should describe the Taj must own genius equal
to his who built it. Description halts between its
mass and its fineness. It makes you giddy to look up
at it, yet it is so delicate you feel that a brick would
lay it in shivers at your feet. It is a rock temple and
a Chinese casket together—a giant gem.

Nothing jars; for if the jewel were away the setting would still be among the noblest monuments on
earth. The minarets at the four corners of the platform are a moment's stumbling-block: they look ir-
reverently like the military masts of a battleship, and

the hard lines where the stones join remind you of a
London subway.   But look at the Taj itself, and the
minarets fall instantly into place; they set off its
glories, and, standing like acolytes, seem to be challenging you not to worship it.   At each side, below
the Taj, is a triple-domed building of sandstone and
marble; the hot red throws up the pearl-and-ivory
softness of the Taj.   The cloisters round the garden,
the lordly caravanserai outside the gate, the clustering
domes and mosaic texts from the Koran on the great
gate itself—all this you hardly notice; but when you
do, you find that every point is perfection.   As for
the garden, with shady trees of every hue, from
sprightly yellow to funereal cypress, with purple blossoms cascading from the topmost boughs, with roses
and lilies, phloxes and carnations—and the channel of
clear water with twenty fountains that runs through
the garden, and the basin with the goldfish.   .   .   .
It is pure Arabian Nights!   You listen for the speaking bird and the singing tree.   And was it not hither
that Prince Ahmed, leaving his brother Ali to cuddle
Nuronnihar in the palace, followed his arrow?   And
is not that the fairy Peri-Banu coming out of the
pleasure-house to welcome him?   Surely man never
made such a Paradise: it must be the fabric of a
dream wafted through gates of silver and opal.

O Shah Jehan, Shah Jehan, you are bewitching a
respectable newspaper-correspondent.   The thought
of you is strong wine.   Shah Jehan, with your

queens and concubines without number, their amber feet mirrored in marble, their ivory limbs mirrored in quicksilver; Shah Jehan, who starved them in the black oubliettes, and hung them from the mouldy beam, and sluiced their beautiful bodies into the cold river; Shah Jehan, with elephants and peacocks; Shah Jehan, returning from the conquered Dekhan, dismounting in the Armoury Square, hastening through the Grape Garden, hastening past the fair ones in the Golden Pavilion to the fairest within the Jasmine Tower!

Shah Jehan—Grape Garden—Golden Pavilion—Jasmine Tower—there is dizzy magic in the very names. And when I turn aside in your garden, shunning your fierce black-and-scarlet petals to bring back my senses with English stocks and pansies, the sight of your Taj through the trees sends my brain areel again. I go in and stand by your tomb. The jewel-creepers blossom more luxuriantly than ever in the trellised screen that encloses it, and the two oblong cenotaphs are embowered in gems. But here it is dark and cool: light comes in only through double lattices of feathery marble. You look up into a dome, obscure and mysterious, but mightily expansive, as it were the vault of the heaven of the dead. It is very well; it is the fit close. In this breathless twilight, after his battles and buildings, his ecstasies and torments, his love and his loss, Shah Jehan has come to his own again for ever.

XV

THE RULERS OF INDIA

THIS short chapter contains nothing new or original. It is merely abstracted from books within the reach of everybody, and inserted here to save you the trouble of reaching them. In India you get a chance of seeing the actual work of Government being carried on—such a chance as is hardly possible at home. What is done in England in the offices of county councils or town councils, boards of guardians or school boards, or often of private companies, is usually done in India by one man sitting in a tent. But the actual instrument of Government works, of course, under a superstructure of higher authority. He, to most observers, is the most interesting wheel in the machine; but to understand the nature and extent of his functions it is necessary to have an idea of the higher authorities also.

The ultimate power in the Government of India is yourself. You, the British elector—subject to the usual formality of getting enough of the other electors to agree with you—can do with India exactly what you please. You control Parliament; Parliament controls the Cabinet; the Cabinet controls the Secretary of State for India, and the Secretary of State controls the Viceroy. And in India the Viceroy is supreme. He controls the Lieutenant-Governors of provinces, and they control the Commissioners of Divisions, and they control the District Officers, who control the people of India.

There is a good long ladder, you observe, between you and the natives of India. In the last resort, if a question of very vital interest arose, you would dispose of their destiny. In the meantime, this House-that-Jack-built of control is only occasionally and partially effective—which is just as well for India. As it is, the Secretary of State, the Cabinet, and Parliament probably have far too much to say about Indian administration. So, at least, thinks everybody in India; for where they have anything to say they are more likely than not—most naturally, seeing that they know next to nothing about it—to say the wrong thing. It is one of the unthinking commonplaces of the day to say that Parliament and the electorate are shamefully apathetic about India; that the thin attendance on an Indian Budget night shows a disgraceful insensibility to the plain duty of a legislator; that our political men should all visit India; and so on, to infinity and to nausea. Doubtless a visit to India might be a useful part of a political education, if the visitor had the prudence to spend most of his time collecting and collating the views of experts, and made no attempt to form independent opinions on subjects where a lifetime's observation still leaves you ignorant. But as for Indian Budgets and Indian questions, it wants only a moment of common-sense to see that those who know nothing of India show their best wisdom in leaving such to those who do.

However, let that pass for the present. Keeping this exposition to the authorities within India, the Viceroy is assisted by a Council, which practically constitutes his Cabinet. Lord Curzon represents the Prime Minister and Foreign Secretary; the Financial member is Chancellor of the Exchequer, and the Military member Secretary for War; two members of the Civil Service take charge respectively of the Home Department and of Public Works; while the Legal member, who must be a barrister of five years' standing, exists for the purpose of drafting bills. Each of these Cabinet Ministers has a permanent secretary under him and an office, as in Whitehall. The Commander-in-chief in India is an extraordinary member of this Council.

For purposes of law-making, the Viceroy's Council is increased by additional members, who are not to be less than ten nor more than sixteen. The duties of these are purely consultative: they have no hand in the actual work of government. Six of these are officials, and about half are natives. Of the non-official members four are nominated by the non-official members of subordinate provincial councils, and a fifth by the Calcutta Chamber of Commerce. This you might call the Parliament of India. It meets round a long table in Government House—portraits of past Viceroys on the wall, a row of dining-room chairs for the public, members sitting down to speak. Altogether, it looks much more like a board of directors than a legislative assembly. The proceedings are not exciting, nor even audible; there is hardly ever a division. No measure can be introduced unless the proposal is first approved in the Executive, or Cabinet, Council. The Legislative Council itself gets through most of its work in Select Committees, which amend or recast bills, after they have been brought in and published, in the light of reports made upon them by the officials in the provinces concerned.

You must bear in mind, though, that the analogy with the Cabinet or the House of Commons is a false one in this particular: the Viceroy, subject to the approval of the Secretary of State at home, can override even the unanimous opinion of either Council. He is merely obliged, in that case, to give his reasons for so doing in writing. But in practice the members of the Council are bound to know so much more of the details of the business than the Viceroy does, that this power is very seldom, if ever, used.

Under the Government of India are the Provincial Governments, which miniature the central authority. There are eight provinces—Madras, Bombay, Bengal,

North-West Provinces, Punjab, Burma, Central Provinces, and Assam. The first two are still called presidencies, and get their Governors from home, instead of from the Civil Service; but the distinction is an obsolete and insignificant one. The next four are ruled by Lieutenant-Governors, and the others by Chief Commissioners; but here, too, the distinction is more nominal than essential. The Governors of Madras and Bombay, and the Lieutenant-Governors of Bengal and the North-West Provinces, are assisted by bodies similar to the Viceroy's Legislative Council. Each provincial Governor has a small staff of civil servants at his headquarters. Civil servants are also at the head of the divisions of each province and the districts of each division, while there is a large staff of what is called the Provincial Civil Service. These officers are not members of the Indian Civil Service, properly so-called, which is recruited by examinations in England, and which, in virtue more of superior ability and force of character than of any privilege, fills most of the higher posts in the public service. The members of the provincial services are almost entirely native. Below them comes the subordinate civil service—clerks, messengers, and the like—who are wholly native.

The institution of the Provincial Civil Service has proved a fairly satisfactory solution of a difficult problem: how far is it wise or possible to employ natives in civil administration? A few years ago the

House of Commons passed a resolution ordering that examinations for the Indian Civil Service proper should be held in India as well as in London. There could hardly be a more childish misconception of the true reason of competitive examination. We do not want scholars to govern India so much as men and gentlemen of good physique, unimpeachable integrity, unbending strength of will, abundant common-sense and tact. Only, as there are more candidates of this kind than there are vacancies, we examine them in Greek iambics and quaternions as the most convenient way of discriminating among them. The more necessary qualities we assume them—and rightly, as experience shows—to possess in roughly equal measure. But we cannot assume that such natives of India as would be likely to succeed in competitive examinations would possess these qualities—rather the opposite. To allow them to compete in such examinations, whether in India or in London, is about as reasonable as to allow the passengers on a liner to draw lots for the privilege of navigating the ship. In the provincial services, on the other hand, promotion is by approved merit, and a native official who has shown his capacity can be advanced to any of the positions usually held by members of the Civil Service itself.

Under the provincial Governors—except in Madras, which does without the grade—are the Commissioners. Each rule a group of districts called a division. Under them are the district officers—variously designated in various provinces—who are the real working members of the Government. A district is the administrative unit of India; it is complete in itself, and its head is responsible for every branch of its working, almost for everything that happens in it. This is the case throughout India.

If, therefore, you want to see the Government of India at its daily work, dealing with the people, raising its taxes and spending them, toiling—as it is always unselfishly toiling—for the benefit of the natives, and them alone, you must seek out the district officer. In a larger unit you will not see the actual work; in a smaller, you will not see it all. The district officer has usually two or three members of the civil service under him. But, as a rule, not more than one of these is a very efficient helper; the younger have yet to learn the vernacular languages and dialects—which are innumerable and infinitely various—and their duties generally. The district officer is the backbone of administrative India.

XVI

THE DISTRICT OFFICER

AT the moment the camel deposited me at his camp he was hearing appeals from the orders of his subordinate magistrates. The furniture of the court consisted of a desk, all in clamps and joints and hooks for taking to pieces when camp is struck, and two chairs. Its officials were three native clerks, cross-legged on the floor with piles of papers and inkhorns, and a red-coated, gold-sashed orderly at the tent door. In the shadow of the tent snored another, also red-coated and gold-sashed, like all Government messengers. A little way off squatted a circle of bottomless-eyed brown men—some fat with gay mantles, some thin with wisps of calico—litigants, appellants, petitioners, policemen in dark-blue tunics, and prisoners in irons. There floated in faint cries from the village, a quarter of a mile away, the pipe of birds and the guggle of camels.

At the desk sat the Presence—British rule incarnate in a young man in long boots and a green waterproof-khaki shooting-jacket, clean-shaven, with an eye and a mouth and a chin. Thus he rules, by himself, his kingdom of 5000 square miles and 800,000 souls.

"Roti Ram" says the cross-legged clerk on the carpet; "Roti Ram" bawls the beckoning orderly at the door. There appears, slipping off his shoes at the entrance, a sleek creature in a flowered cotton tunic, like the chintz in which ladies cover up their sofas. He scoops unctuously at the carpet and brings his hand thence to his turban; then bows his head and clasps his hands in the attitude of prayer. The clerk patters out a flowery rigmarole of mixed Arabic and Persian, blotted only by a few bare necessary disfigurements in the way of Hindi words,—that is Hindustani, the official language of Northern India. When he has finished, the District Officer raises his head and asks three questions in the vernacular; Roti Ram replies, with voluble self-abasement. Then the Sahib utters six words, ending with "Go." Roti Ram takes a scoop at the carpet, and, shuffling into his shoes, goes.

He is a landlord, and had desired to evict certain of his tenants. They had applied to the British assistant to be made permanent, occupancy tenants, or, in the alternative, for compensation. Now the landlord appealed against the rate of compensation allowed; the assistant is young and new to the district, and had fixed it at a rate which his experienced superior, knowing his district like a book, knows the land will not bear. Appeal allowed; Roti Ram happy.

"Mukkan Singh!" "Mukkan Singh!" A wisp of

brown arm and leg in a dirty orange turban palpitates in, and clasps his hands. "O Cherisher of the Poor," he begins, and then falls to weeping. "Stop that," says the Cherisher of the Poor, with sternness; he stops instantly, and in a voice of anguish pours forth his tale. A villain has taken away his wife and married her: he wants to prosecute them for bigamy.

"Where did you marry your wife?"

"O Presence, here—no; in Gurgaon—no; it was in the native state of—but no; the Presence will know that ——"

"Where is she now?"

"O Presence, here—no; in Gurgaon—no; she was in the native state—but no; my wife left my house, O my father and mother, and went first to Gurgaon, and there she and the man remained but a little while, and then—" And then Mukkan Singh's brain gives altogether, and he sobs limply. He is removed and set down at the tent door, and a native clerk with a soothing manner is set by him to extract his story in bits as his senses return. Eventually— Application for warrant to be made elsewhere; Mukkan Singh slightly comforted.

So they file in and out, one after another, confirming the Persian proverb that gold, women, and land are the seed of all troubles. Presently they are all done with for the moment; the sun is dropping down the sky, and their father and mother takes time for a cup of tea. But he is instantly back in his office again; he has yet to hear the points submitted to him from the outlying parts of the district, besides a multitude of petitions. When you hear them, you begin to realise what a District Officer is.

1. A peon, who was a Mussulman, went to serve a process in a remote Hindu village. There the natives detected him about to slay for his supper, with his official sword, a brood of young peacocks, and the defence of the sacred birds resulted in a free fight. The peon denied the impeachment with pained indignation: the fact was, he saw the boys of the village going about to slay the pea-chicks, and, knowing that Hindus held them sacred, was putting them into a tree for safety, when the villagers fell upon him. *Note by the local native authority*—The peon is known to be fond of roast peacock, and is it likely that Hindu boys would kill the holy chicks? *Question*, What is to be done to this peon? Peon dismissed.

2. A lady whose son and son's estate are under the court of wards—"which is practically me," explains the District Officer—asks for money wherewith to celebrate the consummation of the boy's marriage. Recommended that he be declared of age and put in possession of his property.

3. Ten native gentlemen of independent means have promised to subscribe for school prizes to the total amount of £1, 2s. 8d. When it comes to buy-

ing the prizes, only one of them can be induced to pay. What is to be done ? Nothing.

4. A woman has accused a man of looting her house ; it turns out he is her lover, and she adopted this device to conceal the fact from her husband. No charge.

5. An old woman accused a man of stealing two pennyworth of green stuff from her field; it turns out that, having a grudge against him, she has hit on this device to work it off, whereas in fact he took the stuff from his own field. No charge.

6. Two Government orderlies have had their official sashes three years and they are worn out; authority is sought to buy new ones. Granted.

7. A headman of a village has sold his land ; therefore, according to law, he ought not to remain headman, nor to collect the Government revenue, nor to receive his five per cent. commission thereupon. But the times are hard, and he has a brother, a fakir in Boondi, who will give him up his land and thus requalify him. Allowed.

8. A head-headman—one who is set over a group of villages, and gets one per cent. on the revenue raised therein, which is paid out of the revenue of one particular village—points out that, owing to hard times, the revenue of this village has been suspended, and there is nothing to pay his commission with. May it be paid from the revenue of the others in his group ? Yes.

9. A native magistrate has remanded a prisoner for fifteen days, whereas the law only allows a remand for fourteen. But on the fifteenth day a superior magistrate, who has power to try him, will return, and he will be saved the trouble and delay of a journey to the central town. Permitted.

10. There is a leper at Chotapur; what is to be done with him? Look up the latest of Government's innumerable regulations on the point and act accordingly.

11. Some prisoners in Jail for non-payment of fines allege that money is due to them for railway work at Hazirabad wherewith they could pay. Write and find out.

12. On the salt-line—the old barrier across country where the salt-tax used to be collected, the land of which is still Government property—a tree has fallen down. May it be sold by auction? It may.

13. A sepoy on furlough has brought Government cartridges to his village, which is contrary to the Arms Act. Communicate with his regiment.

14. A recruiting party enlisted two men in the jungles of a native state and brought them into the district, where they were found to be possessed each of a sword, contrary to the Arms Act. What is to be done with (*a*) the swords, (*b*) the recruits? (*a*) Confiscated, (*b*) nothing.

15. Certain villagers—having presumably quar-

relled with the village accountant—demand an audit of the books of the village funds.   Granted.

16.   May a headman attach a villager's buffalo in default of water-rate ?   He is able to pay.   Yes.

17.   May a headman attach standing crops in default of land-tax ?   Yes—to the extent of the taxes due.

18.   Government granted 10,000 rupees for wells in this district.   Hitherto, times being hard and demand for water great, it has only been granted for cheap *kutcha* wells (unbricked holes), which silt up in a couple of years.   Only 2000 rupees have been applied for, and in seven weeks the unused part of the grant will have lapsed.   May it be proclaimed that applications for *pukka* (bricked) wells will be received? Yes.

19.   Saltpetre licence requested.   Saltpetre is won by washing the earth that bears it and then evaporating in the sun; as salt is found with it, and salt is a strict Government monopoly in India, Government controls the saltpetre industry to the extent of charging two rupees for a licence.   Licence granted.

20.   Question of liquor licence.   Liquor can only be obtained from Government distilleries, and the price of licences acts as a check on drinking.   This is a case of a joint-concession, of which one partner has quarrelled with the other and wants him ejected. Refused.

21.   May a registrar's clerk, who is the son of a worthy man and is well reported on, be confirmed in his appointment ?   Yes.

22.   A question of tenant-right not contemplated in the Act.   Decided on general principles of common-sense.

23.   Gun licence applied for.   Granted.

24.   Gun licence applied for in same village. Refused.

24*a*.   Two more applicants, who had intended applying in case of the others' success, go away.

25.   An old gentleman with flowing white beard applies for the right of sitting on a chair on public occasions.   This privilege is only granted by Government as an honour, and he produces a pile of testimonials from former Government officers.   The sahib asks him, " District Board *ke* member *hai* ? " which is pure Hindustani.   Recommended that it be granted.

26.   A shivering, threadbare, skin-and-bone greybeard says that his land is about to be sold, in default of payment of debt, by the village usurer.   Law is law : nothing can be done for him.

27.   Village messenger, whose salary is 16s. a-year, complains that his pay is 10s. 8d. in arrear. Advised to get work elsewhere, of which there is plenty.

28.   Village leather-worker, same salary, 9s. 4d. in arrear.   Same advice.

The District Officer

By now the huddle of petitioners outside the tent has melted away. There remains (29) a pile of papers ten inches thick to be signed. " Every one of these means the ruination of some poor devil," says the District Officer; they are notices of proceedings to recover debt. " But I can't do anything."

And that will give you an idea of some of the things on which a District Officer had to keep his eye. Not all, for he has a light time just now: big questions like organisation of town councils, or water-works, or new canals, or famine-works, have let up for the moment. The Presence talks as familiarly of abolishing octrois and suppressing town councils as you do of engaging a housemaid. Nor yet does this give you an idea of all his work; for before this chapter began he had ridden four hours from village to village. A most commendable regulation directs him to spend so many weeks a-year in camp, journeying from point to point in his five thousand square miles. When the day's work is over the sahib strolls into the sunset with a gun, as he has done every evening for years, till the sight of black-buck and partridge has grown odious to him. That moment an army of tent-pitchers hauls down the court, takes the bench to pieces, and the whole thing is off on camels and carts to the next stopping-place. We remain in the living-tent to dine and sleep, for it is still cold at night; but there is a second living-tent already awaiting us at the next halting-place. We tumble out in the darkling twilight and start off through the country.   At every cross-road there await the Presence salaaming villagers and more rule to be exercised.

Here—dismounting by the wayside before a semi-circle of dark faces muffled in shawls against the bitter air of sunrise—he inspects the village registers, there checks the cattle-census returns, there refutes complaints of destitution by pointing to stacks of last year's fodder—which proves by one example the wisdom of going into camp—and at the next turning goes over the new village meeting-house.   I saw that house—a huge double-towered building, higher than that of the next village, they tell you eagerly—faced with white plaster and adorned with wondrous frescoes of men and beasts and crinolined gods spearing dark-blue devils.   On the roof above are revealed more esoteric studies,—a gentleman removing a lady's veil, and a white man drinking—O shame!—out of a bottle.   There the men meet in the hot-weather even-ings to smoke on the roof; here they put up the vil-lage guests at the expense of the village fund.   At one place, by a rare exercise of self-help, they are using the village fund to pay the destitute to dig out the village tank.   The same fund is used for judicious bribes to small officials when the village has a law-case.

Through all this primitive hospitality, primitive corruption, primitive joy and sorrow, moves the Father and Mother of District, granting, refusing, punishing, fostering. Respected, feared, trusted, to his 800,000 he is Omnipotence. I should have mentioned that he is thirty years old, and has been at this kind of work for six years.

XVII

JUSTICE

WE have given India justice—every authority agrees on that point; and, whatever else we may have done or left undone, this alone, we tell ourselves, is enough to justify our rule.

It is quite true, only it requires a little qualification. Most things in India, when examined, assume the features of a huge jest, and justice is like the others. We have offered India justice, only India will not have it. India prefers injustice. We have offered honest administration; India prefers dishonest. So that administration to-day means the light of a few honest Europeans shining in a naughty native world. Justice, when you come to see it in action, means the guess work of shrewd European magistrates steering through billowy seas of perjury.

From many cases in a district court let us take one or two. Din Mohammed and Abdul Kerim are charged, the one with stealing a down-calving buffalo, and the other with killing and skinning the same, well knowing it to have been stolen. The evidence against them has been heard already; to-day is for their defence. They crouch, salaaming, into the tent, shackled together by the wrists, with the other end of the chain in the hand of a blue-tunicked, khaki-breeched policeman. He is about half the size of the prisoners—two splendid fellows of six feet two or thereabout. Din Mohammed's demeanour is defiant: he has been here three times before. His blue-black moustache and beard bristle fiercely; his shining eyeballs are a splash in saucers of dazzling white. Abdul Kerim, inexperienced, thinks that a melting mood may better serve his turn: his crimson-turbaned head droops sideways like a peony in a shower, and his eyes are turned plaintively upwards.

There are three witnesses for the defence. Each stands over six feet, each has a beard and moustache like horsehair and eyes like onyx; they might all of them be blood relations to Din Mohammed—which is exactly what they are. They enter and stand with clasped hands and eyes directed unswervingly towards the top left-hand corner of the tent. Their story is simple and consistent. Din Mohammed bought the buffalo in their presence for seventeen rupees, and they solemnly swear that this is the truth. Every now and then one of the prisoners, standing also with folded hands and rubbing their bare toes together, throws in a word of encouragement or corroborative detail. Cross-examination brings out no discrepancy in their story: time, place, figures, names, tally exactly. And the last of them winds up: " O Presence, I have kept the Fast for forty years and never told a lie."

A judge at home would have no more to say : obviously not guilty. In India, unluckily, there are one or two further points to be considered. As, first, that Din Mohammed is a landless man, and has probably never eaten meat in his life—much less killed a down-calving buffalo, which in a month or so would be giving twenty quarts of milk a-day. Second, that a down-calving buffalo costs at least forty rupees, and up to three hundred—not seventeen. And, third, that Din Mohammed has been convicted of this same offence three times already ; and that on each of these occasions exactly the same witnesses appeared on his behalf, including the Washington who never told a lie, and swore to exactly the same story.

" Bring in the prisoners." As they rattle in, the magistrate looks up : " Din Mohammed, seven years ; Abdul Kerim, six months." Out they go. A district magistrate has no time to address the prisoner at the bar and dilate on the enormity of his offence.

That was a very simple case, and interesting only as illustrating the native idea of evidence. But some are brain-cracking perplexities. For example, a magnificently powerful Sikh is next brought in, his clothes blood-spotted, his jaw broken, and his mouth hideously on one side. As he enters he artistically drops off his turban, disclosing a big wound on his head, and bursts into lung-tearing sobs. When he is quieted, an equally superb Sikh, grey-bearded and patriarchal, steps in to testify against him. " Rushed up with a sword," he begins. "When?" "The fifth of January." "Where?" "In front of my house." "Who rushed up with a sword?" "Jagta did." It is a further amiable peculiarity of the Indian witness that he begins his evidence in the middle, and all pronouns and adverbs and similar embellishments have to be dragged out of him by a corkscrew of cross-examinations.

The case appears to be this. All the witnesses agree that the prisoner rushed up with a sword and assaulted the old man, that the old man's son rushed between and got a cut in the thigh, the which he displays with triumph. Further, that the son then hit prisoner on the hand with a bamboo and got the sword from him—the sword lies on the tent floor, alive to testify the fact—and that the prisoner was thereupon given into custody. The flaw in their evidence is that, whereas it is obvious that the prisoner thereafter got a most tremendous thrashing, and was indeed half killed, every one of the witnesses denies with an oath that anything of the kind happened. On the other hand, the prisoner cannot account for the illegal possession of the sword, which is evidently a cast police sabre: he says it is not his, and that he never saw it before. And the civil surgeon—native—who examined the son's wound, reports that it could not have been inflicted by Jagta, but was probably manufactured by the son himself.

Now, five years ago, Jagta was concerned in abducting the daughter of the old man. He and another were condemned, but having appealed before a native judge and paid him 1500 rupees, were acquitted. Since then Jagta has brought a criminal charge against the old man and his son, supported by abundant evidence, which was adjudged false and malicious, and for bringing which he was fined. The two parties will go on with their accusations and counter-accusations for a generation.

There are, therefore, two hypotheses. First, the old man's party may have fallen on Jagta and beaten him; then, to cover themselves, rushed off to the police, accused him of murderous assault, and bribed them to supply a cast sword to support the allegation. Second, Jagta may have actually made the attack, and got the unacknowledged thrashing in return; and then his friends may have bribed the assistant surgeon to say that the son's wound was self-inflicted. Both hypotheses are in the nature of native things probable; only both cannot be true—and how in the world is the wretched magistrate to decide between them?

And now you understand the nature of Indian justice. The case is dirt-common, and quite typical. Of course the wretched magistrate has to take full notes of all the evidence, of which half must be, and all may be, false. Indian law allows great freedom of appeal—with the possible result that when, after years of trouble, the magistrate has caught the master cattle-lifter of his district, an inexperienced appellate judge sets him free again because the evidence appears equal on each side. In one case out of ten he may be right; but who is to blame him when he is wrong? To give India justice would demand second-sight. India loves litigation: the court is the ryot's parish council—as good as a circus. It would probably be wrong to say that the native does not appreciate honesty in his judges; but he appreciates it mainly with the sporting notion that it is a good thing to be sure that the litigant who cheats best will win. Every day cases come into court in which every word of the evidence is carefully, lovingly fabricated beforehand. Prosecution and defence are alike masterly and elaborate perjuries, for the native—especially in cases where, as usual, both sides are to blame—will never be content without improving on the truth. It is the morality of the country, and you live longer if you laugh at it than if you weep; yet sometimes you get a case that is truly devilish. The false witness begins before the crime is even committed. In the districts about Peshawar especially, where murder is the equivalent of writing to the newspapers with us, men will go to the police, at intervals, for months, to point out that So-and-so hates Such-an-one, has threatened to kill him, is believed to be lying in wait for him. Sure enough, in the fulness of time, Such-an-one is found dead with a knife through his back, and So-and-so is arrested. But the real murderers were the men who had warned the police; so that magistrates will hardly ever dare to convict a man lest he be an innocent victim, and murders have gone up about Peshawar to four hundred or so a-year.

Not a single native is to be trusted. Many no doubt are impeccable; but with instances of dishonesty among the ablest and longest unsuspected, it is next to impossible to be sure of anybody. The truth is, that native opinion does not utterly condemn corruption. The jail authorities encourage prisoners to write petitions that they may get backsheesh from the dealers who provide the Government paper. The police are notoriously corrupt, the officials are corrupt, the officers of the court are corrupt, the very native magistrates and judges are corrupt. A case is adjourned and adjourned and adjourned, every time on a plausible pretext, for months; meanwhile the judge's jackals are out in the villages hinting to the suitor that if he will but agree to this or that compromise, the cause shall be heard and settled at once. As a rule, they take bribes from each side, and then decide the case on its merits. The man of really scrupulous honesty takes the same present from each side, and then—just like our own Lord Bacon—returns the money to the loser.

Only why, you ask, is this allowed to go on? Because, though everybody suspects, and hundreds of natives know, you cannot get a man to come forward and say, "I paid this magistrate such a sum," and prove it.   Of course not, for the man who paid is usually the man who profits.   It is one of the superlative jests of India to see a superior tell the equivalent of a county court judge he strongly suspects him of taking bribes, and the learned gentleman sobbing on the floor and challenging anybody that has bribed him to come forward and say so, yet in no way resenting the charge.   But only last year one of the ablest native judges in the Punjab was found guilty of venality in its very grossest form.   He had taken 1500 rupees from Jagta and his friend; from the brother of a maharajah he had had as much as 60,000 in one case.   His cleverness was such that every one of his decisions looked plausible.   His wealth, of course, was prodigious; and, when the crash came, he was off to Pondicherry: much of his money was invested in native States, and bags of rupees or bars of gold were found hidden in the homes of professional thieves.

" Our pay," said a Government official—retired— " is but the chutni which we eat with our meat."

XVIII

PROVIDENCE AND THE PARLOUR GAME

AMONG the duties of a District Officer, in his general capacity of Father and Mother of the People, falls the inspection of anything in the nature of a public institution that he may happen to come across. In two days I had the honour of assisting at inspections of a jail, a dispensary, a school, a public garden, a treasury, a police-station, a dak bungalow, the registers of half-a-dozen villages, two Arab stallions, and a stud donkey.

When you meet the Government of India in camp it seems the ideal of a single system adapted to a simple country. It appears to reside, not in ink and paper, but in men. The man knows his business and knows his own mind, and Government appears to work in a string of six-word orders delivered at the rate of a couple of dozen an hour. The Briton understands and commands; the native understands and performs; work is done quickly and cheaply, and there is a responsible man to see that it is done.

Unfortunately that is only half the fact. If that were all, India—provided only that its local rulers were both trustworthy and trusted—would be the best-governed country in the world. But there is another side. The rulers, for the most part eminently trustworthy, are only half-trusted. From that comes supervision, regulations, correspondence, clerks by the thousand, writing by the ream, red-tape by the league. The Government of India, in the one aspect the ideal organisation for work, becomes in the other the inevitable and gigantic joke—a cobweb of rules and checks and references, compared with which eight-pack Patience is simplicity and the House that Jack built terseness.

As soon as you leave the tent and come under a Government roof it is this side of the matter that begins to unroll itself before you. At the police-station alone ten books are brought out for inspection. Every single thing that the police does is carefully written down, even to the cleaning of their Sniders. Every pill that goes out of the dispensary is similarly made a note of, together with the recipient's name and religion. At the school every attendance of every scholar is kept, together with records of all passes and failures and long reports from inspectors. Thus with everything.

So far, of course, all is natural and indeed necessary. You would find almost as much paper covered in similar institutions at home. In India, furthermore, the details of administration must needs be largely in native hands, and of responsibility the ordinary native official is neither desirous nor worthy.

Providence and the Parlour Game

Therefore he writes down questions in black and white, and his European superior gives him black and white answers.

It is not only officials who fly to writing as a friendly shelter against responsibility. In all India you will hardly find a native who will take verbal instructions. You send a peon with a letter : he will take no notice when you tell him where to go, but instead will waylay every European he sees in the street and hold out the letter to him, in hopes that the talismanic writing will find its destination for itself. When I first started forth into India I came on a native doctor, or semi-doctor, on plague duty. His instructions were to keep passengers from Bombay in a segregation camp. I assured him, and he must have known, that plague regulations did not apply to Europeans; he replied that if I would kindly wait twenty-four hours on the ground at nowhere-in-particular he would telegraph to his official superior for instructions. When I eventually lost patience, and said I was going on, instructions or not, he asked if, at least, he might telegraph on the number of my ticket. I gave it him : at the sight of a regulation number he quite revived, and of course nobody heard any more of it. Similarly the guard of a railway train writes down the number of your ticket in his notebook—why, Heaven knows. Briefly, the whole ambition of the native is to leave off being a man and to become a sort of pneumatic tube ; and the sole qualification for the native public service is to be able to read and write and to know the way to the post-office.

But, to go back to Government, the records of the police-station and the dispensary are meagre compared with those of the *patwari*, or village accountant. This gentleman keeps a number of books, which together form the minutest record of the economic history of the village. He has a linen map—he lugs it out of his pocket like a very dirty handkerchief—which shows the boundaries, not only of the village lands, but of every field. In his records he puts down the area of land sown with each crop and the amount harvested. In another book he puts down the rent of each field and the land-tax, while any changes of ownership or of occupancy are likewise entered. Everything that the wit of man could hit upon as re-cordable is recorded. So long as the *patwari* does his duty—which he usually does, unless he is paid to do otherwise—Government has matter for an economic history of rural India beside which the collected works of Mr. Charles Booth would be a superficial pamphlet.

To the British mind such a system is suspiciously reminiscent of the given moment at which every child in France is saying its multiplication table; and you will ask, What is the use of it all? Much. For the Government of India—you will hardly guess it from the Wedderburns of the age, but it is most true —is the tenderest-conscienced ruler in the world.

Providence and the Parlour Game

Every thirty years it assesses the land revenue, which
is its principal source of income, and in this work the
village registers are invaluable.   They show, as nearly
as experience can forecast the future, what the land
can pay, and it is assessed accordingly.   The theory
in India has always been that the land is the State's,
and that the State is entitled to the whole of the produce after the cultivator has half-filled his belly from
it.   In British theory this right has relaxed.   In
Bengal and parts of the North-West Provinces it has
surrendered its rights to zemindars by the Permanent
Settlement, which cheats it out of its fair share in the
prosperity of the country.   Elsewhere the settlement
is in the nature of a thirty-years' lease of the land,
granted either to a village collectively, as landlord, or
directly to the cultivator; and in this case it is considered reasonable to take one-half of the net profit.
But in practice the assessment is generally much
lower.   Sometimes blunders are made, and it is much
higher.   There is a story of a landowner who be-
queathed all his land to the officer who had last assessed it—remarking that, as the sahib had taken all
the produce, he might as well have the land itself.
But in the main the settlements are equitable, and for
that thanks are largely due to the *patwari's* register.

Only Government is not content with the register.
The settlement officer has also to furnish a most
elaborate report, beginning with the district's history
from the earliest times, telling you not merely what

grows there and how much it fetches, but also the race of the people and their local superstitions, a great part of their language, and what they look like, and who has the right of sitting on a chair, and whether the post-office is also a money-order office, and how many people died of ruptured spleen, and what the irrigation system was in the reign of Aurungzebe, and before there was any irrigation system at all what there was where the irrigation system now is, and the deuce knows what besides.

If Government were content with that—it is only once in thirty years. But the curiosity of Government is insatiable and feverish. Every year the District Officer has to make reports on every important branch of his administration—huge piles of foolscap an inch thick. If Government were only content with that—but there are a million subjects on which special reports have to be made. If a wretched babu clerk to a medical officer embezzles Government cash, it is the District Officer who really suffers; for he has to write a special report—Sub-head No. 123,456,789 —on defalcations of Government servants. If a member of Parliament asks a question in the House— purely to waste time, as like as not, or to get his name into the " Times "—the Secretary of State asks the Viceroy for the answer, and he asks the Lieutenant-Governor, and he asks the Commissioner, and he asks the District Officer, and he collects information from his native subordinates. He combines their answers into a report, and the Commissioner combines the reports of the District Officers, and the Lieutenant-Governor combines the reports of the Commissioners, and the Viceroy combines the reports of the Lieutenant-Governors, and sends the result home to Whitehall, which it reaches long after the man who started the inquiry has forgotten that he ever made it. And on the top of that some toy ruler in the Secretariat at Calcutta or Allahabad, or somewhere a thousand miles away, will have the idea to get a series of monographs on the home arts and industries of the people, or the natural history of the bullock, or the extent to which natives wear shoes. So the subject is served out to various wretched civil servants like an essay at school, and each writes a book about it which nobody ever reads.

The people who mostly instigate this sort of thing are always talking to you about "the art of government" and "the way to rule men." It is not ruling men; it is a parlour game. Doubtless the information acquired is very interesting; and if India were rich and had a superabundance of British officers with nothing better to do, it would be a most blameless and intelligent way of working off superfluous cash and the energy of the superfluous staff. But India is poor, and it has one trustworthy administrator to every three hundred thousand of its people. So that in the cities money goes for hundreds of babus to copy and register things that do not matter, to for-

ward them and acknowledge receipt of same.   And in
the villages the Father and Mother, who should be going in and out among his officials and his people, becomes a parent who writes treatises on education while
the children play in the gutter.   The Presence might
better be called the Absence.   He must cease playing
Providence to play the Parlour Game.

XIX

THE FOREST OFFICER

THE elephant knows. When the mahout wants to get on to her neck, she takes him on her trunk and bends it till he can walk up her forehead. When you want to get on to her back, she lets down a hind-foot to make one step, and curls up her tail to make another. She knows that a branch she can walk under will sweep you off her back; therefore she goes round, or, if that is not possible, pushes down the tree with her trunk as gently as you put down a teacup. At every ford she tries the bottom, at every bridge she tries the planks: she knows better than you do how much she weighs and what will bear her.

Jerk, jerk, jerk—she seesaws you at every step, for you are sitting on a blanket just atop of her shoulder. Now and again the mahout addresses her in a language, handed down from father to children, that only mahouts and elephants understand, or smites her over the head with the heavy, iron-hooked ankus. It falls with a dull thud on her hairy forehead; it would crack your skull like an eggshell, but it hurts the elephant as a dead leaf would hurt you. Behind her ear you see a crevasse of raw flesh in the armour-plating of hide: that wound is kept open, and through it only can she be made to feel. She just tramples on, now tilted almost on to her head, now all but standing on her tail; over the shallow rivers, along the rutted cart-tracks, till the sun begins to bake and the line of hills in front changes from a wash of blue to a clear-cut saw-edge of shaded greens and browns.

Past a village of leaning mud, past a string of squeaking carts—the elephant knows the bullocks will shy, and tries to skirt round them: they shy none the less, and the cart twists on the yoke-pole and turns clean turtle. The driver is not in the least disturbed: time is plenty in India—jerk, jerk, on we go. Now we begin to climb the lowest slopes—the toes of the Himalaya, whose waists are girdled with clouds and whose heads look over the floor of heaven. We tilt up and down narrow paths, brush past mats of branch and thorn and creeper: now we are in the very forest, the native immemorial jungle. From the elephant you look over a sea of tossing greens curling into a yellow foam of young leaves, or flecked with eddies of rusty brown where the frost has bitten. Nearer are pavilions and cloisters roofed with slabs of blue-blushing creeper-leaf. Across the alleys dart sun-birds, gold-green dusted with bronze, or magpies flashing yellow-plush bodies under black-and-white wings, or tiny blue-satin kingfishers reflected in dia-mond cascades. Then a creaking wooden screech, a crackling in the underwood, and overhead, with his crested prow, his sea-purple side, his long wake of plumes, floats by in full sail the royal peacock. In the intervals the jungle is dead silent.

Another rise, another elbow of cliff, and the elephant, plucking a tuft of grass to shampoo herself with, is kneeling down by a little plastered bungalow on a dry lawn. It is the forest lodge. Here, looking out and down to the blue steak of the river as it scrambles out of the hills and trundles the rafts of deodar-sleepers down to the railway, looking across to the scarred sides of the hills beyond, to the floor of plain on his right and the giant's stairway of mountain on his left, lives the forest officer.

He stands nearer six feet six than six feet, and rides nearer fifteen stone than fourteen ; therefore, drawing the pay of a forest officer, he usually walks. In the corner of his bare-plastered living-room stand a rifle and gun, which he takes out when he walks, in order to persuade himself that he has his recreations. At his feet snores a retriever-spaniel, which he keeps that he may not forget how to talk English. His food comes out of tins, except the jungle-fowl and hares he shoots and the unleavened chapatties his servant bakes instead of bread. Religion in this region allows the shooting of pea-fowl, but because of religion he denies himself beef. He gets up two hours before dawn, that he may waste no daylight in beginning his work at the far end of the forest. After dinner he is too tired to read, though he loves books, and his opinions on them are those of a man who thinks when we are talking. As it is, he nods over the five-days-old " Pioneer "; he cannot keep his eyes open after half-past eight. Thus he lives alone from month to month and year to year. His wife and children and friends are the young trees in the forest. Sometimes in the jungle he comes across another white man, who stays five minutes and talks English over a peg.

If he wants to save his soul alive, he must save it, like three-quarters of the rest of them in India, by work. The work of the forest officer is strange enough to the ordinary Briton: there are forests of a sort at home, but no forestry to speak of. My friend knows nothing except forestry, he cheerfully alleges, and therefore he must cling to his present billet through solitude and fevers, or else starve. In France and Germany they have State forests—ten square miles to an officer with efficient rangers and guards, where the Indian officer has perhaps a thousand with hopeless natives. Eleven million acres— over a third of the area of England—are the domain immediately under the Indian Forest Department, and of late years Government has begun to make money out of them.

The forest officer must save his soul by works, but also by faith. He differs from the other slaves of India in that they can reap the fruit of their labours; he never. The district officer sees his people harvest their crops and Government garner its revenue; the engineer watches his canal make fields out of sand. Of the trees the forest officer plants, the first will not be felled till he has left the service; before the last is turned into revenue his very tombstone will be moss-grown. He plans by night and sweats by day to create what he will never see. Of all India's bondsmen she asks the greatest sacrifice of him; of all she asks the best of their life, but of him she asks his very individuality. He must sink himself to be a mere connecting-link, a hyphen in the story of his wood, taking up that which was old before he was born, and passing it on to be still young when he is dead. Twenty rings in a log—and the life's work of a man!

It is his to follow the working plan. A forest, you understand, is so much national capital, and, like other capital, it must be made to bear interest. If you cut down all your timber, your capital is gone, and your children will want for sleepers and window-frames and firewood—that is what naughty rajahs do. If you fell nothing, you are wrapping your talent up in a napkin. The working plan is designed to draw the annual increment from the forest and to leave the principal untouched. The trees in a particular wood take, we will say, a hundred years to reach maturity; then, if the wood is of a thousand acres' area, you fell ten acres each year. As you cut down you sow again; so that at the end of each year's fellings the forest is divided into a hundred ten-acre compartments varying in age from nothing to ninety-nine.

Simple enough so far; but so far the forest officer's work is only a bit of paper. There are a thousand complications. Some young trees will not grow except in the shade of others, which shelter them from sun or frost or wind; then you cannot simply cut down the forest in strips. It may be that part of the wood is on a slope, and to clear it altogether would untie the binding roots and call down a landslip. In such cases you must have the trees of different ages mixed. Then, again, there are such things as sapling forests, which grow from the stools of felled trees and not from seed; these will be cleared at regular intervals, say, of twenty years—a less impersonal business for the forest officer, for he can actually see his forest grow from year to year.

Whatever the plan, there is only one course for him. Experts argue theories of planting or thinning: he must go out into the forest and look at the trees. No two cases for planting, for thinning, will be exactly alike, because no two trees out of all the millions are: he must go out and judge. So out we will go, under the beating sunshine. First along the fire-lines, where the ground has been cleared to a width that flames will hardly leap over: the cutting of fire-lines around and within the forest is the first precaution of the conservator. In this forest it was at one time neglected; hence crooked trees which have had their sap frizzled up one year and have budded in another direction the next ; now they will never make good logs if they grow for ages.   Then we turn up a nullah—a mad torrent in the rains, now a scrunching ladder of pebble and boulder.   Then aside into the forest towards a sweet savour of wood-smoke : here are half-a-dozen squat hillmen round their earth-banked charcoal furnaces.   They asked the other day for new axes, and the officer inquires, in their Him-alaya dialect, if they have got them yet.   " No, O Presence," says the monkey-whiskered headman. The ranger had been told to serve them out, and has not done it.   Then off through the long grass that brushes your ears, breaking through tangles of bush, dodging under branches, wriggling over meshes of creeper ; a distant tapping sharpens into the chock-chock of axes, then comes a burst of sunlight, and we are in a half-open glade where coolies are felling and cross-cutting.

This particular work was reported by the ranger as finished three weeks ago ; it is still going on.   And there you fall once more across the maddening, be-numbing clog of all work in India—the native sub-ordinate.   In the law-court it is his dishonesty that most strikes you : here it is his indolent incapacity. And, indeed, if you cannot get good native magistrates and clerks, how shall you look for good rangers ?   The ranger is probably a bunnia's son : that shopkeeper-usurer sees that education brings a livelihood, and educates his son for the public service. Such as are not good enough for desks in the civil service go to the Forest School at Dehra Dun, and presently are fledged rangers. For centuries the rangers' fathers have been sitting on the counter of a shop, sticking their fingers into a pile of sugar and sucking them: what should the ranger do in a forest? He hates the place and everything about it. Why should he walk over a lot of beastly stones, through a lot of beastly prickles? Then in the day it is hot in the forest, and in the morning he cannot go out without his food. Why, indeed, should he be asked to walk at all? To walk is an indignity in India.

So he ambles his pony along the fire-line every few days, and leaves the inside of the forest to the foresters and the guards and the coolies and God. And when his officer asks him what has been done, he draws on his voluble imagination. The ranger in this case had ridden within twenty yards of the fellings every day— or said he had—for weeks; he had never taken the trouble to turn in and see how the work was really being done.

A few yards further the beat of axes suddenly ceased behind a bush, and was succeeded by the buzz of a saw. A turbaned head appeared, watching our approach through the boughs; when we reached the spot, two coolies were cross-cutting a log, and a forester sprang up in great confusion, bare-headed. The meaning of that little comedy was obscure to me, but plain to the expert. The man had been ordered to make his coolies use the saw for cross-cutting, which they, disliking, had prevailed on him to let them hack away with the axe. When he saw the Presence coming he gave warning and they flew to the saw; and to prove he had not been keeping Cave he knocked off his puggari, without which no self-respecting native would ever appear before a superior. With an air of bashful confusion he rewound the turban and humbly pointed out that he was making them use the saw.

Thus native assistants assist. The white man is out in the cold, dead hours before dawn, when the beasts are gone to sleep and the birds are not yet awake, when the very trees doze and the forest is a cavern of black silence, stirred only by the plump of heavy dewdrops on to the decaying humus below. The natives are in bed; and when the white man comes in back-broken at sunset he has two hours of asking why they did not do their work and of doing it for them. By this means, despite the neglect of many generations, the forests are slowly filling up with straight, young trees, and the bookshops with works on the gratifying efficiency of our native public services. That is exactly India.

XX

THE CANAL

No rain had fallen for the better part of six months, and the snows were as yet unloosened about the shoulders of the Himalaya. Out of the foothills the Jumna issued on to the endless level, like a thread of blue water on a broad belt of dead-yellow sand and round-worn pebble. Over and under and through scrambled the scanty trickle—a profitless thimbleful, you would say, to the vast plains and dry-lipped deserts below.

Following it through the thickets and over the stones, you come to a road raised on a long embankment; and following that, you find it presently closes in on the river. The stream, confined on this side, appears to gather weight, and slides along the more swiftly, as if making up its mind to a purpose.

Then suddenly you look ahead—and there is no more Jumna! It has stopped—disappeared. Across its broad bed, with pier and buttress, bridge and battlement, runs a long dam, relentlessly solid. Between the piers you see double flood-gates, each with an upper and a lower leaf, and a travelling winch on rails above to draw them up. But at present they are all shut down, and the stream pulls in vain against that curb. Beyond it there is still the broad bed of dead-yellow sand and round-worn pebble—but only a feeble ooze through chinks, a puddle and a gutter-runnel of water struggle to lick over it. What on earth has become of the Jumna?

Next moment you see. Before you, along the right bank, is another weir with many piers and a broad road over it, double flood-gates, and a travelling-winch. The river, now bolting outright, swerves round a curved revetment, rears back from the dam in its front, and plunges madly through the arches of the other. Under the weir it is a lather of foam; a hundred yards beyond it is in hand again, galloping with a swift and solid momentum between its narrower banks. The Jumna has ceased to be the wild stallion of a river; it is broken to man's service—bitted and harnessed into a canal.

From now on it has a double use: it is a highway where there was little road and no railway, and it is a perpetual spring of fertility where there was only sand and drought. In early summer, when the melting snows bring it down in shouting spate from the mountains, the gates are opened in the transverse weir, and it tears along its natural bed as well as along the canal. When the water rises above the lower leaf of the gates the upper can either be raised to let it off or kept lowered to hold it in place. It can be held up at the transverse weir and driven down the canal, or it can be held up at the lateral weir and eased off down the natural bed.

And it takes some regulating, as the white-bearded engineer will tell you. He is simple and courteous and very keen, even after thirty uncomplaining years of canal work—now shiver, now sweat, and always work and anxiety. It is at posts like this you meet the non-commissioned ranks of British India—like this man, living with a working wife, bringing up children with difficulty, pinching the not over-liberal pay to squeeze out the expense of summers in the hills. Such men—there are hundreds of them on canals and railways, in engine-rooms and fitting-sheds—are not the least heavily-burdened of the slaves of India. They hunger for Camden Town as the others hunger for St. James's Street; but there is no three-yearly privilege-leave for them. Their children must be brought up in India or not at all; and to be country-bred in India is good neither for mind, body, nor estate. In big stations there may be a club for them, and tennis with sergeants' daughters; more likely they will be pushed away where there is a white superior to talk to six times a-year and a white equal never. If you come across such, and be expected, you will find the good man in a new white topi, and the good lady in an old silk gown, and tea and Huntley & Palmer's biscuits. Sit down and talk: you seldom have such a chance to do a good deed without any virtue of your own.

The Canal

So here, in his little bungalow, alone—the higher ranks of Public Works Engineers are few, and the few are here to-day, and at the other end of the canal to-morrow, and dead of enteric the next day—keeping his accounts, commanding his coolies, sits the white-bearded engineer, and governs the river Jumna. When the floods come down it is anxious work, for it needs some masonry to stand against that tugging, snorting strain. It takes some regulation to prevent the torrent from savaging banks and bottom and swallowing up gates and travelling-winch and piers and all. To get due warning of such onslaughts they have just laid a telephone-wire miles up into the hills: here is a gauge which, when the water rises to a given height, automatically rings a bell at the head works below.

Even now, when there is a bare three feet of water on the sill, there is plenty of devil in the Jumna. The four natives who man your boat row as you might know that natives would—a slice in, a languid scoop, and a good rest between the strokes; yet you race down, and the boat will have to go back by bullock-cart. You soon forget that you are navigating a canal, for this is as broad as the Thames below Folly Bridge, and curbed with rough stone jetties and streaked with cross-currents into hills and valleys of water like the very Rhine. Now your boat bump-bumps against the bottom, now spins round a headlong corner, now kicks her rudder in the air and digs her nose down a sliding cataract. Now you are caught and all but hurled against a raft of sleepers; for the canal is a main highway of the timber trade. Next you coast round a big island, where tulip-trees mosaic the intense blue with black leafless boughs and scarlet blossoms, where tribes of puff-billed water-fowl, half-duck, half-cormorant, jump off the branches and flap heavily towards the long spear-grass above the sand-shoals. Here is a village alive with calves and staring brown faces; here a soulless flat of poor pasture, where the canal is swilling great fids of bank; here another weir-bridle across the still restive stream; below it, a shoot of beryl-green water and snow-white foam into soberer, profounder reaches below.

So you could float for days, with the water-air cool on your skin and the water-rustle drowsy in your ear. . . . But wake up: this is not Nuneham or Shiplake; this is hard business. This Western Jumna Canal is part of perhaps the most original and beneficent piece of engineering in the world. It flows thus along the watershed between the Ganges and Indus basins for over a hundred miles, giving out water into a gridiron of channels that lead it to the checkered fields, till at last what is left trickles back to its mother Jumna at Delhi. A second branch of it heads out the best part of two hundred miles to Sirsa and Hissar and the sands that fringe the Bikanir desert, where the year's rain is less than twenty inches, and generally fails at that, and two crops out of three must sponge on the canal or die of thirst. This pleasant river of tulip-trees and water-fowl spells life or death two hundred miles away.

This is only one of the great canals with which British rule has turned flood into steady moisture and desert into corn-land, has mitigated bad years and filled to overflowing the abundance of good. This particular Western Jumna Canal, it happens, was there before we came: an Emperor of Delhi—Feroz Shah, in the reign of our Edward III.—cut it and planted it with trees. Only his engineer made the tiny oversight of leading it along the line of drainage instead of the watershed, so that wheels and buckets and oxen were needed to prevent it from drying the land instead of wetting it. Left derelict till our time, it was then realigned; and its perfected principle was applied to nearly all the great rivers of Northern India.

The principle is briefly this. The rivers have eaten out low, narrow valleys for themselves; so that an ordinary dam would not be enough to raise the waters to the upper lands beyond the valleys, while simple channels could not reach them at all except at points low down the river's course: you would have to take off cuttings and lead them over miles of country before they could begin their work. The plan, therefore, has been hit on of intercepting the whole bulk of the rivers as soon as they enter the plains, and carrying it to the watershed that runs parallel with the course of the streams: thence, by gravitation, it distributes itself. Of these canals the Jumna sends out three—one eastward, one westward from Tajawallah to Delhi, and another from Delhi to Agra. The Ganges is intercepted at Hurdwar, whence four thousand miles of main and branch lead it back to the natural bed at Cawnpore; the stream that gathers from tributaries below Hurdwar is again taken up and sent to reinforce the original canal. In the Punjab the Ravi, the Beas, the Sutlej, and now the Chenab, have been similarly shed abroad on to waste places; on the latter especially colonies have come from congested districts to land-grants in what till now was desert. Of the great rivers of the north, only the Jhelum and Indus remain untapped.

These works of irrigation are brilliant, effective, popular, and—the crowning grace of public works—they pay. It was worth the while of Government to make them, even if it were not a father's duty, for the increased land-revenue they bring in; but, apart from that, they actually pay by the water-rates levied from the owners whose fields they give upon. In each village a water-registrar, corresponding to the land-registrar, keeps the account of the fields irrigated, and the headman collects the rent. The Punjab canals already pay over six per cent., though the Chenab works are but just completed; the North-Western Province gets about the same; the patriarchal Western Jumna yields nine.

The Canal

That is good hearing; the idea of charity in Government is hateful to well-balanced minds. But for the true eulogy of Indian irrigation you must go to the cultivator. Forms of Government the cultivator neither knows nor recks of; even justice he does his best to clog with perjury; but he understands and appreciates water on the land. Go into any village and mark the difference between this field and that—the dense, long-strawed, full-eared barley; the dark, thick-podded rape; the dense blue-flowering gram-pulse—on one side: the stunted, bloomless blotches —is it meant for crop or fallow?—on the other. Water is scarce just now; seven or ten days of full canal, then seven or ten of dry, is the usual alternation. The ryot grumbles on the dry days, as tillers of the soil will; but every village has a grey-beard old enough to remember what happened when winter rains failed in the past—in the years before the sahibs bridled the river and brought it to the village gate. And on the full days—go out at evenfall and see the ryot naked to mid-thigh scraping entrances in his little embankments with his antediluvian hoe. First one, then another, rod by rod, till the whole field is soaked. Listen to the glug-glug of the water as the last compartment gets its douse, and look at the great peace on the ryot's face. You can almost hear his soul glug-glugging with the like satisfaction.

XXI

THE SHRINE OF THE SIKHS

THE Sikhs are the youngest of the great powers of India. A kind of Hindu Protestants, their Luther arose about 1500 to fulminate against caste and the worship of idols. Instead of Shiva and Kali, they worship their Bible, which is called the Granth. They abhor tobacco, and it is impiety to shave or cut the hair. Sometimes, when a Sikh plays polo, you may see it come undone and wave behind him like a horse-tail. From Puritans they turned to Ironsides, praying and fighting with equal fervour, wearing an iron quoit in their turbans, partly as a sign of grace, and partly as a defence against a chance sword-cut.

For some three hundred years they fought the Mussulmans, Mogul or Afghan, for the dominion of the Punjab, and won it in the end. The Mussulmans tortured the Sikh teachers to death with their families; the Sikhs sacked and massacred in return. The Mussulmans took Amritsar, blew up the temple of the Granth, and washed its foundations in the blood of sacred cows; the Sikhs took Lahore, blew up the mosques, and washed their foundations in the blood of unclean swine. Fanatics and heroes, they lived only for the holy war, and became the barrier of India against the Mussulman tribes of the North-West. At last, in 1823, the Sikhs were united under Ranjit Singh into the greatest power of India. But he died in 1839; four wives and seven concubines were burned with him, and you can see their tombs under marble lotuses in Lahore. Ten years later the second Sikh War was over, and the Punjab was British. If the Sikh rule was short, their battles have ever been long.

The later history of the Sikhs—how kindly they accepted British rule, which has still treated their religion with more than tolerant respect; how they supplied and supply to-day noble regiments to our army; the splendid services they rendered in the Mutiny, but a decade after their conquest; the un-swerving gallantry and devotion which they have displayed on every field of honour,—all this is part of the military history of the Empire. The very officers of Gurkha and Pathan and Dogra regi-ments admit that the Sikh is the ideal of all that is soldierly.

Ranjit's capital was Lahore, but the holy city has ever been Amritsar. " The Pool of Immortality," it means, and here in the centre of the pool is the Golden Temple. In its present form it is not yet a century old—quite an infant in India. Amritsar, indeed, is full of new things; for, as it is the Mecca, it is also the Manchester of the Punjab. Carpets and shawls and silks are manufactured there, or brought in by merchants from Persia and Tibet, Bokhara and Yarkand. Here you can see modern native India untainted by Europe.

Amritsar wears an air of solid prosperity. Not in the least like the manufacturing towns we know, lacking the machinery of Bombay or Calcutta, it neither shadows its streets with many-storeyed factories nor defiles its air with smoke. But it wears a uniform and thriving aspect, as of a town with a present and a future rather than a past. The Bond Street of Delhi is a double row of decayed mansions propped up by tottering booths; the houses of Amritsar are middle-sized, regular, stably built of burned bricks, neither splendid nor ruinous. The looms clatter and whir in the factories, and the merchant bargains between the whiffs of his hookah in his shop, and Amritsar grows rich in a leisurely Indian way, unfevered by Western improvements.

To the Western eye it is unenterprising and rather shabby. The stable comfort of Amritsar stops short at the good brick walls; inside, the shops are bare brick and plaster. There is nothing in the least imposing about it. "Chunder Buksh, Dealer," says one placard, and it would be hard to say what else he could call himself; for his stock seems to consist of one fine carpet, some brass pots, and a towel. Above him is "Ali Mohammed, Barrister-at-Law," in a windowless, torn-blinded office, which you would otherwise take for the attic of Chunder Buksh's assistant. But compared with the rest of India, Amritsar is a model of wellbeing. It is dusty, but otherwise almost clean; the streets, of course, are full of bullocks and buffaloes, but it seems rare that animals share their bed with men; there are plenty of people all but naked, but it is rather from choice or religious enthusiasm than of necessity. The trousered ladies, strolling with trousered babies on their hips or smoking hubble-bubbles on shop counters, wear silver in their blue-black hair, pearls in their noses, gold in their ears; they jingle with locked-up capital. Finally, there is a Jubilee statute of the Queen, and a clock-tower for all the world like an English borough's. But besides these and the Government offices and the railway-station there is hardly a whisper from the West in the town; and in Amritsar you begin to conceive a new respect for India.

The stream in the streets sets steadily towards the Golden Temple. From the heavy-browed city gate to the holy pool the winding alleys are splashed with all the familiar hues—orange outshining lemon and emerald throttling ultramarine. Following the stalwart, bearded pilgrims, in the midst of the city of shopkeepers you suddenly break into a wide square: within it, bordered by a marble pavement—white, black, and umber—a green lake dances in the sun-

light; and in the midst of that, mirrored in the pool—
you look through your eyelashes, for the hot rays fling
back sevenfold-heated, blinding—gleam walls and roofs
and cupolas of sheer gold.

A minute or two you blink and stare, then you
see that it is a small temple on an island with a causeway leading to it from under an arch. And after the
first blink and stare your notions of beauty rise up and
protest against it. The temple is neither imposing by
size nor winsome by proportion. It has two storeys
—the lower of marble, inlaid, like the marble of Agra,
with birds and beasts and flowers, but with none of
Agra's grace and refinement; all above it is of copper-
gilt. Above the second storey rises something half-
cupola, half-dome, but it is not in the middle; there
are smaller cupolas at the side overlooking the causeway, and others smaller still at the far side. The
whole temple is smaller than St. Clement Danes, and
a little building has no right to be irregular. If the
Taj Mahal, you say, which is three times this size,
can take the trouble to be symmetrical—Well, if this
is the masterpiece of modern India—As for the gold,
it blinds you for the first moment and amuses you for
the second; but you might as well ask beauty of a
heliograph.

Nevertheless, do not go away, for you will hardly
see anything more Indian. Outside the gate they
show you a Government ordinance that everybody
must either conform to the religious customs of the

place or forbear to indulge his curiosity; you bow, and a bearded giant, who might be a high-priest for dignity, takes off your boots and ties on silk slippers instead. You leave your cigar-case behind you: tobacco must not defile the holy place. Then, behind a white-bearded policeman—who performs the triple function of guiding, preventing you from doing anything impious, and clearing worshippers out of the way before you—you start forth to see.

The pilgrims shuffle on eagerly round the pavement to the great gate before the causeway. On a gilt tablet, in English and Punjabi, stands the record of a miracle: how that a great light from heaven fell before the holy book, and then was caught up into heaven again, whence the learned augured much blessing upon the British Raj. Past the gate they press without turning the head, though it is carved and pictured over every inch. On one side of the entrance a marble tablet shows the legend XXXV Sikhs and something in Punjabi. From the gate you issue on to the causeway. It also is flagged with marble, and lined with gilded lamp-posts; but the lamps above the gold are that crass-blue and green-coloured glass of the suburban builder, and more than one hangs broken. So you come to the sanctuary itself—a lofty chamber with four open doors of chased silver. Within sit three priests on the floor, under a canopy of blue and scarlet, before a low ottoman draped in crimson and green and yellow.. The high-priest, eagle-eyed and long black-bearded, reads continually in a loud voice from the Granth; beside him sits one with a gilt-handled wisk and fans the sacred book. At another side sit two musicians: one twangs a sort of one-stringed mandoline, one thrums a tom-tom. Before the Granth lies a cloth; and each believer, crouching in, flings on it flowers or cowries or copper coins for his offering. To the white man they bring what looks like a dry half-orange or candied citron, only white; it is made of sugar, and the white man responds with the offering of a rupee. The walls about this strange worship blaze with blue and red and gold in frets and scrolls and flower-tendrils; above are chambers and galleries of the same and studded mirrors; in one more than holy room are brooms made of peacocks' feathers wherewith alone it may be swept.

That is the great shrine of all; but there is much else. All round the lake are palaces of stone and white marble belonging to the great Sikh chiefs who came here to worship. Before them, on the pavement, men squatting under canvas screens hawk flowers—lotus, jasmine, marigold, or scabious—to be offered before the Scripture. In one of the palaces, which matches the temple with a gilt dome of its own, you see a glass case; within it, under crimson silk, rest the sword and mace of some old Sikh Boanerges, mighty in prayer as in battle. Then there is a tower temple of eight storeys, dedicated to a bygone saint and miracle-worker, the lower chamber aflame with paint and gold. As the policeman enters he touches the step with his finger; a woman in violet trousers flings a flower on to a cloth and ottoman like that of the central shrine; a woman in green-and-gold trousers places a bread-cake before it and lays her forehead on the marble sill; others grovel and shampoo it with their hands. The next thing you come to is a plain shed with a dynamo that supplies the shrines and gardens with electric light. After that a group of naked fakirs, powdered white with ashes, with long mud-matted hair and mad eyes. Then a door, fast closed and seeming to lead nowhither, with a tiny wreath of marigolds hung on it.

Everywhere the same grotesque contradictions— splendour and squalor, divinity and dirt, superstition and manliness. The Western mind can make nothing of it, cannot bring it into a focus. You simply hold your head, and say that this is the East, and you are of the West. In the treasury above the gate are silver staves and gilt maces, canopies of gold and diadems of pearls and diamonds. In the sacred, putrid lake rot flowers. A fakir standing before an enclosure drones in a full voice words you do not understand, like a psalm without any end to it: the refrain, after every half-dozen words, sounds like "Hullah hah leay." Inside the shrine the high-priest never ceases to intone the Granth, nor the other priest to fan it, nor the musicians to tinkle and thrum; and in and out that holy place fly clouds of pigeons, perching on the canopy and fouling the growing pile of offerings before the ottoman. At every turn you come on little shrines with books on silken cushions and prostrate adorers. A calf, unchecked, is trying to lick the gold off the great gateway.

XXII

ON THE BORDER

INDIA ends with the mountains as suddenly as it began from the sea. Out of the stretching plain, in which you could lay down Great Britain and Ireland and France and then lose them, you draw into a narrowing valley. Blue hills shepherd it on either side, not high, but rising abruptly out of the level; over their heads, deep back, lean mounting sheets of perpetual snow.

On the tongue of the valley stands Peshawar. It has stood sentry there ever since cities were, looking forward through the teeth of the hungry mountains, looking back to the gullet of the fat plains. The mountains are lean and swift and bloody; the plains are gorged and lazy and timid; the bases of the hills are the line between, and it is only one stride over it. That curling zigzag of smoke up the hillside is the Khyber, which has belched horde after horde to fatten on the corn and oil of India. On the verandah, where the grave merchant spreads for your approval the carpets of Penjdeh and the silks and velvets of Bokhara; in the trim garden of the club-house, where children are playing with shuttlecocks—you are just an hour from

the rocks where without armed guard no camel-load
is safe from looters, and where stranger or native
alike is shot in the back for his rifle.

Peshawar city is almost as old as the hills, but, in the
true spirit of the border, it makes no enticing show of
riches. It has been sacked and sacked and sacked
again, and looks as if it expected to be sacked anew
to-morrow. The junction of a skein of trade-routes,
it looks as poor and bare and crowded as the most
miserable village. It is one huge caravanserai, a mart
wherein half Asia bargains for riches that must be
enjoyed in safety elsewhere.

So that native Peshawar is like no other town in
India. There is nothing Indian in its aspect, nothing
Afghan nor Persian nor Tartar : it is merely Eastern.
The bazaars and houses are packed as tight as they
can stand. Its shops are bare, even for oriental shops
—square, naked cupboards, three feet above the street,
where the trader unrolls his stuffs, kneads his dough,
grinds his grain, puffs his blowpipe into the charcoal,
or hammers his sheet-metal into bowls and pitchers.
The houses are naked mud on naked wooden frames,
neither painted nor carved—just places of shelter, and
no more. The mosques are no more than places of
prayer for a safe journey : you turn in the street at
sunset and see a row of a dozen men swaying and
kneeling in a three-walled recess no bigger than a
tramcar. Peshawar's only public buildings are the
fort, heaving up its huge mud walls on one side, and

the old palace with its watch-tower on the other. From it you look over the city—compact, cramped, flat-roofed, split by narrow and winding alleys—a frightened herd of houses huddling shoulder to shoulder in the open plain.

The house-tops are fenced round with walls and mat-screens; the poles that bear the screens give the idea of a city that has never stood undisturbed long enough to take down its scaffolding. As the sun sinks over the Khyber all Peshawar comes out on to the roof to breathe the cool. You imagine that the screens are intended against wife-stealers and sharp-shooters impartially, and that Peshawar knows it is safer to take the air on its own house-top than among the knives in the street below. Plain street and house, bazaar and people,—that is all there is of Peshawar. Bleak, populous, as old as time and as young as yesterday, Peshawar remains to-day as Nineveh and Tyre, as Rome and London were—the archetype of cities, the lowest common denominator of habitation.

It is only a caravanserai, yet it is choked with life and business. Going under the needle-eyed city gate you are instantly in a throng as dense as Cheapside's. It is a daily fair: all the peoples of the unhastening East meet within its walls till you can hardly move in the street. They are hammering and embroidering and chaffering to-day as they did yesterday and the day after the founding of Babel. Here and there, before an open upper room, you see the sign of a pleader—a babu alibi-merchant, imported to swell the list of Peshawar's unpunished murders; but, for the rest, the city goes back straight into the book of Genesis. Here is red Esau—only he has dyed his beard that flaming crimson-orange to hide the grey hairs in it—driving in his goats. There is hawk-eyed, hawk-nosed Lot sitting in the gate. Then you lift up your eyes, and behold the camels are coming. To the slim dromedary of Egypt these are as the retriever to the greyhound—heavy, thick-set, furred with soft brown hair, as if they wore tippets and petticoats. The veiled woman striding behind them in dust-stained trousers might be Rachel, the heavy bales of merchandise hiding her father's gods.

From Kabul with apples and raisins and pistachio-nuts, from Bokhara and Teheran with rich-coloured fabrics, come the laden camels, and they wind back up the Khyber heavy with cloth and raw sugar and tools. Then the Peshawar bazaars are not merely exchanges, but manufactories as well. One street is a row of clattering coppersmiths: they ornament bronze vessels with bands and scrolls of white by sheer hammering of the metal. Next are the silversmiths, each with his tiny charcoal furnace on the shop-floor under his nose. They are common to all India, but perhaps a shade more necessary to Peshawar: they turn rupees into the nose-rings and bangles which are the native savings-bank. As you pass out of the gate you are among the waxcloth-workers, and these are more special to the place. Waxcloth is not a kind of lino-leum, but any material—silk, cotton, satin—embroid-ered in wax. You have seen it often enough in Eng-land—white or golden peacocks and palms on blue or crimson; but it astonishes you to see it being made. A boy squats on the floor with a lump of sticky white, like putty, on the ball of his thumb; with a steel-pointed stylus he kneads it up, takes a point-full, as you fill a pen, and begins to draw on the fabric. You would think no skill could ever make the treacly stuff manageable, yet the shaggy stripling—let us hope his hand is cleaner than it looks—draws a peacock's feather in it with nothing more to copy than a spider has in making his web. When it is done and dry, it remains for ever, and you can wash your work of art without bringing off a line.

This for the city; now drive out of the gate over the dusty two miles to the cantonment. The evening sun will slant into your eyes—the European quarter stands forward towards the mountains, screening the city—and the air after sunset will be like cold water on your skin. At the end of February Peshawar has still two months of cool before it. Later it becomes a crackling inferno, but till May it breathes as divine a climate as man could wish to live in. Along the Mall the yellow grass, the palms, and the crimson-purple bells are India; the trees just knobby with new buds, the hedges beginning to redden and cream into roses, the soft breathing of violets are pure spring.

On the Border

The morning air has the nip of spring, the runnels of water from the Swat River canal fill the valley with whispers of its coming. India crumbles and soaks from dry season to wet; this cool leaf-fringed cantonment, with its straight avenues of sheer spring, is new blood in the veins of northern men.

Now, as the patrol was riding one of these same avenues of spring on a windy night in February, there flew a sudden volley out of the dark, and in the morning they found one sowar dead and the other with a bullet through his thigh, and both carbines gone. They were away in the hills, where a true-shooting weapon is even as a tall hat in London. In the blue hills, an hour from the violets, he who owns a Martini or Lee-Metford bears the hall-mark of respectability. He is fairly started in life, a credit to his family, a factor to be reckoned with in society. Presently he will build himself a tower, and then perhaps steal another rifle and sell it. With the proceeds he will buy a wife or two—they are a great deal cheaper than breech-loading rifles—and found a family. It may even be his to bring the feud of generations to an honourable end, by killing the last adult member of the opposing family. So he will die full of years and honour, bequeathing to his first-born a stainless name and a title-deed sighted up to 2000 yards.

A judge on circuit finds in his camp a hook-nosed, white-bearded grandfather, hung like a trophy with knives and swords, with a Webley revolver—the gift of a European well-wisher—and a couple of flintlock pistols in his belt, with a six-foot mother-of-pearl-inlaid, sickle-butted jezail over his shoulder, and behind him two young men similarly armed.

" You kept my petition waiting, O Presence," he explains ; " this night I shall sleep in your camp."

" I'm hanged if you will," says the Presence.

" Do you think I am going back to my tower by dark ? " laughs the old man. " Myself and my son and my nephew are the last of our family, and our enemies have a dozen left still."   So he sleeps in the inviolable camp of the sahib, and goes back to his tower next morning, and pulls up the twenty-foot ladder after him. He has not been out between sundown and sunrise for years—not since he shot his tenth man of the other side—and he never means to. Only one day it occurs to the sahib that he has not seen his old friend for some time, and on inquiry he learns that they got him in the end.

An Afridi subadar-major—senior native officer of a famous regiment—one day went on furlough. His time ran out and he did not return. A week went by, and then another ; still no subadar-major. The officers wondered : it was impossible that a man of his service, of his proved loyalty, should have deserted ; where could he be ? Another week ; and there appeared in barracks a dirty-haired youth with a letter. " I am grieved to overstay my time," wrote the subadar-major, " but what can I do ? I am the last of my clan, and two of my enemies sit outside my tower night and day." It seemed a poor look-out for the gallant officer, and the next on the list for promotion was congratulated by his clansmen in advance. But a week after, unannounced, there walked into barracks the subadar-major himself, chest expanded, whiskers curling with satisfaction. "A wonderful thing, Colonel Sahib," he explained. "I awoke one morning and looked out of my loop-hole, and there—I could hardly believe my eyes—there were both my enemies in one line! So I took my rifle and shot them both with one bullet, and returned hither with all speed."

You will hardly believe it, but that is the normal state of social intercourse among the Pathans. And not only among them across the border, but in the plain also: wherever the Pathan is, there rifle-stealing is the staple industry, murder a social duty, and violent death the common lot of man. On Thursdays, riding past the jail to the meet of the Peshawar Vale Hounds, you will remark on it if you do not see a man being hanged. But in such cases as shooting the man who stole your wife, or shooting the man who shot your brother who stole his wife, or shooting the man who shot your father who shot his brother who stole your mother—why, in domestic matters like this it is not expedient that the law should be over-curious. It is not well to hang men for doing their social duty: a wise Government will temper routine with sympathy.

On the Border

Occasionally, indeed, this attitude is slightly misapprehended. A worthy Pathan was much troubled by the scandalous misbehaviour of a vicious mother. He confided his sorrows to a magistrate, who promised to help him in any way he could. " Well then, sahib, the best plan I can think of is this. One night some brigands from over the border will come down and abduct my mother. I shall complain to you, and you will send Staunton Sahib with police. But they will not find my mother, and we shall hear no more of her for ever."

> " Ah, this thou should'st have done,
> And not have spoken on't,"

murmured the magistrate. But in the end he got the bad old lady locked up for one of her misdeeds, and the son was as happy as if he had scuppered her himself in the character of a trans-border raider.

It is the truth that here, on the thin line between elaborate civilisation and primeval barbarism, where you may begin your morning by trying a duet with a lady on a grand piano and finish it with a tulwar through your belly—here there is more sympathy between white man and native than anywhere else in India. British soldiers pull tugs-of-war against Kohati school-boys, whose fathers may easily have shot their room-mates. British gentlemen sit down to table with Mussulmans—each considering the other irretrievably ripe for damnation, but each knowing the other to be a man.   The Briton was made to do with the barbarian, being—the more you think of it the clearer you see it—half a barbarian himself.   For if the carbine-thieves crouching in the wind-gusts by the roadside are one side of the matter, the squad here at riding-school, the squad there at bayonet-drill, the Sikh recruits practising the double—these are the other.   For the first time in India's history the mountaineers look down over the border at India rich, but India armed and unsleeping.   With us it is as with them: the hand keeps the head.

XXIII

THE KHYBER

THE front-door of India, Bombay, is magnificent; the back-door, the Khyber, is therefore naturally shabby. Out of the rose-hedges of Peshawar a dust-yellow road carries you through a dust-grey plain, heading for dust-drab mountains. India seems worn out—giving up the weary effort to be soil, reverting limply to rock, sand, mud.

An hour your tonga tongles—there is no ready-made word for its combination of rumble, jolt, jump, spin, and fly—straight for the hills, which seem ever to recede. You mark a point between two ridges as the mouth of the Pass; you drive through it, and you are still in the plain; that gap beyond must be the mouth. Then, almost insensibly, you do enter the jaws. Walls of brown rock enclose you on either side; a round hill of brown rock, crowned with a mud fort, blocks you in front; a turn in the road, and a sweeping ridge of brown rock cuts you off behind. Above the walls, beyond the hill, behind the ridge, spring up with every turn other walls, other hills, other ridges, more sheer, more towering, more mazy than the first. You rise and rise, now along the gully of a defile, now sweeping round a rim, now zigzagging up a face; at one moment peeping over a shoulder at the plain behind, the next dashing confidently towards two sky-swallowing, khaki-coloured, black-spangled humps that seem to fill the whole world. Frowning over your head, slipping away from under your foot, letting in vast perspectives of more khaki rock and black bush, shutting up the world into two cliffs and an abyss—the Khyber is a mere perplexity of riotous mountain.

You would say these savage hills could support nothing but solitude—yet here are the mountaineers. A couple of lithe aquiline young men in khaki and sandals rise out of a heap of stones as you pass, and shoulder Snider muskets. On the hill above, under the mud-walled block-house, loll half-a-dozen more. These are of the Khyber Rifles—Afridis who, now that the war is over, have returned without malice and without abashment to their old service of guarding the Pass. They start out of nothing at every wind of the road; on all the lower summits you can just make out khaki pickets against the khaki country.

For to-day the Pass is very full. Above you, in a short cut between two serpentines of the driving road, you see the ordered columns of a British regiment descending; and at the next turn you almost fling a file of its transport mules over the precipice. Spin down the next decline, shave the boulder at the angle, and—Ai! toot! wheeze, wheeze, toot! ai, pig!—we are plump in the middle of two meeting caravans entangled in a commissariat-train. The camels from Kabul barracked for the night at Landi Kotal, those from Peshawar at Jamrud; to-day, which is the open day, they cross in the Khyber. The Pass is now—or was then—open two days a-week, which means that it is picketed by Khyber Rifles while the caravans go through. Twice a-week they go up towards Kabul; twice a-week they come down into India, needing the whole day to make the Pass. This is the sum of the intercourse between India and Afghanistan.

Now comes an hour of steady jostle and shove and bang, of abortive attempts to toot the broken-winded bugle and more successful vilifications of all camels, bullocks, camelmen, bullock-drivers, and all progenitors and collaterals of the same. The down-coming and the up-going camels of course are jammed in a second, and of course the drivers do not care. One laden beast balances himself on the eyebrow of the drop and lifts his eyes to heaven in plaintive appeal against the woes of life; the next huddles under the wall and tries to shove it back with a truss of straw, so as to make more room; the next plants himself directly in the middle of the road and squeals in helpless horror as the tonga barges at him. Struggling down to where the road touches the Khyber Water under the mud battlements of Ali Musjid, we enter the stratum of bullock-carts, just as they have finally decided that the best thing to do is to lie down across the path and let the camels clamber over them. No created thing can wake emotion in a commissariat bullock. Twist his tail, hit him over the head, heave a tonga-wheel—half as heavy as a field-gun's—into his flank: he looks benevolent and remains placidly in the way. When at last the idea of action has penetrated his hide, he methodically hooks his yoke into the nearest wheel with a look of profound meekness, and plunges into meditation again. So the tonga stops and everybody abuses everybody else till they are tired; then they rest a little, and abuse a little more with fresh breath; finally, they unite to unhook the yoke and push the cart on to the bullocks. They, finding the cart moving by itself, are eventually penetrated by an idea again. "It seems, brother, they wish us to move again." "Very well, brother; let us always do what they wish us to do." And so they move thoughtfully on.

The Kabul-bound camels are beneath us now, promenading with dignity along the bed of the stream. It was worth the delay to look at them; for the camel of Central Asia is the flower of his otherwise discreditable family. His cousins of Egypt and India are necessary evils: he is a joy to the eye, and he knows it. They are all neck and leg, all corners and misplaced joints, half-snake, half-folding bedstead: his daintily tilted nose is thrust out of a shower of rich brown silken fur. It cascades from the ears all down his throat to the chest, like a lady's boa, only far longer and finer, and especially far better worn. His shoulders and thighs are clothed in brown astrachan. Altogether he is an animal with contours, not a folding monstrosity; and he knows it. Other camels are tied head to tail on the march: he tramps along serenely under his heavy load, picking his own way, convinced of the superiority which others only feign, not to be thrown out of his business by anything less devilish than a wheeled double centaur with the voice of a bugle.

From Ali Musjid the road seesaws, with a balance of ascent and the pass gradually widens. You begin to see villages—or the dry bones of them. Jagged stumps of towers and rents where walls were print the record of the punishment of the Afridis. When they took our fort at Landi Kotal they stripped off every stick of wood and carried it away; when we destroyed their towers we did likewise: on these stark hills wood, next to a rifle, is the most desirable possession life can offer. As you swing up and down the grades of dust you see now and again the black blot of a cave-mouth in the hills: these are now the villages of the Khyber Afridis.

At last you turn your final corner. In front of you, across folds and rifts in the ground, is a white encampment; to your right you are quite close on a long quadrangular fort, towers at the angles, loop-holes along the tall walls, the Union-Jack over all. Behind it is another encampment. You have reached the quarters of the Khyber Brigade at Landi Kotal. You are on the very rim of British India. Behind the elbow of the road is Landi Khana, whither the Afghan escort brings the Kabul cavaran : the click of a telegram, the call of a bugle, and British troops could be in Afghanistan again.

But we must not talk of themes like these. Meanwhile here are three battalions and a mountain battery and sappers, under the best-trusted brigadier in India, every man as fit as the hills can make him, and football-ankles the only solace of the hospital. It is not exactly active service, but it is the next best thing to it. The surrounding population is obedient in large things and sportive in small. The Shinwari villagers—those are their walls and square, tapering, forty-foot towers sloping up the branching valley northward—are thoroughly friendly : when you observe the easy access to their homes and their young corn just greening the dust-coloured earth, you wonder the less at their virtue. The very Afridis southward submit to the General as their arbiter. They have a custom, when they plough, of meeting in jirgah, and there each man lays down a stone before him ; while the ploughing lasts the stones are down, and all blood-feuds sleep. The other day, the war with the Sirkar being over, and a feeling abroad that the rifles had been silent too long, they came to the General Sahib for permission to lift the stones and open the each-other-shooting season. " The first village that begins will be destroyed," said he, and they went away sorrowful, but obedient.

Only in small things they are a law unto themselves: you could hardly expect them to deny themselves the exercise of rifle-stealing with a whole brigade of Lee-Metfords and Martinis before their very eyes. So on dark nights the promising young Afridi creeps down towards the sentry, who, if he is sleepy, will be found next morning with a knife in his back instead of a rifle. As a rule, he is not sleepy. Then there are shots, and perhaps shots in return; but, what with the dark and the hillman's cunning, and the danger of shooting at large in camp at night, it is seldom that a rifle-thief is bagged. There was a story of a British sentry who was both knifed and beaten over the head with the butt of his own rifle; but he clung to the sling like a Briton, and the Afridi went empty away.

All things considered, you had better be wary when going home after dinner in the Khyber camp. Within the perimeter let your " friend " follow closely on the Ghurkha's " Hahlt, huggas ther ? "—outside it they shoot first and challenge afterwards. Better take the air by day—say, on a route-march with the Ghurkhas. Khaki jackets and short baggy breeches that leave a bare knee above the putties, black belts, and hunting-horns on their buttons like our Rifles', bayonet on one hip, and broad-bladed kukri on the other, a tiny round cap worn over the ear, and leaving the sun to get through the close-cropped bullet-head if he can—the jolly, flat-faced little mountaineers will repay you for more than a morning's march with them. They leap from stone to stone like he-goats till you are right up, up below the clouds, and the Khyber country and Afghanistan are unrolled below you.

You see, and at length you understand the campaign against the Afridis. Gad, what a country! Not a level yard for miles, and miles, and miles! Not a fair field of fire within the whole horizon. Nothing but a welter of naked khaki-coloured mountain. Shale scree giving on to precipice, ridge entangling ridge, height topping height. You toil up a knee-loosening face to the summit, and there is another summit dominating you; up that, and there is another, and yet another, and another. No end, no direction, no security—nothing but exposure and sheer toil. From the white steeps of the Hindu Khush in the sky to the back-dotted wild-olive bushes beside you—not a green thing, not an open place, nothing but hard, sterile, unorientable fanged impossibility.

Only down there, on the other side, the Kabul river threads the mountains in its mail of sunshine. There is level ground and green corn-fields in the valley; there is Dakka, the first Afghan town; and there, in that spreading pool of green, the hazy shimmer must be Jellalabad. How many marches? Is that blur their cavalry lines? It is easy to be wise about the

forward policy from your arm-chair; but go up with
a regiment and look out from your own barren peaks
on to the green plains over the border. You will understand what a frontier feels like, and why frontiers
have a habit of not standing still.

XXIV

THE MALAKAND

THE flagging ponies gave one last hoist to the tonga, in the afterglow six miles of upward-straining road lay behind us along the huge mountain like a pack-thread. We turned an elbow of cliff, and behold it was night. Off the empty hillside—bare precipice above, bare abyss below—we were suddenly in a dense wood of black trees, among shadows and echoes; and all about, above in the sky, plumb below in some bottomless pit deep, deep beneath our feet, camp-fires played on white canvas. Where were we? Which was back or front, above or below, head or heels? The world seemed to be tilted up on end.

"Is the house of the Sahib near?" says I, in my pure Urdu. "Near, O Presence." "Where?" For answer the half-soldier, half-footman pointed above his head. Exactly in line with the ventilation of my helmet I saw a light hanging between two stars. It was about ten yards as the crow flies; as the man climbs it looked ten miles. Surely the world was tilted up on end. This was the Malakand.

Four years ago nobody except political officers had ever heard of the Malakand, or knew whether it was a mountain, a river, or the title of a local chief. For four years past it has been the most frequented name on all the Frontier. It is a pass lying a little to the east of north of Peshawar, almost due north of Nowshera, and forty-eight miles from it. The Malakand opens—if " opens " is the word for such a tangle—into almost the only part of the North-West Frontier which we had been able to let alone. The tribes beyond it—in Swat and Bajaur and Dir, and all the other uncouth places with uncouth names—were content to stew in the blood of their own feuds, and prudently we let them stew.

Before 1895 our frontier-post was Mardan— " Mardan, where the Guides are." Here, ever since its foundation, that famous regiment has been quartered in the intervals of campaigns which have consistently added to the lustre of its record. The only corps in India, except the Ghurkha battalions, which has permanent quarters, the Guides have made Mardan less of a station than a regimental home. Here are its family heirlooms—the mess-walls covered with heads of buffalo and ibex, antelope and mountain-sheep, with banners taken from the enemy, and queer Greco-Buddhist statuary excavated out of the neighbouring hills. Here is the regimental cemetery—full now, and overflowing into a new one—and an arch and little garden tardily erected by Government to the memory of the handful of the Guides who died at their post round Cavagnari in Kabul. There is home-

liness in the little swimming-bath in the officers'
garden, as there is romance in the fort with sentries
of many types—here a Sikh, there an Afridi, a
Ghurkha, a Rajput, a Dogra—for " God's Own " is
welded of the pick of all the fighting races of India.

In enormous long white trousers sepoys and sowars
walk placidly about their home and the home of their
fathers: for the fighting native puts down his young
son for the Guides as you might at home for the
Travellers'. You come across a native officer of
forty-two years' service—straight away to before the
Mutiny—a smiling little old gentleman, whose dyed
beard only just matches the mahogany of his skin.
He regrets, politely, that the Guides were not able to
be present at Omdurman, and remarks, as an in-
centive to my future efforts, that he himself saw a
war-correspondent killed at Landakai. Every officer
or man you meet has the air of a gentleman taking his
ease in his own house. Mardan is the concrete
epitome of the spirit that makes a regiment—the only
satisfactory translation I ever met of the words *esprit
de corps.*

Through Mardan in 1895 advanced the force which
brought the Malakand into frontier politics. Chitral
was to be relieved, and the relieving force, taking the
directest road, had to force the Pass, and we have held
it ever since. But Chitral was relieved from the
other side, from Gilgit, and the reward of our interference with the Malakand was the furious assault

upon it and the fort of Chakdara beyond, which inaugurated the great frontier war of 1897 and 1898. Now it makes one more of our garrisons beyond the old frontier of India—garrisons where no man knows whether he will wake up to-morrow to find peace or war. Whether such posts make in the end for the one or the other, who is to decide? Without their deterrent, say some, you would have the tribes on you to-morrow. Without their menace, urge others, you would never have had the tribes on you at all. Unfortunately both may be true, and the result, insecurity, is one and the same.

In the morning it was possible to look over the position—but easier to look than to comprehend. You will find it put clearly both in word and plan in Mr. Winston Churchill's "Story of the Malakand Field Force"; but no putting short of actual sight can do justice to the supernatural complication of the Malakand. "It would take the whole British army to hold it," said a good judge; "and then I don't quite see what the plan would be." Try to arrange a box of tin soldiers on a rockery, and you will get some idea of it. There is, indeed, a tennis-court, but that has been made artificially; otherwise there is not level ground for a billiard-table. From the top of the place where I eventually landed to the bottom, where I saw the coolies' camp-fires, you could easily pitch a stone; yet to walk from one extremity of the position to the other would take you hours. The road comes up the Pass, but where it ought to debouch on to a plateau it winds through a sieve of deep holes. What ought to be the diverging sides of the Pass are terraces of hills, each one commanded by the one behind it. What ought to be the sloping, opening valley beyond the Pass is choked by a handful of rocky hills promiscuously flung all about it. As a military position, you can say this of it, that if you have enough men to hold higher hills than the assailant, keeping touch, you ought to be able to hold it; and if the assailant has enough men to hold higher hills than you have, keeping touch, he ought to be able to take it—which amounts to saying nothing at all.

This luminous theory may explain why the authorities build forts on this hill, and then pull them down and put them up again on that; why they first put the troops here, then there, then take them away altogether, then bring them back and reinforce them. But we may leave that to them, and turn to the only proper occupation on a frontier—going on. Over sky-lines, round corners, you must still be going on to see what there is on the other side. Round the corner of the right-hand wall of the Malakand you can just see a peeping tent or two; as you scramble down, these enlarge into the camp of the Movable Column—a brigade stationed down in the Swat Valley, beyond the Pass, ready to move at any moment against any enemy that may appear. Further on—you are moving up a broad valley with rigidly enclosing walls—the driving road stops at a bridge. Under it is the turbulent slither of the Swat; beyond is the fort of Chakdara.

This is the sentry on the main road to Chitral. The bridge is India all over: piers of stout stone—it must need it all when the Swat comes down in spate —carry stout cables; but the long bridge that is hung from them is tacked on with wire, buckling in the middle, swinging in the wind. The fort is of a type already familiar—heavy gate, a horn-work to protect horses, towers and loopholes, signal-station at the top, blockhouses on the immediately covering hills. In the barracks that form one side sweat and frizzle half a battalion of Punjab infantry. The bullet-dints of the last siege can still be seen on the walls: the next may begin to-morrow.

For our last bit of frontier push a few miles further up the Swat. It is a queer valley historically—a valley with a past. Many think that it was by it that Alexander the Great, the first and best of frontier generals, descended to the conquest of the Punjab; certainly the ancient Buddhists occupied it in great importance. You find their sculptuary—half-Indian types, half-Greek—under almost every mound from here to Mardan, and west and east into Bajaur and Buner; their hemispherical shrines crown appropriate hillocks, both here and in the Khyber; either they or Alexander made the road—too stiffly graded for these degenerate days—which still runs alongside ours. The conclusion from all of which is that the Swat Valley is capable of far more importance than it has lately claimed. The Buddhists were great traders, and this may have been one of their main highways into Central Asia, as it was Alexander's into India. What has been may be again.

Of the riches of the valley there can be no question. A gridiron of canals, drawn from the Swat, has turned it into one teeming rice-field. In this hard land it is luxury to drop your eyes from the bleak mountains to the vivid green. After the summer there are loads on loads of rice to export, and cloth and tea to bring back. If we only had the administration of the valley,—but as we canter over the stony bed of a tributary we are suddenly in the midst of them. Here are the Swatis, who two years ago found Paradise by thousands in the attempt to slaughter our countrymen, come out to bid us good day, and escort us against any possible harm. Then they were enemies; now they are local levies—irregular, very irregular, forces of her Majesty, who supplies them with their sabres and Sniders. Next year, or next week, or to-morrow —well, never mind to-morrow.

The shaggy group—perhaps fifty of them, a dozen parish councillors on short-barrelled country-breds, and the rest ambling along on foot—belongs to the tribe of the Yussufzais, or sons of Joseph. Everybody on the frontier firmly believes that they are the lost ten tribes of the House of Israel. Their vices suggest it, and certainly they look it. Powerful beaks, thick outward-drawn lips, floating raven-wing hair and beards, eyeballs a trifle close together—only not the eyes of your Jew—eyes hard as flint-stone. I was told that there is a place named after the Yussuf-zais on the borders of Persia and Beluchistan, although nobody in that country to-day knows that such a tribe exists. That is suggested as one of the halting-places of the Israelites on their travels eastward. It would be a queer irony if one-half of the kingdom of Solomon had turned to the Jews we know and the other half to these wild beasts of hillmen. Never mind who they are: they are uncommonly amiable to-day, and would die for the Sahibs as a matter of course. So we troop along to the spur of Landakai, whence the Upper Swat Valley pushes its emerald tongue yet farther into the mountains. The Swatis discourse of the fight there little over a year ago, when our people and theirs respectively killed each other; they discuss the points of the engagement with calmness and absolute impartiality. The game is over now, and they bear no malice. To-morrow, when the reliefs go up to Chitral, when the Mad Fakir comes down again—then they will have another try at cutting our throats; but always without malice, and in the best spirit of the game.

XXV

THE FRONTIER QUESTION

THE frontier question is like the frontier country. Toilfully surmount one branch of it—and it is commanded and controlled by another. Struggle through the pass of one problem—and it opens on to a worse tangle of others.

Take a typical case—Chitral. At the first reconnaissance nothing could be simpler. Obviously, for a host of reasons, we ought to keep clear of Chitral. An invasion of India in anything like force from that side is all but inconceivable. The country, as well as the country between it and India, is infernal, the inhabitants devilish. Before we began to meddle they were content to exercise their devilishness upon each other. Our interference has brought us two costly and profitless wars already; it threatens a fresh one every spring when the Chitral garrison is relieved. It clogs our finances with the permanent expense of the Chitral and Malakand garrisons and of the Malakand movable column, which is necessary to cover the reliefs by threatening the tribesmen's villages; for we no more hold the road to Chitral than we do the road from the Cape to Cairo. Our interference hampers our policy by the consciousness of a perpetually vulnerable point. Decidedly we ought never to have gone to Chitral; ought never to have stayed there; ought, if we must stay there, to have communicated with it, as originally, from Gilgit. The whole business is a palpable, costly, ghastly blunder.

Thus triumphantly we crown that height. And then, unfortunately for our comfort of mind, we begin to observe fresh heights to be crowned above us. As, for instance, the following. It is quite true that India could never be assailed in force, especially by an army bringing guns and transport, from Chitral. Yet it has a strategical importance—contingent, but, assuming the contingency, vital. From Chitral down the Chitral and Kunar valleys a comparatively easy road runs to Jellalabad. Therefore, if we were fighting Russia, as many think we should do, along the Kabul-Kandahar line, even a small force descending that valley from Chitral could turn our flank, work round our rear, break up our whole position. That for one point. For another: we had to go to Chitral, because if we had not Russia would have put an agent there, who would have made it his business to stir up the tribes against us; so that we should have had the wars of '95 and '97 just the same, only worse. For another point: even though we thought it was wrong to go to Chitral, and though Sir George Robertson was wrong to meddle with its dynastic quarrels, could you leave him to be cut up? For another: even though Lord Rosebery was prudent in refusing to hold Chitral or make the road from the Malakand, can you, having once advanced against Asiatics, safely retire ?

The more you look at it, the more it mazes you—point topping point, and argument crossing argument. And that is only the very tiniest fraction of the whole frontier question. There are a dozen places like Chitral, each with a tangled problem of its own ; and above all are the greater questions—the influence on India proper, the defence against Russia—with all their branches.. And the peculiarly exasperating feature of these difficulties is that every action we take seems to leave them more confounded than before.

We went to Kabul in 1840-42 and 1878-80, each time with great expense and loss. Yet you find men in India firmly convinced that we must go to Kabul again when the Amir dies, and again when the next Amir dies, and so on to an infinity of dynasties. What policy could be more heroic or more impotent ? You know not whether to call it bravery or despair ; and there are other men who, recognising this, say that the next time we go to Kabul we must stay. It comes to this : we went there twice to preserve a buffer against Russia ; and now, the third time, we are to destroy that buffer by our own act. It is precisely thus that the frontier lures you on.

Similarly with the recent war. When you speak of " the war " in India now, you can only mean one

war—the Tirah - Mohmund - Mamund - Swat - Bajaur-
Buner campaign of '97 and '98. There is a great
deal of disappointment and a little bitterness in India
about "the war." Civilians, as a rule, execrate it
root and branch; soldiers feel that perhaps the most
difficult campaign in history, and deeds certainly never
surpassed for endurance and valour, have been scantily
recognised at home, where popular applause and official reward have been reserved for the luckier heroes
of easier enterprises. The feeling is most natural;
but the blame, if there is any, lies not with the British
Government nor the British public. They inevitably
reward and applaud campaigns, not according to their
difficulty, but according to their results. When "the
war" was over, what was there to show for it—for the
greatest exertions of the largest force which the empire
has put into the field for a generation? Only the
prospect of more, and similarly inconclusive, wars in
the near future. If more could have been done with
the force, then any blame must lie with the generals.
If all was done that man could do, then the blame is
with the Indian authorities who embarked so huge a
force on an enterprise which could never justify its
employment.

Yet that is not quite fair either. For the great
campaign, though nobody pretends that it achieved
results commensurate with the force squandered upon
it, did at least issue in some tangible gain. The tribes
did not come out of it so well as they seem to have

done. Probably they suffered less loss in men than we did; certainly, though there was a hollow pretence of disarmament, they were not disarmed. Yet, in one way, they were vastly impressed. The Afridis, for an example, had always held themselves invulnerable in Tirah; a British force marched through their valleys, destroying crops and villages at will.

Briefly, we proved that at any time we choose we can exterminate the Afridi nation. We can occupy their valleys in unassailable force, destroy everything, and drive men, women, and children into the winter snows to starve and freeze to death. The knowledge of that—and they know it well enough—is a warning even to their levity against more than ordinary misbehaviour in the future. But then—another height to complicate the position—the extermination of the Afridis is just what we do not want. Setting aside the atrocity of it, we want to keep the Afridis for our own use. The fighting races of India proper are even now, in some opinions, falling off; with settled government and canals, with just taxation and courts of appeal, they are certain to deteriorate in the long-run. In the recent war, say many good judges, by far the best of our soldiers were Afridis fighting against their own people; and as long as they stick to the national industry of rifle-stealing and mutual murder, they are likely to remain so.

But now—it will make your head ache—comes another dominating height. Will the Afridis stick to the industries that foster their present martial qualities? Already firearms of precision are so common among them that private war is becoming more than a joke. With a jezail it was a question of stalking your man and bringing him down with a long, long aim at 500 yards. With a Lee-Metford you sit in your tower, and as soon as your enemy comes out to cut a cabbage in his garden—bang! you get him easily at 1000. Even Afridis will find life impossible under these conditions in the long-run.

Meantime, since we do not wish to exterminate the Afridis, and it is poor fun fighting them on their own ground in their own style, the course appears to be to treat them well, and, if possible, enlist the whole nation of them. Training in our army will not make them any more dangerous at their own style of warfare—they are perfect at that already; if anything it will put them more on terms with us. So far so good; but there are a thousand little folds in this ground also—as what relations we are to maintain with them and how, what we are to do for the safety of the Khyber route, and so on, and so on. We might easily lose ourselves in these—so perhaps we had better not venture in.

At the back of everything remains Russia. You may reply that Russia could not invade India, that never were we on better terms with Russia, that Russia proposes disarmament, and many other things. All that—forgive me—is childish nonsense. Russia knows quite well that we shall not invade Central Asia, that the Amir will not invade Central Asia; yet at this moment she has just finished a railway that brings her within a week of Herat. If that road is not for aggression, what is it for? Trade? Partly, perhaps, but the trade will never pay the working expenses. For the sake of trade it is even proposed that we shall agree to couple up our Indian railways with Russia's Central Asian. Russia and Germany link railways at the frontier, you say; why not Transcaspia and India? Simply because Russia and Germany are approximately equal in military force, and are bound to respect each other. Our military force is out of proportion inferior to Russia's, and we must redress the balance with every advantage of position we can keep or take.

Then, what to do? The whole question turns on where you intend to fight; though it is astonishing how few people in India, even soldiers, are clear on that point. Russia could not invade India through Afghanistan at present: difficulties of transport would be insuperable. Therefore, if you advance to the line of the Helmund to meet her—through difficult country and savage tribes—you are wantonly throwing away your only good card in the game. On the other hand, if you elect to fight along the border mountains, Russia can swallow Afghanistan piecemeal. First, she can establish herself and accumulate stores, supplies, and beasts to carry them, in the valley of Herat; next in the valley of Kabul; then suddenly she is at the gate of India, and once more you have discarded your winning ace.

One more complication: while we are fighting Russia in front, what would be happening in our rear? We must fight on the Helmund, they say, because a defeat on the present frontier would mean revolt in India. But a defeat on the Helmund could no more be hushed up than a defeat on the Indus: it would only take a few hours longer to reach the bazaars. But then, they answer, the danger is in letting the disaffected know the Russians are so near. The reply is that if we were beaten on the Helmund they would very soon be equally near, and that the only way to keep them out is not to be beaten at all. Therefore we should fight where we are likest to win.

The best way out of the tangle is to make it clear that the moment Russia goes to Herat we fight. We fight as best we can. If Russia comes straight for India we should beat her; if not, we try to wear her down elsewhere; in no case do we make peace till she retires to her old boundary beyond Herat. But will the British people fight to the death for Herat, seeing that it is not theirs, and they do not know where it is? Accustom yourself to the thought, O British people! For in the long-run it is a choice between this,—conscription for service in India—and how would you like that?—or else the loss of India altogether.

XXVI

OF RAJAHS

"His Highness," perspired the babu, "trusts that you are in the enjoyment of good health."

"Thanks to the beneficent climate of his Highness's dominions," I replied, " I am in the enjoyment of especially good health."

With such momentous words opened my first serious interview with a Rajah. As I drove up to his palace on the hill I noticed an elephant or so left casually standing about at the corners of his crooked streets. This was his ingenuous way of hinting to the mind of the stranger at his rank and wealth and importance. An elephant is a peculiarly royal beast, as a peacock is a royal bird, and without one, at least, of each no Rajah is complete.

At the door of the stucco palace a dishevelled sentry presented arms with even more than the usual fervour. After a moment I understood—and perceived coming down a corridor slowly, slowly, and quite noiselessly towards me, a small human figure. It wore a white turban, a tabard of lilac silk lined with salmon satin, a long muslin scarf round the neck, snow-white linen drawers, tight yet shapeless,

and white cotton socks. It came up, always quite
noiselessly, appearing to be moved rather than to
move : I saw a brown face, melting black eyes, a
long-haired, fine-haired, oiled, black beard.

The figure took my hand in a hand that seemed
made of soufflet, and with the same mysterious, un-
moving motion led me across a high-roofed hall, with
chandeliers like forest-trees and the paint peeling off
the skirting-board, into a verandah that overlooked a
reeling chasm of torrent-bed and a towering heave of
mountain beyond. He set me in a chair beside him,
the interpreter opposite, then turned and fixed his
eyes on me. If the movements were inhuman the
eyes were unearthly. Eyes weary beyond satiety—
eyes utterly passionless and purposeless, as if their
owner neither desired anything nor intended anything, had either never had any interest in the world
or had quite finished with it. Looking into those
black pools of sheer emptiness, you wondered whether
he were a new-born baby or a million years old; you
almost wondered if he were alive or dead.

That was the Rajah. And then, in a voice that
seemed to fall among us from nowhere, he told the
fat-cheeked, gold-spectacled babu to tell me he trusted
I was in the enjoyment of good health.

Awhile the conversation floated at this level, and I
began to think that this Nirvana-eyed Rajah was—if
one may so speak of princes—a fool. But presently
the babu's circumambient periods began to coil them-

selves round a definite subject, and the Rajah was instructing me on the political question of the hour. It does not matter to you what the question was; it did not matter to me. The interest to me lay in comparing what the Rajah suggested with what I knew to be true. In black and white he said nothing, but he hinted worlds. The suggestions were so subtly nebulous that you could hardly be sure they meant anything at all; the subject seemed to be in the air rather than in his conversation. I found it quite impossible to speak a language so evasive, and had to fly to brutal verbs and nouns. He accepted my remarks, though with deprecation of their bluntness; so that at least I had the satisfaction of knowing we were both talking about the same things.

But the astonishing and inhuman feature of his talk was that he continually conveyed to me views of the questions of the hour which I knew to be false, which he knew me to know to be false. At least he knew that I came with the Resident, and might have known that I would ask him about things and believe what he said. Yet, without the least encouragement, he insinuated and insinuated and insinuated away, till I felt almost a traitor to sit and listen to him. He cannot have thought I should take his side, or that I could be of any service to him if I did; but that appeared to matter nothing. Intrigue was his nature, and in default of a better confederate he kept his hand in by trying to intrigue with me.

And then suddenly, without a flicker in the eyes of either Rajah or interpreter:—

"His Highness hopes that on your return to your country you will write to him from time to time, and give him your advice on affairs of State."

I gasped. "His Highness has heard much of your good name and high reputation," pursued the bland, relentless voice—he had first heard and forgotten my name three hours before—"and he is sure that your opinion on the government of his country would be very valuable to him."

And while I still gasped, his Highness motionlessly rose, handed me out of the chair with his soufflet touch, and prattled in English, "Do not forget me."

I shall not forget him. Nor yet the Commander-in-Chief of the army—a mild little man with a stammer, who sat on the extreme edge of his chair. Nor the Chancellor of the Exchequer and Lord Chancellor—the two officers combined in one beaming babu, who told us how he intended to decide cases which had not yet come on for hearing. Nor the feudal chief, a relative of his Highness, educated in England, who wanted to raise money. "But you're very well off, surely?" said the Resident. "I regret to have to state, sir, that such is not the case," replied the descendant of a hundred bandits. The next functionary—so clumsy is destiny—complained that "I got plenty pay, sir, not got no work."

Happy State, you cry. You will say so still more

when you hear that there are only two acute questions of party politics at present before it : (*a*) Whether a certain member of the royal family ought to be allowed to shoot pig, instead of preserving them for sticking ; and (*b*) Whether a nilghai is a cow. A nilghai, as you know, is not a cow, but an antelope ; it destroys crops, and the Opposition press a bill to legalise the shooting of it. But, on the other hand, urges the Government, it looks like a cow, and there is a strong body of tradition in favour of regarding it as such, and therefore holy. So the matter has been referred to arbitration. A college of saints at Benares has ruled that a nilghai is not a cow ; but it is quite capable of ruling, on—and for—a sufficient consideration, that, though not a cow, it is as it were a cow. Meantime party feeling runs strongly—as does also the nilghai.

But, indeed, the native State is, in its way, a paradise. As long as the Rajah behaves with tolerable decency, and his people are not quite outrageously overtaxed or disorderly, he can do exactly what he likes. In the old days, if he shut himself up with opium and nautch-girls, a neighbour would come and take his country ; now the Government of India instructs the Resident to use his influence on the side of virtue, and meanwhile sees that the frontiers stand fixed. Then his subjects might rise against misgovernment ; if they did it now British troops would come in to uphold him. A few years ago the Thakurs of Bikanir—the feudal nobles, mostly of royal blood—did actually set about to depose their king for incompetence and exaction. This has ever been the Rajput method of constitutional government—but the Sirkar sent a column to put the Maharajah back again.

But when the Maharajah goes too far—squanders his revenues, or hangs his subjects up by the toes—the Sirkar sends him a Resident with power to do more than lecture on the beauty of virtue. The Resident becomes an administrator. Mysore was governed thus for over fifty years; now, restored to a wise Queen-mother and a promising prince, it is the most flourishing native State in India. Kashmir was on the verge of bankruptcy a few years ago; now, under the Resident as virtual Prime Minister, with officers lent from British India and a carefully selected Council of State, the land revenue has been increased and the burden of taxes decreased simultaneously, the army decreased but made efficient, the Customs revenue and forest revenue doubled, and Kashmir's feet are on the road of prosperity again.

Of Rajahs there are very many kinds, and much thought and care have been expended on the theory and practice of their production. The Government of India, while usually leaving them to themselves, has made an exception in the case of their manufacture. It is exceptional that a native State passes to an adult heir—a Rajah's life is not a healthy one : the average age of ruling princes appears to be about seventeen—and the Government of India educates the minors. For young Rajput chiefs there is the Mayo College at Ajmir; rulers of wider influence usually have a Governor told off to them from the Indian Civil Service or Staff Corps.

The question is, what sort of man you should aim at producing. The old-fashioned good Rajah—the conservative, pious ruler, on good terms with his Resident and his subjects alike, but impartially disliking champagne, sanitation, bookmakers, female education, and trousers—was perhaps the most satisfactory, certainly the most dignified, type; but he, alas! though still extant here and there, must shortly die out. With him, as a compensation, will probably perish the old-fashioned bad one, the intriguer and blackmailee, the tormenter of subjects and would-be assassin of Residents, who took greedily to champagne and bookmakers and—now and then—trousers, but hated sanitation and female education none the less. Of the new generation the most familiar type is the sporting Rajah. In what was practically the final of this year's polo championship, the Patiala and Kotah teams were each captained by the Maharajah. Other young chiefs are not less eminent in the saddle, and the Maharajah of Patiala is a keen and useful cricketer. The Nizam of Hyderabad is, or was, almost the best shot in the world. At his best the sporting Rajah is probably the best solution of the difficulty of keeping a man manly when you deny him his hereditary pursuit of war.   At his worst—and there is a worst—he becomes a bad imitation of the less dignified kind of sporting peer.

In both cases it is hard to get him to take the least interest in the affairs of his subjects.   After all, why should he?   If a second Akbar were born in India we should not let him rule in his own way, and he would in that case rather not rule at all.   It is childish to blame the Rajah for being oriental.

Thus seesaw the native States of India—over a third of its area, over a fourth of its population.   Up with a good Rajah, down with a bad ; most up with a very bad who brings in a British administrator. Many of their people would like to be annexed to British India; others prefer things as they are— especially everybody even distantly connected with the public service.   We might annex them—there is never any lack of pretext—and we might leave them entirely alone to serve as awful examples, and make our subjects contented by the contrast.   Instead of that we do—as always in India—the straight and disinterested thing.   We are tolerant of the Rajah as long as he is possible, and succour his people when he is not.   Thus—as always in India—we get no thanks from either.

XXVII

THE COMPLETE GLOBE-TROTTER

WITHIN the hour of your landing India begins playing its jokes upon you. You drive through piles of palace and masses of palm to a hotel whose name is known throughout the world. A Goanese porter receives you, and requests you to inhabit a sort of scullery on the roof. I do not exaggerate a jot. I have seen the European cell in a remote district jail, and it was very appreciably larger, lighter, cleaner, cooler, and more eligibly situated than the first room I was offered in an Indian hotel.

As the first, so was the second, and the third, and all of them. By the time I left the country I had been in almost all the best hotels of India. Four, throughout the 1,800,000 square miles, might indulgently be called second-class; all the rest were unredeemedly vile. When they were new they may have had the same pretension to elegance and comfort as a London public wash-house has; but by now they are all very old, and suggest anything rather than washing. There can hardly have been a depreciated rupee spent upon the herd of them. The walls are dirty, the carpets shabby, the furniture rickety, the food uneatable, the management non-existent. The only things barely tolerable in an Indian hotel are the personal service and the bedding, both of which you bring with you of your own.

The apartment in which I originally recorded these opinions was furnished as follows. A table with a deep crack across it; a bedstead with a mattress covered with dirty ticking; a wardrobe papered inside with advertisements from the " Pioneer," now black and peeling off in strips; two chairs, both of which had holes in their cane seats, and creaked and rocked on their joints when you sat on them; two occasional tables, both broken-legged and sloping perilously; and a decayed hat-and-coat rack with one peg missing and two loose. There was a sort of sackcloth carpet, stained, creased, and littered with bits of straw. All the French windows were warped and refused to shut; over one hung two wisps of torn and coffee-coloured lace curtain. The walls were of green distemper, blotchy and coming off; in the ceiling was a cobwebbed hole, which once held a chandelier, and now held vermin. Many squirrels and mice were running up and down the floor. This was a shade worse than usual, but only a shade. All these things you expect in an Indian hotel; and at the touring season of the year you are lucky if the swollen babu in the office will let you in at all.

And after all, what do you expect ? Why should there be good hotels in India ? In Bombay, it is true, a really good hotel is wanted, and would pay : they say that one is on the point of arriving. Everybody that comes to India comes to Bombay, and nearly everybody can afford to pay to be comfortable, or at least clean. There are always people, more or fewer, passing through ; also many bachelors will be found to live in a good hotel, for the Parsis have cornered all the possible bungalows. If you get custom enough to pay a good European proprietor to own, and a good European manager to manage, there is no reason on earth why a hotel should not be as good in India as in Egypt.

But for the rest of the country, what can you expect ? If a hotel is in the plains, it will be empty in the hot weather ; if in the hills, it will be empty in the cold. The European population of India is sparse and scattered, and of measureless hospitality. The white man sees less of hotels than of tents, of dak bungalows on lonely, half-made roads, or rest-houses by lonely, half-empty canals. His work is always hanging on his back, and will not let him travel at large ; if he goes for a day or two into a town, it is to a friend or to the club. So the hotel languishes. Presently the European owner sells it cheap to a native, and he puts in first a Eurasian manager and then a babu ; and the owner will not spend a pie to renew the furniture or new-stain the walls, and the manager will not spend an hour to see that they are clean. Presently the place comes to look like a haunted house crossed upon a byre, and the Indian hotel is complete.

So that the tourist wallows in discomfort. He and she are, like tourists in most other lands, dazed by the unfamiliar into all-accepting meekness. Most of them did not know where India was till they arrived there. They carry in their pocket-books a piece of paper, whereon Mr. Cook, pitying the lost sheep, has written down the names of the places they are to go to, with the times of the trains by which they are to arrive and leave. They bring native servants—or is it that native masters bring them?—who show them such sights as can be compassed without walking, and then smoke and doze under the back verandah of the hotel, while their wards smoke and doze under the front. As a rule the tourist is too broken-spirited even to dress for dinner; how, then, should he complain of a hotel? He would sleep with his feet on the pillow if that were more convenient to his servant, and remark on it next morning at breakfast as a new peculiarity of Indian life. At intervals of days an observation will strike a spark on the petrifaction of his mind: he will flicker with intelligence and remark, " What a number of tombs and mosques and temples there seem to be in this country!" If you counter with the suggestion that there are a good many gravestones and churches and chapels at home, he agrees; but then that is a civilised and highly-populated country. As for India, he opines that the population must have been much greater in those days—"those days" stretch, roughly, from 0 to 1700 A. D.—for that in these days the country parts seem quite deserted. There are, as a matter of fact, only 240,000,000 people " in the country parts "—and the Anglo-Indian is disappointed because the tourist does not appreciate his work !

India, to put it summarily, does not exist for the casual stranger, nor yet for the European at all, but for the native. You may say, broadly, that everything which only the European wants is bad, while everything the native wants is good. The native has taken up with enthusiasm the recreation of railway travelling, and the Indian railways are accordingly admirable. They lack only one point of excellence, and that is exactly what the European wants and the native does not—speed. The white man is often in a hurry, the native never : the Indian train strolls accordingly at a decorous twenty miles an hour. The sahib may get impatient, but it is lightning to people whose national conveyance is a bullock-cart. The native troubles himself nothing about time-tables : he goes to the station before sunrise and sits down till the train comes; and the amount of native traffic is astonishing—astonishing even though it costs him about a farthing a mile. The station-yard and the road beyond are a fair by day and a doss-house by night; at the opening of the gates the roaring, jabbering platform recalls the breaking of the crowd when the Lord

Mayor's Show has gone by. The third-class carriages are even as crates of fowls: some stand on the seats, some lie on the floor. You see only a jungle of heads and legs and arms projected vaguely out of nowhere. At night the compartment is a heap of sack-coloured bundles that might indifferently be men or mail-bags. Your own Indian railway carriage is not unlike the Indian house. It has space and all indispensables for existing in a bad climate, but little of finish or embellishment. In Europe the sleeping-car mimics the drawing-room; in India, where often the very drawing-room is but a halting-place in a perpetual journey, a sleeping-car is merely a car you can very well sleep in. To it, as everywhere in India, you bring your own bedding and your own servant to lay it out. You take your meals at stations by the way; if there is no refreshment-room at the right time and place, you bring your food with you. The European train is like a hotel; the Indian like a camp. Your servant piles in your canvas bundle of bedding, your battered dressing-case, your hat-box, your despatch-box, your topi, your stick, your flask, your tiffin-basket, your overcoat, your cricket-bat, your racquet, your hunting-crop, your gun, and your dog; you insert yourself among them and away you go.

The Indian train may not be sumptuously caparisoned, but it is workmanlike to the uttermost hat-peg. On the metre-gauge lines you are a little cramped at night, inevitably; on the broad-gauge there is far more dressing, washing, and shaving space than on any line in Europe or America. Against the hot weather screens of boarding hang from the carriage roof to midway down the window; these stall off some of the dust, while most of the windows are smoked to cool the glare. Ice can be had at important stations during the hot months. In the more civilised parts a boy with ice and mineral waters actually travels in the train with you. As a rule there is a servants' compartment contiguous to your own; on the South Indian Railway they have a sort of ticket-window through which you can bid him minister to you. Another vast convenience is the railway waiting-room. You arrive, let us say, at six, and take a cup of tea; while you drink that a shave and a hot bath are preparing in the waiting-room; while you take those, breakfast is cooking in the kitchen. You go forth and do what you came for. Then, having an hour to spare, you can sit down and minister to the public mind from a better chair and table and room altogether than, I doubt, you will find in any hotel in India.

In short, your Briton is not at all the conservative creature that at home he would make himself out. Put him down where he has more or less of a clear field, and he will adapt and invent and contrive and tolerate the usefully ugly with the best of them. The small convenience, for example, of carriages coloured according to their class, now timidly nibbled at in

England, has long been familiar to India : first-class is white, second dark green, third native-colour. Only one fault can I think of in the regulations for Indian travel—there are no carriages reserved for men. Consequently ladies enter in with their husbands, which at bedtime brings embarrassments. Once I have actually had to ask the stationmaster to put on an extra carriage solely for me to hide my blushes in.

For the rest you may look forward to your Indian travel with much confidence. Besides the train there are other delights,—the ferry-boat in the aching cold of dawn, the row-boat on the racing canal, the ekka over dust-ruts, the tonga and trotting bullocks on a metalled road, the tonga and hill-pony over precipices, the double-saddled camel over sand-drifts, the elephant over everything that comes in the way. The tonga is a low, two-wheeled dachsund of a cart, with the build of a gun-carriage, wherein you wedge yourself between back seat and tail-board and travel among the hills, with good ponies and luck, at an average of eight miles or so an hour. It is better sport than an automobile, as the ponies are seldom broken, and sometimes have to be hauled into the desired course with a whip-thong twisted round the car and then prevented from flinging the whole thing over a cliff if Allah so wills. The ekka—which is for natives only—is a painted ice-cream barrow with an awning above it and a pony before. The elephant—well, you may have seen him, and though for my own part

I never considered him as a serious beast till I knew him personally in India, you have already heard the little I know on that subject.

As I was saying, you will enjoy your travelling in India, if you have so many friends there that you never need put foot in a hotel. If you have not, you had much better go somewhere else, and leave India to worry through by itself.

XXVIII

THE HAPPY HOMES OF INDIA

ONE letter of introduction, discreetly managed, will furnish you with lodging, board, drinks, fire, mounts, shooting, fishing, carriages, servants, books, flowers, and clothes from one end of India to the other.

I never heard of anybody who was shameless enough to do it—I did hear of two Frenchmen who went forty days on the strength of letters from a native prince neither of them knew—but I am certain that, discreetly managed, it could be done. It would be better, though not absolutely necessary, to have a suit of clothes to start in, and it is not usual for your host in giving you his introduction to your next host to add a railway ticket. Short of that, Indian hospitality is limitless.

You get out at the station and find a bearded Mussulman salaaming over a letter. The letter informs you that the bearer will do everything—and he does. He puts you into a carriage, and an attendant or two he has brought with him, after a short, shrill controversy with your own servant, grapple with your luggage. On the easiest of springs and cushions you roll along broad, straight roads, arcaded with trees, the dust carefully laid by half-naked watermen sluicing out water through the necks of the goatskins on their backs. From time to time you pass gateways; but, unless it is evening and lamps are lit, you can only guess that there are houses behind the trees. Presently you swing through one of these: there appears a broad house, too high, it seems, for one storey, too low for two, with pillared front, verandahs on all sides, and a *porte-cochère.* They take you to a vast bedroom as lofty as the big saloons of a grand hotel, laid with matting and rugs, with at least one long, cane-seated lounge-chair with forward-jutting arms that will serve indifferently as table or leg-rest. In the matted bathroom adjoining your hot water is waiting for you. A servant, or two, or six, will hasten at your command, while your own bearer is struggling up with the luggage, and bring you anything you may be pleased to desire from a newspaper to a joint of mutton.

Next morning you find that the house stands in a compound: even Government offices and banks and shops possess it. It is a large walled or hedged enclosure, part garden, part mews, part village. The Indian garden is almost the most pathetic thing in a whole land of exile. In the morning the bullocks will be hauling at the creaking well, and all the little baked squares of light grit wallow under water. The native trees and shrubs and plants—huge leaves, garish petals, heavy perfumes—flourish rankly. But the poor little home flowers—the stocks and mignonette and wallflowers! They struggle so gallantly to pretend that they are happy, to persuade you that this is not so very far from England; and they fail so piteously. They will flower in abundant but straggling blossoms; but the fierce sun withers the first before the next have more than budded. They make no foliage, and they are drawn into leggy stalks, all out of shape. It is a loving fraud, but a hollow one. The very wallflowers cannot be more than exiles.

In the mews, past the big carriage Walers, the Arab hacks and polo ponies thrust trusting heads over bars in hopes of carrots, or pluck impatiently at their heel-ropes. Then there is the village—a whole village of servants in every compound. The principle of division of labour, of one man one job, has been taken up by the Indian servant with a grasp and thoroughness that would move the despairing envy of a modern trade-unionist. Every kind of work requires its special man, so that a normal Indian household is something like the following. The sahib's bearer or valet, 1; the memsahib's ayah, or maid, 2; the khansamah, or head cook and caterer, 3; the cook's two mates and the scullery-boy, 6; the khitmagars, or table-servants, 8; the tailor, 9; the dhobi, or washer-man, 10; the bhisti, or water-carrier, 11; the sweeper, 12; the gardeners, 15; the syces, or grooms, 19; the grass-cutters—for in Indian not only must you have a groom to each horse, but a grass-cutter to each groom—23. Some add a dog-boy, but that savours of luxurious ostentation; as a rule, the sweeper will kindly consent to fill up some of his leisure with the care of dogs.

But that is not all, or nearly all. If the sahib is in Government service, you must add from one to three munshis, or clerks, and from two to four chaprassis. These are a kind of cross between messengers and lictors : their scarlet coats and sashes are symbols of the presence of the Sirkar. A small man may have no more than two; a Lieutenant-Governor will have four tongas full, and a Viceroy, I infer, a special trainful. How many red chaprassis there must be in the whole of India it beggars statistics to compute. That brings us up to a household of thirty. If the sahib is in camp, as nearly everybody in India is for a part of the year, he will probably have a double set of tents, of which one goes on by day to be ready for him next morning. That means an extra bhisti and an extra sweeper, say a dozen tent-pitchers, and the same number of camel- or bullock-drivers. Grand total, fifty-six persons to attend on one married couple.

Arrogant satrap! you cry. But it is not the satrap's fault. On the contrary, his household is the curse of his life and of his memsahib's. As each servant takes a new wife, he wants space in the compound to run up a wicker-screen round her; hence, and from other sources, perpetual quarrels. Perhaps the sahib, as yet unbroken, desires to have half as many servants with double the work and double the pay. He may argue and beseech and swear: he might as well hold a public disputation with a bullock-team. The servant prostrates himself and says, "O Presence, it is not the custom."

If you question the memsahib of the ordering of her household, you will find that she knows very little about it. She knows that the bearer is supposed to dust the drawing-room and does not, and that the khansamah presents a monthly account. This account is almost the most wondrous thing in India. A khansamah who knows his business fits it to the sahib's income with undeviating precision. Servants at home know everything; in India they know yet more. The quiet men who wait at table know more English than they pretend; usually there is somebody in the house who can read English letters. Anglo-Indian life is all under verandahs, behind open windows, transparent blinds, and doors that will not shut. Also every servant knows every other servant, as well as the clerks at the bank and in the Government offices; therefore a man will first hear of his impending promotion or transfer from his bearer. And when he is promoted, his wife, hoping to save money to eke out the ever-nearer retirement pension, will discover that the expenses have risen in exact proportion to the rise of pay. "The Presence has more pay now," says the virtuous khansamah. "Does it become the Presence to live like a mere assistant-commissioner? I have seen many sahibs, and I know what is fitting."

Where does it go to? Do not ask, but count from time to time the bangles on the ankles of the khansamah's leading wife. You will notice that they enlarge and multiply. The word for this process is *dastur*; in French it is spelt *mes sous*, and in English "housekeeper's discount." You may say confidently that no money changes hands between the sahib and a native without it has borne commission. "What is the price in the bazaar of a tin pail?" the memsahib asks of a chaprassi. "God knows. I am a poor man. Yet by making inquiries it can be known." So he disappears round the corner, where waits the pail merchant, and by making inquiries it is known. Every man has his pice.

But if the rich man's expenses increase with his pay, the poor man's remain steady. The pinched married subaltern gets exactly the same food and servants and everything else as the plump commissioner. The Indian servant may be a tyrant, but he is also a providence. He asks no more than your all: give him that honestly, and he will see that you want for nothing. His honour is in his sahib and his sahib's establishment. It is his pride that he never steals contrary to custom: he will take half a farthing commission on the expenditure of 2d., but he is safe as the grave with your whole month's pay in his pocket. When the exile is over, and the sahib returns across the black water, the bearer weeps quite sincerely. "Behold I am grown old in the service of the Presence. The Presence is my father and mother: what now shall this dust-like one do?" Then one day, in the riced-and-buttered ease of his native village, he hears that his old master's son is on the way to India. God knows how, but he hears it. And when the boy lands at Bombay, an old man creeps up to him bearing a chit from his father. "Behold it would be a shame to me if any but me should be the Presence's bearer, seeing that I have many times held him on my knee when he was so high." So he is the Presence's bearer. The old man, who had retired rich for life from a general's establishment, begins again in a subaltern's quarters and serves the young sahib till his infirmities will let him serve no longer. Then he goes back to his village again with a pension, and sends his son to serve the Presence instead.

The bearer and khansamah may well take loads on themselves, for there are agonies in Indian housekeeping which must fall on the memsahib alone. How would you like to do your shopping at a thousand miles' range? Except in Madras, Bombay, and Calcutta there is hardly a possible shop in India. You must think what you want, and order it a fortnight in advance; even so, it will probably arrive a fortnight late. And then, if people are coming to stay over Christmas. . . . I have heard of a Resident's wife who had to send two hundred miles for a flock of sheep for the needs of her house-party, and then the local Brahmans intercepted them and put them in the pound; and religion ordains that what has once been in the pound can never be slaughtered.

There are other sorrows. Go into the Indian drawing-room: it is shady and cool and charming, but nearly always it seems a little bare. The rest of the furniture—the pretty nothings—are packed in boxes at depots in Calcutta or Bombay or Pindi. The piano is staying with a friend, and the silver has not yet come back from the bank. Leave one year and transfer the next, camp next month, and an imperative change to the hills for the memsahib the hot weather after that—the Indian house is ever a place of transition. It is a mere caravanserai—a double exile. The Anglo-Indian has not even a fixed place of banishment. It is not enough that the mother must send away her children: she may not even live with her furniture.

In this fugitive encampment on alien soil the very order of meals is shaken. When it is hot you rise before dawn and take your *chota hazri* of tea and toast. Then for your ride, your bicycle spin, your game of racquets in the first hours of the sun. Then home to dress, and then breakfast, and then a day's work through the long, long heat and glare. Tiffin you have no stomach for, and so you wait for tea.

The Happy Homes of India

After that life is bearable again: there is air if you only gasp hard enough. There is the drive by the Hughli at Calcutta, on the shore of Back Bay at Bombay, on the Marina at Madras. Then for men the club: in smaller stations the club is free to women also. All prepare for dinner with billiards or badminton, which is battledore and shuttlecock over a net. Then dinner under the punkah; or maybe it is dance night, and everybody forgets hot to-day and hotter to-morrow and the whole weary year.

Sunday brings little respite. Man has his week's arrears of work. For woman, if she cares, there is church at the big station; and in the small the little Scotch missionary, or the Resident, or the Deputy-Commissioner reading the service in a drawing-room to his wife and his assistant and the engineer's wife—the engineer is out on the canal, and the doctor is a native—the railway-man and his wife and his children. It does your heart good to see how the missionary enjoys his sermon—the one taste of theological Scotland in his week of stupid scholars and stupider patients; it does you good to hear the railway-man growl out the hymns of his childhood.

There is one day yet more sacred than Sunday—mail-day. Nobody makes calls that day: nobody is to be seen; next day is a sort of lazy holiday. Everybody hates mail-day, they tell you; nobody misses it. Across five thousand miles. . . . Still it is something.

XXIX

THE CASE OF REBELLIOUS POONA

BALKRISHNA, Wasudeo, and Ranade lie in the central jail, two miles out of Poona. This is in June, and they have been there since early March; some day between now and the reading of these pages they will have been hanged by the neck until they were dead.

They are the last—some think; others think not the last—of the gang which on Jubilee night in 1897, headed by their elder brother, Damodher, murdered Mr. Rand and Lieutenant Ayerst. Since then two of the witnesses against Damodher, who was hanged, have been murdered; attempts have been made on others; and Wasudeo—aged seventeen, and a student, if I mistake not, at the same college which educated this year's Senior Wrangler—crowned his career by firing a pistol at the magistrate in open court. These crimes, added to trials for seditious writing and speech, such as those of Tilak and the brothers Natu, to difficulties between soldiers and people over plague work, and to reckless calumnies about the behaviour of British soldiers at that time, have given Poona the most evil reputation in India. Here is one centre in India which seems thoroughly and irreconcilably disaffected. A Poona Brahman is the type all over India of serpentine cunning and malignancy. "Poona was always a nasty place," I remember hearing an old engine-driver say years ago, when I hardly knew where Poona was. "It seemed different from other places, somehow. You didn't know what those chaps were up to. You didn't quite know where it was, but there it was. It was a nasty place." That sums up the general opinion about Poona with most accurate vagueness. Nobody quite knows what it is, but everybody is quite sure it is something. So Poona has a bad name, and from time to time bits of it are hanged.

There ought, you feel, to be some definite and tangible reason. But if there is I do not know it; and, though I have sought, I have not met the European or the native that can tell it me. Except for the murders, and the obviously widespread sympathy which permitted and screened them, Poona seems to have done no wrong beyond Calcutta or Lahore; except for the fine imposed by the quartering of extra troops on it after the murders, Poona seems to have suffered nothing beyond Bombay or Madras. Yet, when you leave searching for specific causes and fall back on general grounds of discontent, the case becomes plainer. Poona is the ancient capital of the Marathas, and there are a score of reasons why the

Marathas should chafe under British rule more than any other people of India.

We must go back, after the fashion of the official reports, to the days of Aurungzebe. You must bear in mind that it was from the Marathas and the Sikhs, from Hindus not from Mussulmans, that we actually conquered India. At the beginning of the eighteenth century the Mogul empire began to fall to pieces with the death of Aurungzebe. The Marathas and Sikhs were the Hindu reaction. Spreading from Western India, the Marathas overran the whole peninsula from the Punjab to Bengal. They made the Emperor of Delhi their prisoner, and governed and raided in his name; Maratha chiefs founded the dynasties of Scindia, Holkar, and Baroda; but the head of their confederacy was always the Peshwa of Poona. In 1789 they captured Delhi itself. According to the ordinary run of India's history they would in due time have been subjugated by some hardier race from the north. But the Sikhs formed a temporary barrier against the Mussulman hordes; and the death-blow of the Marathas therefore came from the other side—from the sea and the British. In two desperate wars, not unshadowed by British defeats, they lost, first Delhi in 1803, and then, fifteen years later, Poona itself. After about a century of rule the Maratha empire collapsed as swiftly as it had risen.

Other provinces of India were ceded to us or conquered from alien lords; the Marathas lost their all in war. So, later, did the Sikhs; but while the Sikhs have long since reconciled themselves to our dominion, the Marathas have never forgotten how high they were less than a hundred years ago, and who it was that brought them low. They lost more than others, and they feel the loss more. For others we were a change of masters; them we brought down from masters to slaves.

The case of the Marathas offers an unhappy and unique combination of everything that can embitter subjection. They were gallant warriors, if wanting stamina; they were also patriots, devotees, and a people of an extraordinary acuteness of intellect. The Rohillas, whom we conquered, were as gallant warriors; but they were adventurers, not a nation. The Ghurkhas, from whom we captured provinces, were both gallant and patriotic; but they were careless of religion, while to the straitly Hindu Marathas the very existence of British rule is a compulsion to daily impiety. The Sikh is brave, patriotic, and religious; but he is simple and unlettered, and easily forgets a beating in the satisfaction of having fought a good fight. The Maratha, more introspective, hugs the smart of defeat. The Bengali vaunts as acute a mind —at least until it comes to action,—but he has forgotten what it is to be free. Each has his compensation, except the Maratha. His empire, his nationality, his religion, his honour, his beautiful language—we have taken away his all.

The Case of Rebellious Poona

It is not our fault. Some of his complaints are even grotesquely self-destructive. For example, he seizes greedily on English education to fit himself for political and journalistic attacks upon us, and in elaborate Macaulayesque periods complains that the English tongue is killing the Marathi. Another of the Brahman's grievances is that he is poor; yet when he gets a Government post that would be great wealth for one, he divides it into pittances for a score of brothers and sisters, and uncles and aunts, and second-cousins, who all come to live in his house. This is his religion, and it is a most unselfish one; but it is his doing, not ours. Yet with all their illogic his complaints are sincere. The Maratha really does think himself most ill-used. He seems to bear a vinegar disposition on his very features. The type is very well marked as you meet it on descending from the north—a shaven head that looks small and square under its peony turban; a skin so darkly brown that it almost amounts to a scowl in itself; brows that press down on the gleaming eyes in a perpetual frown; a small, rather formless nose, often almost snub; a black or grey moustache that turns down stiffly over the corners of a tight-drawn mouth,—a face full of character, but of bad character. The harsh brows and precise moustache convey somehow a look of sour self-righteousness. The Maratha looks as if he were ever brooding over wrongs most undeserved. "These people," he is saying, "will all be damned when I am in heaven; and yet they rule me, and I cannot shake them off."

That at least is certain: he cannot shake us off. The Government of India had a bad turn of nervousness after the Jubilee murders; but it is safe to say that there will never be another Indian Mutiny without aid from outside; and if there were, it would not be the Marathas who could profit by it. Failing that, their discontent finds its vent in what a Brahman I consulted on the subject called " a vague feeling of unrest—with undercurrents." He himself was of the moderate party who favour reforms in Hinduism and constitutional methods of political agitation—agitation for what, they have not yet quite settled. The extremists—such as the now notorious Tilak—are the undercurrents. They find a vent for their vague feeling of unrest in kindling religious animosities among the common people. The common people, of course, have long ceased to sigh for the glories of Shivaji, hero and traitor, or for the great days of raid and empire: it was not they, we may conjecture, who got the best of the loot. But they cling like limpets to their religion. Compared with Orientals, we Western people do not know what religion is: Hinduism prescribes and enters into every single act in the lives of those who profess it. It tells them what to eat, what to drink, wherewithal to be clothed, whom to marry, whom not to touch with so much as their shadows. You may call it unspiritual—religion fossilised into unmeaning, stupid custom—yet it is their all, and they prize it beyond life. The Hindu, in a sense which the West cannot even comprehend, does all things to the glory—or the reverse—of God.

Now a simple thing like travelling in a tramcar is quite sufficient to defile a Hindu, if a defiling person happens also to be in that tramcar. Therefore you will see that the kind of improvements we have introduced into India are fertile of religious offence, and might in the long-run be fatal to Hinduism in its traditional form. That is why the better kind of Brahman favours a modification of the creed—it is really a life rather than a creed—and the worse sees his opportunity in doing all he can to keep it as rigid and formal as possible. A short while ago, for example, a quarrel occurred in Poona between Hindus and Mussulmans. In other parts of India Hindu processions are not allowed to pass mosques with cymbals and tom-toms during the festival of the Moharram. In Poona it had not hitherto been forbidden. But now the Mussulmans applied for its prohibition, and, in accord with the usage of other cities, jingling and tom-tomming was prohibited during that explosive and fanatical time. Thereon Tilak and his friends must get up a sort of Moharram of their own—a Hindu festival very similar to the Moslem one, except that it has no history and no meaning.

It happened not to matter, and now both sects join without prejudice in each other's tom-toming, as before the quarrel. As usual, nobody suffered but the doubly-deafened European. Yet this illustrates the attitude of the extreme Brahmans. Their game is to load the overloaded religion with more and more meaningless observances, in the hope that they may somehow one day lead to strife. To such the outbreak of plague in 1897 and the employment of British troops on house-to-house examination was a golden chance. The use of them may or may not have been wise. A knowledge of the Marathi language and of Hindu domestic ceremonial is not among the accomplishments for which we pay Atkins a shilling a-day, and he may have been wanting in tact. He generally lives away in cantonments, and his appearance in force in the native city was by itself disquieting to the timid coolie. On the other hand, somebody had to do the work, and with sanitary work even the most Europeanised native is hardly ever to be trusted.

If the Brahmans had been honestly desirous of doing good to the people they would have volunteered to go round with the soldiers and keep them from unconscious offence. Some of them, to their great credit and to everybody's satisfaction, have since done this. But at the first they preferred to let the public health go hang, and make mischief, wherein they succeeded richly.

But it seems that the worst of it is over now. Balkrishna, Wasudeo, and Ranade will be hanged by the neck until they are dead. There is an idea that the murderers of Rand and Ayerst were only the instruments of a more powerful backer—somebody who furnished money and ideas, but not his carcass. But those who know best think that though there was much sympathy with them—though they went to people and said, " We are going to kill a sahib," and they only replied, " Isn't it a bit dangerous ? "—they are the last of the gang. To be sure, Tilak's paper called them brave and unselfish youths; but he is the kind of man that prefers hallooing capital crimes from a distance to putting himself inside the meshes of the law. The Maratha Brahman, for a native of India, seems singularly unwilling to die. A simple ryot, the other day, had said good-bye to his relatives, and was pinioned, when suddenly he asked to speak again to his brother. " Recollect," he said, " it's twenty Kawa seers of barley that man owes me. Not Dawa seers "—as you might say imperial pints, not reputed. Then he turned and was hanged without moving a muscle. Another man, a Pathan, was being hanged, when the rope broke. The warder bade him go up on to the scaffold again, but he objected. " No," he said; " I was sentenced to be hanged, and hanged I've been." " Not so, friend," argued the warder; " you were sentenced to be hanged until you were dead, and you're not dead." It was a new view to the Pathan, and he turned to the superintendent, " Is that right, Sahib ? " " Yes, that's right." " Very well; I didn't understand;" and he went composedly up the steps and was hanged again like a man. But it seems that the Brahman, being a more complex creature, does not match this superb indifference. When Damodher saw the black-railed scaffold his knees were loosened; when they came to fit the noose he collapsed in a heap, and had to be supported into heaven like a coward. His three followers received their sentence with bravado, but now behind the bars they were beginning to go the way Damodher went. So that it appears likely that the punishment of this gang will prove an effective deterrent against any attempts to imitate or avenge them.

For the rest, plague looks like becoming a regular cold-weather visitor to Poona. The hot-weather sun killed it this spring; but the odds are it will recur. In any case, the able officers recently in charge of the segregations have quite soothed the people's nervousness. So it may be that the Government and Poona will rub along together again for a space, as they often have done before for years together. But you need not expect the Maratha to like it, and you cannot expect the Government to give him back India. He will go on looking vinegar, and there is no help for it.

XXX

THE JAIL

"THREE yellow, five red, two blue," chanted the convict behind the growing carpet. "As thou sayest so let it be done," chorused the convicts sitting in front of it, as they slipped the thread within the warp. Opposite them, and further up the long factory, and further back and opposite that, rose more chants, and after each the vociferation, "As thou sayest so let it be done."

It was a queer sight to come on in the middle of the central jail. It sounded from outside half like breakers on a shingly shore, and half like a board school at the multiplication-table. "That sounds like noise, you know," said the superintendent; "but really it's honest toil." Inside was a long aisle of looms with many-coloured carpets gradually creeping up them. One man called the pattern—the number of stitches to be plaited in of each colour; with a roar the brown-backed criminals, squatting in a row over the carpet, picked out their threads and worked them in. "Eight green, two pink." "As thou sayest so let it be done."

The Oriental, as you know, cannot work in concert unless he chants in concert too. And he has a wonderful ear for his own uproar. Here, for instance, on the floor were two men bending over the same pattern-carpet. One was dictating to a gang on one side, the other on the other; they were at different places, and as each bawled out a direction to his men the others were revelling in their " So let it be done." Yet there was not a mistake in either, though the carpets were only just beginning : each gang must have caught every word. At the big fifty-seven-foot carpet, of course, the directions were hardly needed : it has been a-making for many months, till the leader reels off the colours and numbers by heart, and the dozen workers, each opposite his strip of pattern, put in the stitches like automata. All the carpet-workers are picked men : it is not every malefactor that has the brain to take in the directions, or the eye to distinguish the colours, or the hand to put them in. Such as have prize the work, for it is the only task in the central jail at which you are allowed to make a noise.

It is different with the half-hundred or so of habitual criminals behind the inner wall which isolates them from the comparatively innocent. Their labour lies in pumping up water for the whole jail. In two shifts—half a day each—they tug and strain at the cranks—chocolate bodies, stark naked but for a wisp of loin-cloth, and shaven heads with one tiny tuft left on the top—and only punctuate their toil by grunts. These are all men past reformation ; many of them are born thieves, and thieves for life. We talk of born thieves at home, but our hereditary crime is a casual accident compared with India's. India has its castes and tribes of thieves, and every member of them is born to robbery as naturally and inevitably as you are born to your father's name. They glory in their calling ; but even if they did not, they could follow no other. To steal is not merely a social duty, with its own traditions and its language, which is never divulged to the outsider, but a very religion, with its own thieving god. For a member of these tribes to be honest would be an impiety. Only occasionally and accidentally can they earn an honest living as watchmen against their brothers. For India believes literally in setting a thief to catch a thief, although to catch he has no need, because his brothers abstain so long as his employer gives satisfaction. Meantime, the watchman himself steals only as much as is necessary to keep his hand in, and generally returns the loot immediately. He cannot afford to let himself get rusty, especially if he be a bachelor; for the religion will not allow him to be married till he has achieved the qualifying number of larcenies.

But even these inbred criminals, together with amateurs who equal their unwearied ill-doing, are not in this prison set to purposeless labour, such as is our crank at home. There is an overflow-pipe, which shows in a moment when everything has been filled, and if the water rises in that half an hour or an hour before the day's end they knock off triumphant. In any case, pumping water is just the work whose utility the native understands. It is better than grinding the air.

The pump is only for the definitely depraved. But every convict on entering must work through a spell of heavy labour—stone-breaking for road-metal or corn-grinding. The jail, like most at home, is all but self-supporting : the assassin grinds the flour for his own supper. The mill is like that at which two women shall be grinding when one is taken and the other left—a couple of grindstones with a hole and a handle in the upper one ; the men's tasks lie in a stone bin beside each, and they grind away—a row of full-muscled, flour-dusted, bronze statues. On the other side of the circle the kitchen swelters in the sun—a curving bank of coppers and griddle-plates. Up about their rims stroll bare-footed, bare-bodied attendants, and prod caldrons of hissing cabbage and cauliflower with baulks of timber. " Better vegetables than most sahibs get," says the superintendent ; and if an unrepresentative sahib may judge, it is so indeed. But the bodies of the prisoners are the diet's best recommendation—plumper than the ordinary villager's, thinner than the ordinary bunnia's. India has the convenience that every native's poverty or wealth is inscribed on his belly.

The Jail

It seems a grim joke to talk of a prison as an Arcadia; yet these plump, industrious jail-birds somehow gave more impression of happy usefulness than a dozen villages. It was so compact, so well ordered, so well directed. In the next circle were a couple of yards full of bamboo-workers—the men sitting under the verandahs with chisel and hammer; inside the sheds the long double-row of bare sleeping-banks—hard, but scarcely harder than their beds in the villages, and, Lord! how unspeakably cleaner! While dacoity was flourishing a number of Burmans came to this jail; they were set to work on their beautifully delicate bamboo tables and chairs and screen-work. There are only half a dozen or so left now—little, button-nosed, yellow faces among the amber ones—but there are enough to teach the Hindus, and do the finer work. It was pleasant to see the pride with which they displayed the latest masterpiece; pleasant to go into the next yard and see the old, old men—too frail to serve out a life sentence of twenty years in the field-work of the Andamans—dozing out the afternoon over a pretence of twisting yarn.. "This is the yard I don't like to show to a visitor," says the superintendent. "There's almost sure to be some breach of discipline—an old chap gone to sleep."

Yes, it was a pleasant sight, this jail. For you must remember that the prisoners are not merely better housed and better fed and better—though hideously —clothed than they would be in their villages; they also have no sense whatever of guilt. This prison leaves no flavour of crime in the mouth. There is no evil conscience and little sullenness. The convict really cannot see why the Sirkar should take that little affair of killing the co-respondent so seriously; still, it must be accepted as part of the general madness of sahibs, and, after all, the place is not such a bad one.

It sounds queer to the home-keeping mind—and perhaps queerer still that most of the warders are murderers. A simple society like most in India has no exaggerated respect for human life, and kills where we merely assault or revile; therefore the murderer, judged by the standard of criminal intention, is often less guilty than the authors of what we call minor crimes. A first offender can rise by merit to be a watchman in a blue-and-white cap, and then to be a warder in lemon-coloured breeches. Every prisoner, by a combination of good work and a blameless walk, can purchase remission of sentence, and pay which means to him a handsome capital to re-commence life with. And the murderer-warders do their work very well, especially considering that some of the prisoners are millionaires compared with themselves. One great point is that many of them are utter foreigners to the mass of the convicts. Here is an Arab from Aden, there a Shan from Mogaung in Upper Burma, there a Pushtu-speaking Pathan from the North-Western border; in the European quarter is a Greek from Zanzibar. It is a microcosm of India, which remains conquered because it is divided.

At certain seasons of public rejoicing Government follows the good old oriental custom of opening the prison doors—only ajar, and with circumspection. "We haven't recovered from the Jubilee yet," mourns the superintendent: "lost all our best men." Everybody released on that auspicious occasion was carefully interrogated to make sure that he understood why. As the result, that one simple soul explained that after sixty years of reign the Rani had a son. Another, more sophisticated, opined that the Rani had at last been allowed by her grateful people to retire under the long-service regulation. A third argued bluntly that it was his right. "People were released in '77 and '87; so, of course, I ought to be in '97."

And for the end, there is one spot more which is not Arcadia—the European quarter. There is not very much of that, thank Heaven! and what there is is not full, and of those there some are not Britons. Yet there are a few Britons—and in the drawn faces and the eyes that dodge past you what a difference from the Arcadians! You look down yourself and hurry on, and almost blush when next you meet the first-class assassin in lemon-colour.

It is all but Arcadia—and then, as always, comes the strange, malignant, hardly human twist that appears in the native's mind just when you are beginning to love him. In jail it takes the form of false witness and most astonishing malingering. The other morning the superintendent, on his round, saw through a grille a quarrel between a warder and a Brahman. That afternoon the Brahman brought a complaint against the warder, and twenty unanimous witnesses to prove what the officer's own eyes had showed him to be false. Another had been struck by a warder, and next morning appeared covered, not only with weals, but with raw strips of flesh torn away also. The doctor was puzzled, till an ancient warder whispered, " Examine their pyjama-strings, Sahib." So each man had to bring up the string that runs round the waist of his drawers, and the tenth or so was found covered with blood and skin. The man had spent all night at this torture merely to make the case sure against his enemy.

Not less inhuman was the group who pierced their thighs with bodkins and strings soaked in oil and dung, giving themselves agonising tumours to avoid a moderate day's work. Or the men who conceal pills to make them ill in holes cut in their flesh—it is too sickening to detail. A little needed comic relief was furnished by a Sikh, who evidently got forbidden opium, though nobody could tell how. At last it was observed that his hair—a Sikh's religion forbids the cutting of his hair, so this is not done, even in jail —was curiously sticky. It was washed, and the results analysed, whereon it turned out that the night before imminent conviction the Sikh had soaked his head in a strong solution of opium. He absorbed enough to last him for months, and sucked it off his hair by night.

XXXI

HYDERABAD, DEKHAN

I AM in quite a new India—the Dekhan. I can see it very characteristically from the temple of Parbati, above Poona—characteristically in every way.

A highly educated Brahman shows me eight-armed goddesses and elephant-headed gods, compared with which a penny doll is artistic and spiritual; then adds in his gusty Marathi head-voice, " Here-is-the-historic-window. From-which-the-Peshwa-surveyed-the-battle - of-Kirkee. Which-resulted-in-his-conquest-by-the-British. You-can-command-an-extensive-view." And if I loiter—" Command-the-view ! " he urges encouragingly. I hastily command it—Poona city and cantonment and the lines of Kirkee, all cloaked in trees, looking immense, like all Indian cities. They lie on a rumpled carpet of grey-brown, sunburned down, with a ring of low, grey, stony mountain enclosing it. Only here and there, where there is water, the grey is lit up with vividest green—emerald lines where a canal runs, or emerald squares of irrigated field. And here and there are spots of vermilion and red-lead—the wonderful gold-mohur-tree, whose blossoms clothe it in spring, and glow ever more fiercely with the fiercer sun, till it looks like a tree hidden in butterflies. Uneven, colourless tableland, undecided shapes of colourless mountain, gemmed here and there with dazzling green and scarlet—that is the type of the whole vast triangle of the Dekhan.

On the way to Hyderabad you roll through nearly four hundred miles of it with scarce an incident. It looks like a tableland, as it is; at this season it also looks worthless land, as it is not. Potentially, say men who ought to know, the Nizam's territory is of the richest in India. You notice at once the wealth of cattle—thousands on thousands, satin-skinned, melting-eyed, humped little beasts, with long horns that stand straight up over their foreheads like the frame of a lyre. The scantily watered soil grows few crops, but it affords copious pasture of the frugal Eastern kind. The people are astonishingly well-to-do. A plague-officer told me that he visited a small town off the railway, where hardly a white man had ever been, and found there the most prosperous population he ever saw. Everybody had enough of everything; and, as this land was well irrigated, the one agent of Ralli Brothers, the great merchants of India, enjoyed a lucrative monopoly in cotton. These happy villagers, on the first sign of plague, had independently isolated themselves—shut up their houses, and put up a temporary town in the fields. They deserve their prosperity. Besides the crops and the cattle, enthusiasts believe there is enough gold in Hyderabad State to cut the throat of Klondike and beggar the Rand. I have heard the same of Utah, Tibet, Madagascar, the Libyan Desert, and the bottom of the sea; yet who knows?

At a station, through the sun-shutters, there swept a sudden volley of yells, imprecations, shrieks, groans, gibbers. The native of India can make himself heard when it is a question of giving or receiving the third part of a farthing; yet surely but one race on earth can make such music as this. I looked out, and—yes: it was Arabs. A gang of half a dozen, brilliantly dishevelled, a faggot of daggers with an antique pistol or two in each belt, and a six-foot matchlock on each shoulder. For Hyderabad, you must know, is full of Arabs. They serve as irregular troops there, and it must be owned that if irregularity is what you want, no man on earth can supply it better. Presently there got into the carriage an Arab chief, a big man in breeches and gaiters, a revolver and a fez; his family have been feudal lords under the Nizam for generations. The fez appeared to be the fashionable head-dress hereabouts; even the railway guard wore one over the black curls that greased his official collar. I observed that the railway tickets in this country are stamped with a crescent. Next I noticed a Sikh with his hair tied into a bob; then a vulture-beaked Pathan; then a group of half-a-dozen soldiers in ill-fitting khaki, each with a different badge on his chain-mail epaulettes. The civilian, hugging his corded bundle cased in a blue-and-red-striped rug—the badge of the Indian third-class passenger—also cherished under his arm a cavalry sabre. Everywhere I breathed Islam and the Middle Ages: was I not coming to Hyderabad, the last stronghold of medi-evalism in Southern India?

Its threshold is of a piece with it. The train had caught the local atmosphere, and was forty minutes late. For an hour we had been running through his Highness's huge preserves—grey leafless bush and coppice, spangled with gold-mohur-trees. Now on either side rose dump-heaps of grey-black boulders as large as houses—obelisks, walls, hemispheres, mush-rooms, uprights and cross-bars, formless jumbles as if a baby Titan had been playing at Stonehenge. Little lonely domes appeared below them, then flat-roofed houses, then broken lines of suburbs. Next came a broad blue lake, with round-headed trees low on its farther shore, and a long white palace at its far end—a mirage made substance. Then a broad plat-form, full of men, armed with Martinis and match-locks, bayonets and scimitars, in khaki and blue and amber and green and carnation. Then broad streets, with broughams and servants in gold-lace, with bul-lock-carts and beggars in ashes. Then a hotel with a large compound and a deep terrace in front, two flights of broad steps to the door, the naked slate of a dismantled billiard-table within, dinner laid outdoors for eight, and I the only guest. There was spacious profusion in every detail of Hyderabad.

Next day—of course with two horses, and one footman to fold his arms on the box, and another to run in front and push cattle out of the way—I drove out to see Golconda. Although the diamonds were never found there, and are cut there no longer, the opulent name of Golconda suits well with Hyderabad. What is there now—the fort and tombs of the kings who reigned here before the Nizams—is not less barbarically vast. You drive among the littered Titan toys till you find yourself heading for one higher hill. It looks like the rest of them—a dump-heap of the world's raw material—till suddenly you are driving through a lofty arched gate with guard-houses. Inside are lines, some ruinous, some alive with soldiers and soldiers' families; you drive and drive through a great city. Presently another tall gateway, with more guard-houses; you go through, and are at the foot of the hill.

Then you see it is only half a hill and half a building. Men have filled up the gaps in God's dump-heap. You climb between walls that eke out cliffs, turn descents into scarps, slopes into ramps, make curtains of cromlechs and bastions of rocking-stones. They are true cyclopean walls—huge unfaced stones laid as they will fit, without mortar. You doubt which is the ruder and more massive—man's work or Nature's. But when you struggle to the top you see that Nature is avenged on her improvers. Nature's chaos still stands; man's is as chaotic, and less stable. From the roof of a ruined palace you look out over a tossing sea of broken masonry. You can trace the line of the rough outer wall, still hardly broken, dwindling and narrowing below you, dipping into a depression, climbing again as a thread across a rise—the mummied skin of what was a teeming city. Within it the bones sear and gape and crackle under the pitiless exposing sun. Palace and mosque, armoury and treasure-house, they are all gone. Only remains a shapeless waste of stones, almost as rough, and not so substantial, as the huddled granite that was before them and remains after. Two miles away rises a heap of boulders about as high; two miles from either you could not tell which was fabulous Golconda and which was creation's lumber.

Nothing remains whole, except the tombs. Great domed chambers, square without, octagonal within, vague wistful suggestions of the Taj without its beauties, they lie grouped in the plain below, stripped of their embellishments, crumbling and forlorn, kept standing by the alms of the kings that have succeeded to their glories. Ghosts of the dead past—and that is all there is of Golconda.

But Golconda is nothing to us that we should weep for it; which of us ever heard of the Kutb Shahi kings, of Mohammed Kuli and his beautiful favourite, Bagmati? Come, instead, into living Hyderabad.

Hyderabad, Dekhan

Scale the sheer elephant that awaits you, and seesaw along streets as gay as a ballet. A mingling of incense and cinnamon, sugar and civet and dirt—the pure smell of India—deliciously fills the air all about you. There is little dirt either: the regular terraces of houses—you look into the upper-storey windows as you pass—the plain tall arches across the roadway, the four elaborate minarets whence diverge the four broad, thronged main streets: it is all orderly and bright and spacious, as befits Hyderabad—an Asiatic Place de l'Etoile.

Along the street comes a tiny boy held on to a pony. He lifts a vague salaaming hand towards the fez that sits above his solemn little yellow face. Behind him is an escort of half-a-dozen lancers, and you naturally conclude that he is of the Royal family. But he is only the son of one of the nobles, and the lancers behind him are his father's. Everybody who is anybody in Hyderabad has a little army of his own. In the city and cantonments—it is a dozen miles from one end of them to the other—are eight distinct kinds of troops. These are the British and the British native, the Hyderabad contingent—four cavalry regiments, four field-batteries, and six battalions, maintained and officered by us for the Nizam in return for the province of Berar—the Imperial Service Troops, the Nizam's regular troops, the Nizam's irregular troops, the Nizam's female troops, and the private feudal irregulars. Of the irregulars, many represent corps originally raised and led by French officers; some of them still preserve a kind of French in their words of command, which only one native in Hyderabad understands. The Arab irregulars are brought over to serve their time, and then sent back to Arabia; there is one at this moment who is a subaltern in Hyderabad, but as soon as he crosses the British border gets a salute of nine guns: he is a sheikh in his own country, near Aden. As for the woman's battalion—alas! I could not see it paraded, since it is quartered in his Highness's zenana. But think of it —of the sheer joy of riding on an elephant through a city where they still maintain a Royal Regiment of Amazons!

As you pad-pad along through the panorama of Indian types and the spectroscope of Indian colours, the sound of tom-toms floats up. Down the street, beyond the four minarets, you see an elephant, then a squibbing flame, and the scent of black powder is in the air. A fight? No, a wedding, which is even more Hyderabadi—a procession that seems to stretch through the whole ten miles of city. First half-a-dozen men letting off fireworks and tapping tom-toms, then a towering, red-coated, gilt-tusked elephant bearing standards. After that a band, and then the family troops. The infantry had a semblance of uniform—a flat Ghurkha cap with " 1 " on it: presumably they were the bridegroom's First Foot. But the irregular cavalry was superb, riding two and two all over the street like a circus—big Afghans, desert pilots from Arabia, Rathore Rajputs, and sheer black savages from Fashoda way; boys and old men in grey beards and spectacles, half-bred Walers and country-bred rats and living skeletons almost too lame to hobble, lances and sabres and carbines, and flintlock pistols and yataghans and switches. Then more elephants, more troops, more musicians, and the bridegroom under a great crimson canopy. Tom-tom-tom-tom —squeal and clatter from a horse that hates elephants —fiz-z-z-z from a squib.

Hyderabad seems too good to be true. It is not so much a city as a masque of medieval Asia.

XXXII

MADRAS

AT last !   I arrive in Madras, and here at last is the India that was expected—the India of our childhood and of our dreams.

The endless corn-fields of Hindustan, the rolling dry downs of the Dekhan—and then in a night everything has changed. The air is moist, the sky intensely blue. You drive on broad roads of red sand, through colonnades of red-berried banyans and thick groves of dipping palms. In pools and streams of soft green water men fish with rods, only their black heads above the surface; at the edge slate-coloured baffaloes wallow to the muzzle.

And the people are just as you have always seen them in your mind. Naked above the loins, petticoated below, any colour from ochre to umber, sharp-featured and quick-eyed, with heads close-clipped before and streaming with ragged locks behind; the fat Brahman under his white umbrella, and the moist-backed waterman under the jars swung from his bamboo pole,—they pass by in a perpetual panorama of India—popular India, missionary India—India as you knew it before you came.

Madras

It never struck me before, but it is certainly so:
our picture of India at home is the reflection of
Madras. You never thought of India as barley-fields
and big men in sheepskins ; but toddy palms, rice-
stalks standing in water, lithe little coolies in loin-
clothes—all these you have known from a baby. The
reason is that Madras is the oldest, the most historic
province of British India, and the nursery does not
change its ideas lightly. Moreover, the nursery looks
for its Indian literature mostly to missionaries, and
the missionary has taken a far firmer hold on Madras
than elsewhere. I am convinced that Little Henry's
Bearer was a Madrasi.

The loyal nursery clings to Madras ; the rest of
India calls it " the dark Presidency," and affects to
despise it. Nobody can deny that it was the first
province where British arms began to overthrow all
comers. Who can forget Clive and Dupleix, and
Coote and Hyder Ali, and Tippu and the Nabob of
Arcot's debts ? But they say up North that Madras's
future lies all behind it. I came there against the
strongest advice of the very best authorities on the
Khyber and Waziristan—came, saw, and was conquered.

For to the transient loiterer Madras appears by far
the most desirable of the great cities of India. In
Madras there appears to be room to live. In Bombay
you camp in a tent ; in Calcutta you contract your
elbows in a boarding-house. In Madras houses are

large, and stand in compounds that are all but parks. The town spreads itself out in these for miles and miles: you might call it a city of suburbs. You can drive out six miles one way to a garden-party, and three the other to dinner. Looking down on it from the top of the lighthouse on the High Court, Madras is more lost in green than the greenest city further north. Under your feet the red huddled roofs of the Black Town are only a speck. On one side is the bosom of the turquoise sea, the white line of surf, the leagues of broad, empty, yellow beach; on the other, the forest of European Madras, dense, round-polled green rolling away southward and inland till you can hardly see where it passes into the paler green of the fields. Down below, though the streams and the Black Town fester poisonously enough, you never seem to be in a crowd; there is room to see the people. Madras, further, is never very cold and never very hot, never very wet and never very dry. Space, green, white and scarlet and yellow blossoms on the trees, the night-breeze from the sea, the very mosquitoes so strong on the wing—they give you the feeling that Madras, so far from dead, is consistently alive, and not merely tiding over from one season to another.

Nor can the wandering eye detect signs of mental darkness. The railway that brings you into Madras has more comfortably arranged carriages and fills you with better and cheaper food than most, if not than any, in India.   The railway that takes you out again, southward, gives by far the best travelling of any metre-gauge line I have tried.   In Madras, it is true, you are conveyed away from the station in a sort of perforated prison van, but that happens in Calcutta too and Delhi.   Your hotel is without honour in its own country, but in Bombay it would be even as the Ritz in Paris.   The native enjoys cheap, rather rapid, and very crowded transport, such as he loves, in electric tramcars.   Wherever space needs to be economised, the wire and its uprights are carried along the edge, not the middle, of the roadway, and the trolley-arm leans over to follow them.   Also Madras enjoys a telephone service; while as for shops—the leading tailor, who also sells lamps and tinned apricots, employs his hundreds, and the leading chemist's might be mistaken for the town-hall.

Then where is the darkness?   It is geographical. Madras has many virtues, but it has fallen into the fatal vice of being out of the way.   Before the age of railways every considerable city in India was in the way, was its own centre.   Madras had, to a great extent, its independent government.   But now, when rails have knit the country together, and the centre of it oscillates between Calcutta and Simla, Madras is left away in a corner.   The Calcutta mail goes almost to Bombay before it turns north-eastward : either to the winter or to the summer capital it is nearly four days' journey.   Madras swims strongly in its backwater, but in the main stream nobody cares. Other voices make what they call public opinion; other hands clutch the money that is to be spent; other armies fight the wars. The function of Madras is to pay. Its lands are all held direct from the Crown, there is no permanent settlement, and the assessment rises steadily. Madras raises the revenue, and the North spends it; and the more loyally Madras pays, the less constrainedly the other provinces squander.

Within the last weeks an event had happened which ought some day to change all that. The East Coast Railway had been opened for traffic between Madras and Calcutta direct. As yet the many rivers on the way are not permanently bridged; the line is still in sections; the trains are very slow and grossly unpunctual, even for the East. But when time has shaken it into shape this railway should bring Madras as near to Calcutta as Bombay or Lahore is. Then the whisper of Madras may penetrate even to the throne, and the very Financial Member understand that a province would fain receive as well as give. Certain material benefits should follow, too. Coal will come down from Bengal or Hyderabad to replace the failing supplies of firewood. In time a line will be built from Madras to Paumben, opposite Adam's Bridge. Near there lies the island of Rameshwaram, which is the holiest place but two in all India. The others are Benares and Puri, Juggernaut's seat, near Cuttack. Between Puri and Rameshwaram the myriads of pilgrims will throng the East Coast Railway, to its own benefit and that of Madras. Later, it may be, the line will be carried right over Adam's Bridge into Ceylon. Then Madras would stand on a direct route from Europe by Colombo to Calcutta—a route that, since the P. and O. meets competition at Colombo and none at Bombay, should be somewhat cheaper, less plaguy, not appreciably longer, and, when it saves the change at Aden, decidedly more comfortable than the present way by Bombay. If that comes about Madras will have its chance of coupling up with the world again.

Meanwhile there are advantages in being remote. Distant from seeds of war and sedition, Europeans and natives appear to live better together here than elsewhere. The native of the Madras Presidency is all new types. For the most part he is Tamil, small and intelligent in the northern part, robust and rowdy in the southern, long-haired, all but naked, speaking a language whereof Sundaraperumalkoil is a fairly representative mouthful. From the west, on the Malabar Coast, you hear tales of still stranger men and manners,—of Malayalis and Kanarese, Christians with Portuguese names—they were converted in blocks by the Viceroys of Goa, and each block took the name, Albuquerque or D'Souza, of its apostle—Arab-mixed Moplas, Syrians, black Jews and white Jews, two distinct breeds, in Cochin. In this Presidency, too, and especially on the sequestered west coast, you can see what Brahmanism is like when wholly undiluted with Islam. There a Brahman is so holy that nobody ever sees him : he has his home and garden and temple all inside his own wall. He goes abroad, when he must, in a closed palanquin, and its bearers shoo every caste-less man off the road. If a low-caste man has got nearly to the end of a long narrow bridge and meets a Brahman's palanquin, he must turn back and with-draw into the fields out of pollution-shot. In this country the very measures of distance are fixed by the spiritual infecting-range of various lower castes : in-stead of speaking-distance or a stone's-throw they talk of the distance a man of such or such a caste must get out of the path when a Brahman comes along. More than that, only the eldest brother of a Brahman family marries ; the rest have the right by custom— which is law and religion added together and multiplied by a million—to range at large among the women of lower caste. Until lately custom ordained that the Brahman was not responsible for the maintenance of his children by such women—as a rule he never so much as sees them. The magistrate who first dared make a maintenance order in such a case was, to his honour, a Brahman himself.

But all that, of course, is outside the city of Madras. In Madras itself the native is perhaps better educated than anywhere else in India, and—what by no means goes with education—is neither captiously discon-tented nor complaisantly submissive. The newspapers splutter a little occasionally, but you must remember it is not always easy to say quite the correct thing in a language not your own. For the rest, they appear to be by far the best-written of the native journals. Here again Madras has the advantage of its age. Whether education in Madras—notice that education always means higher education, not primary, which hardly exists—has not gone too far is another matter. I went one day to the Convocation of the University: when the Chancellor said, "Let the candidates step forward," the whole great ball rose and moved a pace to its front in battalions of B.L.'s and B.A.'s. Are they all wanted? The supply of B.A.'s exceeds the demand even in England: what then of Madras?

But never mind that for now. The air of Madras does not agree with problems. It is enough to be in the India which you had divined and have found at last—to breathe its air and moisten your eye with its green. About Madras, too, you can notice what in chattering Bengal and the fighting Punjab you are apt to miss. There, alone on the field, picking at the earth with a single careless hand on his plough or standing, a lean, naked figure among the sleepy goats, you see the bed-rock of native India. The man who neither chatters nor fights, but does what the Brahman tells him, looks languidly to the land and the stock, and pays taxes. He is essential India.

XXXIII

THE SALT-PANS

THE Assistant-Commissioner wore a khaki uniform,
a braided jacket, and a crown on his shoulder-strap;
yet he did not look like a soldier. He looked over-
worked and underfed. His eyes were pools in pits
of socket; the bones cropped out of his cheeks and
chin. He looked like a man who was always travelling, eating sparely and irregularly of jungly food,
often down with fever, oppressed by unrelenting
anxiety.

Being in the Salt Department, it is not wonderful
if he was all this. Salt, as you know, is a Government monopoly in India: Government controls its
production, prevents its illicit manufacture, and sells
it to the consumers. For these functions it needs a
considerable staff of Europeans; and the European
of the Salt Department is the pariah of white
India.

Not that he is looked down on like a pariah; as a
rule he is simply not looked on at all. As a rule he
is dumped down on a salt-marsh with no white man
within a journey of days. His work makes him
unpopular among the natives about him: naturally

they do not see why they should not scrape up the salt which God has evaporated and spread at their feet. His work is cruelly hard. At any minute of the night he has to get up to inspect the guards posted round the factory, or hurry for hours to surprise illicit manufacturers. Now he toils forward on horseback, now he flounders afoot through marshes and sliding sand-dunes, now crouches in a sluggish boat on a rank canal. When he falls ill—and of necessity he is often put down in festering fever-beds —he will likely enough have to shiver and sweat for a week in a canal-boat before he can so much as see a doctor. Month by month, blistered with sun, quivering like a leaf with ague, no time to lie up, his English tongue going rusty,—and by way of compensation for his lonely labour he receives £125 a-year when he begins, and after fifteen years or so will perhaps be enjoying £300.

However, this particular Assistant-Commissioner was by way of being a lucky man. His district is only 6000 square miles, against some people's 12,000. When he is at home, which he is almost one month in three, he is only fourteen miles from Madras; the trains of the new East Coast Railway are seldom over three hours late, so that you can generally reckon on doing the twenty-eight miles there and back in a day. Also there are two European inspectors at his station, which is one of the largest salt-factories in the Presidency.

The Salt-Pans

You land on to a railway embankment of red sand, and look about for the buildings and the stacks of the factory. You will see nothing of the kind: it is less a factory than a salt-farm. But first begin at the beginning. You get into a punt and embark on what seems a great lake; it is really a backwater of the Bay of Bengal. Once upon a time this was a sanitarium for Madras. The shores of the backwater are densely planted with caserina, a fir imported from Australia, which will grow to firewood on dunes that will nourish nothing else. Out of the black-green depths of these plantations appear crumbling ruins of the half-classical end of last century. Here is the abandoned Government House; beside it moulders the derelict club. Half-a-dozen villas are still owned by residents of Madras with a view to boating and fishing; but hardly a soul ever comes to boat or fish. For all this dates from the days before railways; now people spend their hot weathers in the hills about Ootacamund. And now the old sanitarium—whether the caserina plantations blanket it from the sea-air, or the new railway bridge has unprisoned all the filth at the bed of the backwater—has developed into a fever-nursery instead. Nobody remains except the salt-officers: it is part of their business to have fever.

At the lower end of the backwater the turquoise waves curl in snowy foam over the bar, and swish in through the breach in its middle. At the point— they tell you with a kind of grim pride—lies a salt-inspector, who died alone of cholera on a Christmas Day. He was buried in a piece of canvas before his colleagues came back in the evening to hear that he was ill.

The factory itself is on the opposite shore, and farther inland. When you land again and climb over the railway embankment, you see it stretched at your feet—a few little white shanties on the horizon, and nothing else. Nothing but a great flat of broken, dull-brown, muddy soil. When you get down on to it you see less still. Nothing grows except a red thing like a stone-crop and a few coarse grass tufts on banks and tumbling hillocks. Under wan, lustreless clouds the ground looks barren of all goodness, numb and despairing. You slither along through slime, and presently find that the whole place is seamed with watercourses — broad channels like canals, with ditches and runnels taking out of them. The soil is marked into checkers by little banks. It is like richly irrigated land under a curse of utter sterility. Water all about you, earth under foot, yet everywhere this melancholy and haggard desolation.

That is the farm—a farm watered with brine, whose crop is salt. With relief you come upon something doing—a few poles and bars, black like gibbets on the bleak horizon, with men about them. Nearer, you see that they are water-hoists. . A cross-bar balances on an upright; at one end hangs a palm-fibre bucket; a man standing on the bar shifts back and forward, and seesaws the bucket into the water and out again; another on the ground empties it into a channel. This leads it to the flat checkers; and here are a couple more naked men paddling in the shallow brine as for their lives. Stamp, stamp, stamp, up and down, back and forward, across and across, in a kind of combination between a treadmill and a palsied step-dance. They seem so gravely concentrated on nothing that at first you think them mad, then learn that they are making the floor. They stamp and stamp and stamp it down hour by hour, day by day, till it is as hard as concrete. Then with floor and banks the pans are complete.

They let the brine stand first in deeper, then in shallower, pans, and evaporate in the sun for about ten days—until the intensity of its saltness rises from three by the halometer, or whatever it is called, to twenty-five. Then the salt is precipitated at the bottom of the pans and raked off with broad wooden hoes like squeegees. The natives are as light-handed as they are heavy-footed; they never break the floor which they made with their own soles. The salt drawn off is dried in the sun on the ridges of the pans, then broken up, then put into sacks, then put into boats, and taken to Madras to be sold. And that is all about it.

That is all—except crushing sun and blinding white glare and all-penetrating salt-dust for the salt-officer. In the hottest part of the hottest days other men get under roofs : that is just the time that he must be out all day in the sun. The factory is a chessboard of twinkling brine and snow-white salt, more scorching to the eye than flame. While his eyes are being toasted before a quick fire, salt-drifts are banking up in them and in his ears and his nostrils and his mouth. He looks round, and, like Lot's wife, becomes a pillar of salt. With it all the few salt-officers I have seen appear to grumble almost less than anybody in India. They say it is a healthy life—as long as you are well: when you begin to be unhealthy at all you are quickly very unhealthy indeed. Perhaps one reason for their comparative contentment is that they are justly proud of their department. For in salt, as in most things connected with revenue, Madras sets an example of efficiency and honesty to the whole of India. The salt revenue, you understand, is Imperial—goes, that is, to the treasury of all India, though it is collected by the provincial Governments. Now the salt-tax is very unpopular; therefore a timid and dishonest provincial Government will be lax in putting down illicit manufacture and pressing the sale of the licit product. Thus it keeps its subjects in good humour, and after all it is not the province that suffers, but India as a whole. The Bengal Government, for instance, has long winked at contraband salt-scraping all along its coast; as the result, it sells its people only two-thirds or so of the salt they use, and defrauds the Government of India of £666,666, 13s. 4d. or so a-year.

The Salt-Pans

In Madras, on the other hand, Government sells 16 ½ lb. of duty-paying salt per head of population per annum. It has been pronounced on good authority that man needs 16 lb. of salt in a year; so that the Madras Government can congratulate itself that its subjects do not deny themselves of an ounce of necessary salt, and that, at the same time, the State profits by every ounce consumed. Furthermore, this result appears to be attained without hardship to the natives. Of prosecutions initiated by the department in the last year, over ninety-nine per cent. have resulted in conviction; during the same time, charges have diminished by twenty-three per cent. Finally, there were only eight cases of assault on servants of the department. That, in a country where the only known expression of genuine public opinion is riot, goes to prove that the salt-tax, and the salt administration, and the salt-officer are not so unpopular as they are sometimes painted.

Where the white salt-officer probably is unpopular is among his own native colleagues. A young man sends down a bottle of illicitly distilled spirits—he is excise officer for liquor purposes also—to his native superior. It is his first case, and he is pleased with himself—till he meets the native. "What was in that bottle you sent down?" "Arrack, of course." "Ah, I thought so. When I got it there was nothing in it but sweet-oil. However, don't worry; I've emptied it and filled it up with arrack and sealed it.

I'll swear it had arrack in it all the time, and we shall convict the fellow all right."

It is rather hard for the young man to have to begin his official career by ruining a man who only meant to keep him out of trouble. Still, that is just what the young man is there for. There are fine openings for bribery and put-up cases in the salt and liquor department. Here, as elsewhere in jesting India, the native draws the British rate of pay and the Briton supplements the native's work as well as doing his own. He has to guard the guardians.

XXXIV

THE GREAT PAGODAS

Southward out of Madras you still run through the new India, the old India of the nursery. Now it is vivid with long grass, now tufted with cotton, then dark-green with stooping palm-heads or black with firs; anon brown with fallow, blue with lakes and lagoons, black with cloud-shadowing pools starred with white water-lilies. Presently red hills break out of the woods, then sink again to sweeping pastures dotted only with water-hoists and naked herdsmen.

Then in the placid landscape you are almost startled by the sight of monuments of religion. A tall quadrangular pyramid, its courses lined with rude statues, a couple of half-shaped human figures, ten times human size, a ring of colossal hobby-horses sitting on their haunches like a tea-party in Wonderland—they burst grotesquely out of meadow and thicket, standing all alone with the soil and the trees. No worshippers, no sign of human life near them, no hint of their origin or purpose—till you almost wonder whether they are artificial at all, and not petrified monsters from the beginning of the world.

These are the outposts of the great pagodas of

The Great Pagodas

Southern India—those sublime monstrosities which scarce any European ever sees, which most have never heard of, but which afford perhaps the strongest testimony in all India at once to the vitality and the incomprehensibility of Hinduism. The religion that inspired such toilsome devotion must be one of the greatest forces in history; yet the Western mind can detect neither any touch of art in the monuments themselves nor any strain of beauty in the creed. Both command your respect by their size : that which is so vast, so enduring, can hardly, you tell yourself, be contemptible. And still you can see nothing in the temples but misshapen piles of uncouthness, nothing in the religion but unearthly superstitions, half meaningless and half foul.

The nearest approach to a symmetrical building is the great pagoda of Tanjore. Long before you near the gate you see its tall pyramidal tower, shooting free above crooked streets and slanting roofs. Presently you see the lower similar towers, so far from the first that you would never call them part of the same building. In reality they are the outer and inner gateways—*gopura* is their proper name—built in diminishing courses, garnished with carving and statuary. From a distance the massive solemnity of their outlines, the stone lace of their decorations, strike you with an overwhelming assertion of rich majesty. But you are in India, and you wait for the inevitable incongruity.

The Great Pagodas

It comes at the very gate. The entrance is not under the stately gopura, but under a screen and scaffolding of lath and plaster daubed with yellow and green grotesqueness—men with lotus-eyes looking out of their temples, horses with heads like snakes, and kings as tall as elephants. There is to be a great festival in a day or two, explains the suave Brahman; therefore the gopuras are boarded up with pictures beside which the tapestries of our pavement-artists are truth and beauty. You walk through scaffold-poles into a great square round the great tower, and with reverence they show you that colossal monolith, the great bull of Tanjore. I wish I could show you a picture of him, for words are unequal to him. In size he stands, or rather sits, thirty-eight hands two. His material is black granite, but it is kept so piously anointed with grease that he looks as if he were made of toffee. In attitude he suggests a roast hare, and he wears a half-smug, half-coquettish expression, as if he hoped that nobody would kiss him.

From this wonder you pass to the shrines of the chief gods. The unbeliever may not enter, but you stand at the door while a man goes along the darkness with a flambeau. The light falls on silk and tinsel, and by faith you can divine a seated image at the end. Next you are at the foot of the great tower, and the ridiculous has become the sublime again. Every storey is lined with serene-faced gods and goddesses, dwindling rank above rank, a ladder of deities that seems to climb half-way up to heaven. Then the Brahman shows you a stone bull seated on the ground, like a younger brother of the great one. " It is in existence," he says, throwing out his words in groups, dispassionately, as though somebody else were speaking and it were nothing at all to do with him—" it is in existence—to show the dimensions— of four other bulls—which are in existence—up there." You lay your head back between your shoulder-blades, and up there, at the very top, among gods so small that you wonder whether they are gods or only panels or pillars, are four more little brothers of the hare-shaped toffee-textured monster below.

Reduplication is the keynote of Hindu art. The same bulls everywhere, the same gods everywhere, and all round the cloistered outer wall scores on scores of granite, fat-dripping, flower-crowned emblems, so crudely shapeless that you forget their gross significance—but all absolutely alike. Next the Brahman leads you aside to piles and piles of what look like overgrown, gaudily painted children's toys. This is an exact facsimile of the Tower, reduced and imitated in wood. It is all in pieces, but at the festival the parts are fitted together and carried on a car. Every god sculptured on the pyramid is represented in a section of this model, waiting to be fitted into his place. Only what is richly mellow in tinted stone is garishly tawdry in king's yellow and red lead

—and again you tumble from the sublime to the infantile.

Next, a little shrine that is a net of the most delicate carving—stone as light and fantastic as wood; pillar and panel, moulding and cornice, lattice and imagery, all tapering gracefully till they become miniatures at the summit. It is a gem of exquisite taste and patient labour. And the very next minute you are again among flaming red and yellow dragon-tigers and duck-peacocks, and the one is just as holy and just as beautiful to its worshippers as the other. From which objects of veneration the Brahman passes lightly to the domestic life of the frescoed rajahs of Tanjore. "This gentleman—marry seventeen wives —all one day—doubtless in anxiety of getting son." It is quite true. The Rajah, having but three wives and no child, resolved to marry six more young ladies, and collected seventeen to choose them from. But the fathers and brothers of the rejected eleven were affronted; and rather than have any unpleasantness on his wedding-day, his Majesty tactfully married the whole seventeen, nine in the morning and eight in the afternoon. "And here," pursued the Brahman automatically, showing a tank, "he will let in water— and here he will play—with all his females—and all that."

That is all, except to write your name in the visitor's book. As I went in to sign, I noticed a band of musicians standing at the door and thought no more of it. But as my pen touched the paper, suddenly reedy pipes and discordant fiddles and heady tom-toms began to play " God Save the Queen." A huge chaplet of muslin and tinsel, like a magnified Christmas-tree stocking, was cast about my neck; betel and attar-of-rose were brought up in silver vessels, and flowers and fruits on silver trays. The pagoda keeps its character to the end: the compliment was sublime—and I ridiculous.

Yet the temple of Tanjore is the most simple and orderly of all its kind. Visit the great pagoda of Madura and you will come out mazed with Hinduism. All its mysteries and incongruities, its lofty meta-physics and its unabashed lewdness, seem to brood over the dark chambers and crannying passages. The place is enormous. Over the four chief gateways rise huge pyramid-towers, coloured like harlequins, red tigers jostling the multiplied arms and legs of blue and yellow gods and goddesses so thick that the gopuras seem built of them. In the pure sunlight you almost blush for their crudity, just as you would blush if the theatre roof were lifted off during a matinée. But inside the place is nearly all half-lighted, dim, and cryptic. You go through a labyrinth, that seems endless, of dark chambers and aisles. Now you are in thick blackness, now in twilight, now the sun falls on fretwork over pillared galleries and damp-smelling walls. But as the light falls on the pillar you start, for it is carved into the shape of an elephant-headed

Ganesh, or a conventionally high-stepping Shiva. On you go, from maze to maze, till there is no more recollection of direction or guess at size: you are lost in an underground world of gods that are half devils; you hardly distinguish the silent-footed, gleaming-eyed attendants from the stone figures. Some of the fantastic images are smeared with red-lead to simulate blood: all drip with fat. A heavy smell of grease and stagnant tank-water loads your lungs.

You feel that you are bewitched—lost and helpless among unclean things. When you come out into the sun and the cleaner dirt of the town, you draw long breaths. If you could understand the Hindu religion, you tell yourself, you would understand the Hindu mind. But that, being of the West, you never, never will.

THE RUPEE

IF you would learn about the Indian currency question do not go to India. I would not say that you will become the less able to understand it, but you will hardly become more so. If you stayed there for twenty years and kept a trained eye upon the question in all its bearings, your knowledge would probably be very valuable; but if you wish to understand the question in the space of a month or two, your time would not be well spent in going to India: you had much better stay at home and read Blue-Books. For the Englishman in India, knowing something of India, is the first to admit that he knows nothing about its currency question. He will probably be able to tell you a few of the inconveniences of having such a thing; but beyond that the native himself is not more unintelligible.

The rupee is a little thing, but it is at the bottom of the whole matter. The case is just this: if it were only the rupee and nothing more, all would be well—there would be no Indian currency question. Unfortunately the rupee is, or was until the Indian Government saw to it, also a bit of silver. At one

and the same moment it was, and still is to some extent, a piece of money and a piece of merchandise—
indissolubly, inalienably both. Now that imperative
dual function—perhaps we ought rather to say that
function and that attribute—is more than the little
rupee is able to bear. Could it succeed in shaking
off one, all would be well. To rid the rupee of its
incubus—that is the aim of all these years of strenu-
ous wrangling. That must be the aim of any legislation which is to abolish the Indian currency question. Which must go, then—the function or the attribute? The attribute, clearly. The rupee must
continue to be money ; there is no great reason why
silver, the article of merchandise, should be rupees.
What is wanted is to make the rupee a rupee, and
nothing more. If that cannot be done, the rupee
must give place to something else.

Let us try to be a little more explicit, less dog-
matic. Money, economists tell us, is a medium of
exchange and a measure of value. One of the req-
uisites of an efficient measure of value is stability.
A commodity which is worth so much this year and
perhaps half as much again next may be a good
speculation, but is certainly an extremely bad measure
of value. It is not pleasant to find that to get quit
of your bill you have to pay half as much again as
you expected. Rather than run the risk of that
people will do no business at all. But so it is, or
much the same, with silver. Whether that is the

fault of silver or of gold need not bother us. The point has its value as providing an outlet for the dangerous controversial energies of metallists, both mono- and bi-, but has not much to do with the Indian currency question. The fact remains that the value of silver as measured by gold is unstable.

That brings us to another rub. The value of silver as measured by gold might be as unstable as it liked, for anything India need care, but for India's dealings with the rest of the world. At this moment not only does the Indian ryot, who is most of India, not know that there is any such thing as a currency question—he would not know it in any case—but he is really very little the better or the worse for the particular circumstances which have produced it. But India has a great foreign trade, and India has a great foreign debt, and India employs a great many foreigners to manage her affairs. Now most of India's foreign trade is with gold-standard countries— that is to say, countries which measure their values in gold. Most of the money she owes was borrowed in gold; and her managers come from a gold-standard country, and want their pay in gold. It is her contact with the moving West that, monetarily speaking, worries India.

The rupee, being what it is, has followed silver. When silver has become cheaper in terms of gold the rupee has become cheaper with it. Whether the value of the rupee has followed that of silver exactly, or whether it has not, the argument is the same. Moreover, properly speaking, it is the exchange value of the rupee, rather than its value as a piece of silver, upon which the whole question hinges. Other factors than the gold price of silver contribute to the exchange value, at least since the closing of the mints; but neither need they be considered at this point. Silver is the main factor anyhow, and for the last quarter-century silver has been almost constantly on the down grade. One may say that the decline began in 1873, when Germany, flushed with the French millions, discarded silver and took to gold. In self-defence the countries of the Latin Union, which, by keeping their mints open to both gold and silver at a fixed ratio, had done so much towards keeping silver at its then accepted gold level, were forced to desert it. Probably also a very much more powerful factor in the fall, and therefore in its results, was the enormous development of silver mining. The average world's output of silver during the five years 1871–75 was rather more than 63¼ million ounces; by 1892 the year's output had increased to over 153 million ounces. At the same time the wealth of the world, as computed in money, increased very fast. Silver became inconvenient in itself as a basis of monetary systems. Moreover, every secession from the ranks of the silver-standard countries made the preservation of a silver standard more inconvenient, unprofitable, and dangerous to the residue. Desperate efforts were made to arrest the swift descent. International conferences were tried in vain. The unblushing and successful efforts of the silver men in the United States have cost that country millions upon millions of dollars. Yet all to no purpose. Silver, which stood at 5s. the ounce in 1872, had fallen below 3s. in 1893; the rupee exchange fell during the same period from 2s. to 1s. 2½d. Country after country was throwing silver overboard and taking up gold in its place.

The year 1893 is one to be remembered in the monetary life of India. It is marked by the closing of the mints. Until 1893 anybody could bring as much silver as he liked to the Indian mints and receive rupees in exchange. In 1893 that right was abrogated by law. The position, as we have seen, was becoming serious. The rupee was down below 1s. 3d.; there seemed every likelihood of its falling lower still. Worse than all, there was no possibility of forecasting with any certainty what the rupee might or might not do. If it was to fall, nobody knew how far or how quickly; on the other hand, the fall might be varied by temporary recoveries. The fall which had already taken place had brought the Government to the verge of bankruptcy. The uncertainty was playing havoc with trade. True, a receding exchange had brought prosperity to some industries, but at the cost of the introduction of that speculative element which is highly deleterious to sound trading. Furthermore, the field for the disposal of silver was becoming so restricted that India ran the risk of becoming a dumping-ground for the world. But what chiefly made the position impossible was the impossible position of the Government—that was the main factor in the closing of the mints.

In every year the Government of India has to remit a very large sum of money to England, partly to meet home charges, partly to meet the interest on the sterling debt of India. This is done by selling in London drafts payable in India, which are bought by persons who want to pay away money in India. These Government drafts are put up to tender. The higher the tender—that is to say, the higher the price in sterling which the Indian Government can get for each rupee which it undertakes to pay in India, the better it is for the Indian Government—the fewer will be the rupees that the Government will have to collect in India; or, if you like, the rupees which it has will go all the further. When the rupee exchange fell from 2s. in 1872 to 1s. 2½d. in 1893, that meant that with each rupee of revenue the Government, instead of being able to discharge 2s. worth of obligation in England, was only able to discharge 1s. 2½d. worth. Imagine what that means when millions of pounds sterling are concerned. Sir James Mackay told the Indian Currency Committee in May of last year that had the rupee exchange stood at an average of 1s. between the closing of the mints in 1893 and March of last year (as it easily might have done had the mints remained open), instead of where it did, the cost to the Government and the Indian taxpayer would in all likelihood have reached another nine millions sterling.

The decline and fall of the rupee has borne very hardly on those Englishmen in India who are paid a fixed number of rupees—civil servants, officers of the Indian army, and so forth. Not that the purchasing power of the rupee in India has varied a great deal; it has not. But many of these men are obliged to send home a part of their income to their wives and children; still more, put by what they can out of pay none too lavish as a nest-egg to fill out the pension when they get home again for good. Were salaries fixed on the basis of a low rate of exchange there would be no ground for complaint. But they are not; nor indeed has it been possible to fix them so when exchange has been oscillating as it has. It is annoying to find that while you have been sleeping a third of your savings has run away down the gutter of a falling exchange. Again, when a rupee was falling lower every year the value of rupee pensions, fixed at a higher rate and paid at a lower, fell with it. It is annoying to have to reduce your wine bill in your old age through no fault of your own.

The railways are very much on the same footing with the Government—those, that is to say, which are built with English capital, which are most of them. They borrowed their capital in sterling, took it out to

India in sterling, must pay interest on it in sterling. But the native pays for his ticket with rupees or fractions of rupees. The lower the rate of exchange the fewer are the pounds, shillings, and pence that the native's rupees produce, and the less the railway company has left over to provide dividends for the shareholders. Of course many of the railways enjoy some sort of Government guarantee: if the dividend which such a company itself is able to pay fall below a certain point the Government makes itself responsible for the difference. That is very well for the company, but it makes the plight of the Government the more unpleasant. Moreover, it only makes the company's case a little better than it otherwise would be, for their British capital is wasting all the time. A sovereign brought out with the rupee at 2s. could only go back as 13s. 4d. with the rupee at 1s. 4d.

On the other hand, there is a section of India's foreign trade upon which the effect of a low and falling exchange is in a sense the very opposite. I refer to the exporters of Indian produce and manufactures—tea and indigo planters, cotton spinners and weavers, coal and gold miners, and the like. A good many of these people, usually companies, are like the railways in this respect, that they work with capital brought out from England: their interest must go over in sterling. They are also like the railways, in that the bulk of their working expenses is paid away in rupees. But, to their infinite advantage, they are unlike the railways, in that they are paid for their produce in the same currency in which they have to pay their interest. This does not apply to Indian exports to China, but it applies to her exports to Europe, Australia, the United States, and Japan. The advantage is obvious. So far from having to scrape together increasing myriads of rupees for the purpose of discharging their obligations, they are really for the moment much more comfortable when the rupee is falling than when it is even standing still. A sovereign's worth of tea, for instance, sent to England will bring back fifteen rupees with the exchange at 1s. 4d., but only ten with the exchange at the old rate of 2s. Now whereas, as we have seen, prices and wages in India itself change very slowly, if at all, a sixteen-penny rupee will make a sovereign go about half as far again as a 2s. rupee ; so that your planter has five rupees to play with, and can either pay a bigger dividend or reduce his prices, besides having no need to worry about expenses. He has usually done a little of each. It is not surprising that the planter and spinner have steadfastly stood by the low rupee. Yet as recently as last June the chairman of one of the Indian tea companies was congratulating his shareholders on the steadiness of the rupee in the region of 1s. 4d., because had it remained at 1s. 2½d. the stimulus to planting would have proved so violent that over-production and its consequent evils must certainly have resulted.

The Rupee

One other effect of a shifting rupee remains to be considered—its effect upon the introduction of capital into India. India is a country of vast natural resources, materially speaking, but those natural resources are very far from being fully developed; and nowadays vast resources can only be developed with the aid of vast capital. The accumulations of capital in the world are greater than ever before : never in the course of history has the available capital been more abundant; never has capitalistic enterprise been more vigorous. Yet there are people who say that India is hanging back in the march of what we call progress for want of these things. The restrictions or safeguards—the term varies with the point of view —imposed by the Indian Government have had something to do with it, though one of the earliest incidents of the new Viceroy's rule was their partial relaxation. But something of the blame undoubtedly rests with the rupee. Who is going to send capital to India when, for aught he can tell, in the course of a few months it might automatically, without the slightest action on his part, begin to vanish ? That, as we have seen, is the effect of a falling rupee. True, during the past few years the rupee has firmed up, and bids fair, in the view of sanguine minds, to remain firm. But that is not good enough for your capitalist. He is as fearsome as a scalded cat. Therefore, ironically enough, this improved exchange, so far from bringing capital into the country, has had the opposite effect of taking it out. "We'll get our money back while we can," the capitalists have said among themselves. The exchange can hardly go much above 1s. 4d., thanks to the Government measures of 1893, and it might go down again as it has done before. Meanwhile India languishes for want of capital.

In 1892, then, things looked black. Silver and the rupee had fallen far, and bade fair to fall further. A brand-new International Conference failed of a bimetallic consummation. The Indian Government wrote home asking permission "to close the mints to the free coinage of silver, with a view to the introduction of a gold standard." In a word, the Indian Government was sick of drifting; and small wonder. Silver was all very well in its way, there was much to be said for it; but the game was not good enough, single-handed or nearly so. If the Indian Government had its way silver would go overboard. Lord Herschell's Committee thought it might have its way, and overboard silver went. The splash was terrific. The metallists swarmed round the spot where it fell, and cannonaded each other soundly in bloodless controversy. But silver was gone under and could not be raised. The sound of their cannonading was loud and long; but most of it was eminently premature: they hit each other for what they thought might result from each other's policies. Five years afterwards, in 1898, the hubbub had hushed a little, and the Indian Government, encouraged by the comparative stability of the rupee, and urged by the instability of commercial conditions, proceeded relentlessly with its design for the replacement of silver as the standard metal by gold; whereupon the Home Government appointed a committee to look into the matter.

The committee sat long and laboriously, and in the fulness of time the fruits of its labours appeared in the shape of three immense Blue-Books and an extremely able and lucid report. The Secretary of State approved; the Indian Government is probably only anxious to do the same, despite the somewhat summary treatment which its own proposals received at the committee's hands. By the time, therefore, that this book reaches the world, the Indian currency question will probably be in a fair way towards settlement; for the time being, let us add—for caution's and the silver men's sake.

What, then, is the plan which is to lay this ghost which has walked so long? In the first place, the committee declares for gold out and out. The British sovereign is to be a legal tender and a current coin in India. The Indian mints will take in all the gold that comes their way, giving sovereigns or rupees in exchange. At the same time, the rupee will continue to be an unlimited legal tender concurrently with the British sovereign, and it is to be worth 1s. 4d. If, as the committee desires, an effective gold standard be thus established, " not only will stability and exchange

with the great commercial countries of the world tend
to promote her existing trade, but also there is every
reason to anticipate that, with the growth and confidence in a stable exchange, capital will be encouraged
to flow freely into India for the further development
of her great natural resources."   May the committee
see true !

H. S.

XXXVI

THE ARMY AND MUTINY

Our army in India is maintained as a defence against two dangers—invasion from without and rebellion within. The double character is inevitable, but at the same time it is a source of military inefficiency. It involves a radical contradiction. Two-thirds of our force in India consists of native troops. To guard against Russia our policy is to make these as highly efficient as troops can be made. To guard against mutiny our policy is to keep them inferior in efficiency to our own white troops. In dealing with the British troops Government is in a similar dilemma. To make them efficient against a disciplined enemy they should be trained together in large armies, wherein officers can learn to move and combine masses of troops of all arms. To make them an efficient police against internal disaffection—so it is argued—they should be spread as widely as possible over the country,—should present everywhere to the natives the spectacle of white troops within easy striking distance of any point, and in command of all important strategical positions.

It is obvious that the consistent pursuit of one

policy means a proportionate weakness in the other. If one danger is decidedly the more urgent of the two, then wisdom demands that the provision against the other should be frankly sacrificed. It seems to be the opinion of many good judges in India that the time has come to do this—to make our military policy truly military, and leave internal politics to politicians.

The danger of another Mutiny, it may confidently be said, is vanishing every day. But even if it were not, the measures taken to guard against it are obsolete. The great Mutiny owed its temporary success in the first place to the difficulty of moving up loyal troops over the enormous distances of Northern India. The railway only ran from Calcutta to Raniganj—120 miles out of the 900 to Meerut; the roads were bad and transport scarce. The mutiny at Meerut broke out on the 10th of May; Havelock could not march from Allahabad till the 7th of July. These difficulties will never have to be encountered again. Now, by steamer and rail, troops could reach Meerut from Aldershot far sooner than then they could reach Meerut from Calcutta. That fact, known as well to natives as to Europeans, is a strong deterrent against rising; and it would furnish the strongest weapon against any rising that might occur. The force to defeat a new Mutiny would not be garrisons shut up in isolated towns, with small columns turning from the relief of one to that of another, but strong columns, transported rapidly by rail, and swiftly crushing each force of rebels as it began to gather head. The first requisite for such a mobile column would be good regimental training and tactical efficiency.

Now an instance of what is being done to secure this. The first battalion of the Royal Warwickshire Regiment arrived in India last October. It had just made the campaign of Khartum. Fully maintaining the reputation of the old Sixth, it was acknowledged by all to be among the best of the uniformly fine regiments employed on that service. The men were of a good average of service, weeded by a summer in the Sudan, braced by war. Their drill, discipline, and shooting were consistently excellent. Such a regiment was fit for anything. When it arrived in India it first learned that it had been sent there by mistake or prematurely : it was not wanted anywhere. Finally, half of it was dumped down in Fort George, with no ground for manœuvring or shooting within miles, and the other half at an obscure place called Bellary, three hundred miles away, to guard an old fort of Tippu Sultan. What devotion or ingenuity on earth can prevent that regiment from deterioration ? It is impossible to keep even the separate wings at their present level of efficiency ; but even if it were not, how can a battalion keep itself fit to take the field when its two wings are stationed three hundred miles apart and never drill together ? How can even a proper regimental feeling be maintained when officers and men are forced to grow strangers? What is to become of the men, plunged into a languid climate after severe exertions, conscious that their soldiering is no longer a thing in earnest? What is to become of the senior officers, deprived of their chance of learning to handle a regiment. Or of the junior, first whetted by war and then compelled to find their chief interest in something other than their profession?

This is only a single incident in a deliberate policy. The 1st Seventh Fusiliers are divided between Nussirabad and Neemuch, the 1st Norfolk between no less than four stations on the Bombay side, the 2nd Royal Irish between Mhow and Indore, the 2nd K.O.S. B.'s between Cawnpore and Fatehgarh, the 1st East Surrey between Jhansi and Nowgong, the 2nd Royal Sussex between Sialkot and Amritsar, the 2nd South Staffordshire between two stations in Burma, the 1st Dorset between Nowshera and Attock, the 2nd South Lancashire between Jubbulpur and Saugor, the 2nd Welsh between Ahmednagar and Satara, the 1st Black Watch between Sitapur and Benares, the 2nd Oxfordshire Light Infantry between Ferozepur and Mian Mir, the 1st Essex between Shwebo and Bhamo, the Royal West Kent between Rangoon and the Andaman Islands, the 1st Middlesex between four stations in Madras, the 2nd Connaught Rangers between Meerut and Delhi, the 2nd Argyll and Sutherland Highlanders between Bareilly and Shahjahanpur, and the 2nd Royal Munster Fusiliers between Dinapur and Lebong.

Nineteen British regiments in all split up into pieces, and thus deprived of their best chance of efficiency! It is incredible that the political situation demands this dispersal of units; it is impossible that the military situation should not be weakened by it.

Many of the native regiments are similarly sub-divided. But with them the principal drag is their armament. None of them have the Lee-Metford rifle, wherefore they were often called on in the late frontier war to face an enemy better armed than themselves. In a Russian war they would have to do the same under much severer conditions. In such a war it is very probable that the Anglo-Indian army would be inferior in numbers; should it be allowed to be also inferior in weapons?

I know that this is a subject of great difficulty and delicacy. It is an axiom with many people in India that the native troops should always be kept one stage behind the British. Only we should beware lest in making them safe to ourselves we issue in rendering them equally safe to our enemies. That is surely the greater danger of the two. After the Mutiny care was taken to weaken any fresh tendencies to revolt by instituting class company regiments, combining men of different race and creed. A regiment thus divided, it was thought, would be less likely to combine against its officers. But of late this system has been abandoned, and the newer units are class regiments—all Sikhs or Pathans or Dogras, or whatever it may be. This reversion to the old system, while presumably stimulating regimental keenness, may be taken to show that the Indian Government no longer feels any acute apprehension as to the loyalty of the native troops. Indeed it may be said confidently that such apprehensions are no longer justified in the very least degree : there is no doubt at all of the faithfulness of the native army. It may be true that a Mussulman can never quite surmount a feeling of antipathy—at any rate of strangeness—to a Christian, or a native of India to a European. But it is also true that if the breach between races forbids intimacy, it leaves room in the army for comradeship, and even nurtures the personal devotion of men to officers. It is not quite easy to see, therefore, why the native army is not armed with the very best weapon available. In any case, a beginning might be made with the Ghurkhas. They are foreigners in India, as we are. They have neither caste nor religion, and therefore associate far more easily with Europeans : the friendship between Johnny and Tommy has long been a commonplace of mess-room anecdote. In any rebellion it is as certain as anything can be that the Ghurkhas would be on our side though all India were against us. Why not give the Ghurkhas Lee-Metfords ? And if the Ghurkhas, why not the Guides, the Sikhs, everybody ? The French trust Senegalese with repeating-rifles : cannot Britain do the like in India ?

The Army and Mutiny

It is only natural that the tremendous experience of 1857 should still be something of a nightmare to the Indian Government. "We are living on a volcano." "It has happened once; it may again." You hear such phrases nearly every day. I have even heard it said that if all the ryots were ever to rise in a body, British rule would collapse utterly and in a day. Personally I should be inclined to back one battalion of British infantry, given time and ammunition, against all the ryots in India. But even if the ryots are far more formidable than they seem, they do not want to rise, and there is no reason to suppose that they ever will rise. A faction fight or a religious shindy now and again—certainly; that is the ryot's Exeter Hall. But about his rulers he neither knows nor cares; and if he did, he would never agree about them with the other ryots; and if they all did know and agree, they would only conclude that they are very much better off under the existing Sirkar than they ever were, or are likely to be, under any other. Where the ryot is poor he is no poorer than he was. Where, as in some parts, his wife and children carry on their persons enough jewellery to keep them for five years, fearing neither raiding troopers by day nor dacoits by night—what should impel this man to risk his life and property in hope of a mere change of rulers?

Native India, relatively to our own force, is not militarily stronger than ever it was, and is perhaps even more divided. What disaffection exists is mostly confined to the superficially educated, who have far less influence even with natives of their own race than an English professor of political economy has with our ploughmen.   Among other races, being for the most part of weak and unwarlike stocks, they command only contempt.

There is no danger of a second Mutiny in India, unless the British dominion should ever be seriously challenged.   But if there should ever come a great and doubtful war in the north—what then?   If Russia came against us on the frontier, it is certain she would also do her utmost to stir up risings behind us.   Even so, in our own provinces good officers, with police and volunteers, would probably keep their districts together.   The critical point would be the rajah.   Nearly all native princes to-day are irreproachably loyal; but you cannot guarantee a hereditary house against a disloyal son in the moment of supreme temptation.   With this in mind, many men wag their heads doubtfully about the new institution of Imperial Service troops.   There are over 20,000 of these— —armed, drilled, and equipped nearly as well as our own native regiments.   Doubtless these forces, which owe no direct allegiance to the Empress, should not recklessly be created or increased.   But nothing great can be done without taking risks.   The object of these forces is partly to increase the military strength of India, partly to give legitimate and congenial employment to the rulers and gentlemen of the native states.   If we fail in our dealings with these, the Imperial Service troops are a weakness ; if we succeed, they are an accession of strength.

If our aim were to avoid risks, we should not be in India at all.   Being there, our boldest policy is also our safest.   To weaken our native forces through distrust of their loyalty is only to invite the attack we fear.   To be strong against attack is at the same time to ease the strain on loyalty.

XXXVII

THE IMPERIAL BABU

"But you English have the best of everything in India," said the Brahman; "you can surely afford to be generous."

"O, have we?" says I. "Now what, for instance, have we the best of? Money, pleasure, leisure, satisfaction in work?"

He smiled the wonderful Indian smile, inscrutable and irresistible, winning and fawning at the same time. "You have," he said, "the consciousness of being the dominant race."

That is exactly what we have; and that is all we have. It is a very fine and enviable thing to own. And yet even that is half-fallacious; for the real ruler of India is the babu.

India is governed by natives of India. The last word, doubtless, is with us—with the Secretary of State and the Viceroy and Atkins in his grey flannel shirt. But then the last word in government is hardly ever said. The first word and the second and the third are those that make the difference to the subject. The minor, everyday machinery of rule is the native's. Nearly all the lesser magistrates are natives, and a large proportion of the judges. In the executive part of Government—revenue-assessment and collection, engineering and public works, the medical services, the forest department, the salt department—there are a handful of white men to order and a host of brown ones, half-supervised, to execute. At the centres of Government—the provincial capitals, and Calcutta or Simla itself—where you would expect to find British influence at its strongest, the babu clerks in the Government offices exert a veiled but paramount influence. And the very heads of everything—Lieutenant-Governors and sometimes very Viceroys—uninfluenced by clerks, bow before the prattling philippics of the native press. Theoretically India is helplessly dominated by Britons: actually native influence is all but supreme.

You will call these assertions preposterous, and I shall not be able to call leading officials of the Indian Government to corroborate them. The cause of the British in India is not a popular one, either there or here; yet there is hardly a Briton of experience in India, if I may judge by samples, who will not admit privately that these assertions are mainly true. To the stranger from England it is far the most striking and disquieting discovery that India has to offer. The cry of recent years has been for more Indian influence in India's Government; then you find Englishmen admitting the existence of abuses, incompetence, corruption in the services they are supposed to direct, lamenting them, breaking their hearts over them, but utterly powerless to purge them away. You find men giving orders which they all but know will not be executed, because it is physically impossible to go themselves and watch over their execution. Higher up you find men longing to get work done for India's benefit, but clogged and strangled by meshes of routine, which exist solely to furnish salaries for more and more brothers and nephews of native clerks. You find a Lieutenant-Governor refusing to take measures against plague solely from fear of abuse in the native press. Then you realise that it is not more native influence that is wanted in India, but less—not fewer Britons in the services, but more.

The white man's say becomes daily less, the black man's daily more. The reasons are not on the surface, but, when stated, they make things clear enough. The first, perhaps the most potent, is the new swiftness of communication between England and India. You would expect that to increase English influence, but in India you soon grow inured to paradoxes. The nearer India comes to England the less will Englishmen have to do with it. When Warren Hastings went out in 1750, the voyage to Calcutta lasted from January till October. Hastings, once in India, had to make India his home, his career, his life. It was worth his while to study the ways of the natives and to write Persian verses. At this time there were none of the conveniences—the ice, the railways, the hill-stations—which make life in India tolerable to white women; most of the Company's servants lived with native mistresses and some married native wives. It was not edifying, but it made for comprehension of the East. Money was plentiful, Europe and retirement were far away; the Company's servants spent their income in India and lived in style. Old natives will still tell you of residents and collectors who kept more elephants than now men keep polo-ponies. Above all, the white man in the Company's days was something apart and mysterious and worshipful in native eyes. No man knew whence he came or whither he went; no man pretended to know his ways. He was a strange and superior being—all but a god.

Now London is sixteen days from Calcutta. The modern civilian takes three months' leave every third year and a year's furlough every ten or so. He is married to a white wife, and his white children are at home; he looks forward to reuniting his family when he gets his pension, and then—he will be but forty—to letters or politics—a new career. For this and his periodical flights homeward he saves his money, so that the native is less impressed by the white man's magnificence. The British merchant and barrister expect an even shorter period of exile—a competence in five or ten years, and then the beginning of their real work at home. Nowadays the great Indian merchant lives in London; in Bombay and Calcutta are only salaried partners and managing clerks; Parsis are far richer and more influential than these. Instead of a man's life, India has become an apprenticeship, a string of necessary, evil interludes between youth, leave, furlough, and maturity. You might imagine a burglar so regarding the intervals which the exigencies of his profession compel him to spend in Dartmoor.

The consequences of the new order are inevitable and pernicious. The Anglo-Indian does not shirk his work; to say so for a moment would be the grossest slander. No class of men in the world toil more heroically, more disinterestedly, more disdainfully of adverse conditions. But while his zeal does not flag, his knowledge fails to keep pace with it. Partly this is due to the dislocation of his work by frequent returns to England; partly, and more, to the fatal tendency of the Indian departments towards red-tape and writing. The officer knows well enough that the more time he spends at his writing-table the less efficient he will be among the men he has to rule. He knows that if ever our rule were in danger, the man who kept his district together would be the man who knew his subordinates and whom his people knew; but he also knows that his future career depends far more on his reports than on his personal influence. Can you wonder that he devotes himself to what pays him best? He would be more than human if he did not. Being only human, he has to pay for his devotion to forms and minutes in loss elsewhere. The new generation of Anglo-Indians is deplorably ignorant of the native languages; after a dozen years' service the average civil servant can hardly talk to a cultivator or read a village register. Of the life, character, and habits of thought of the peasantry—always concealed by Orientals from those in authority over them—the knowledge grows more and more extinct year by year. Statistics accumulate and knowledge decays. The longer we rule over India the less we know of it.

Summarily, our knowledge of the natives grows less and less, as the natives' knowledge of us grows more and more. For while the very march of civilisation seems to conspire with fate against our comprehension of the masses of the people, on the other side is the babu, each day more superficially fitted and more greedily willing to serve as middleman between the ruling race and the uneducated mass. In old days few natives knew English; now there is a yearly swarm of graduates only too eager to make things easy for the European official. In Madras, where the native tongues are especially difficult and English education especially diffused, there is hardly an official who can talk freely with the uneducated: the babu interpreter is master of the situation. Other provinces are going the same way. It is so easy to ask your clerk, " What does he say ? "—and so easy for the clerk to earn a couple of rupees by putting things before the Presence in the right way.

The divinity that hedges a sahib is slowly breaking down. There are so many sahibs nowadays that they have ceased to be wonderful. And they are not all like the old sahibs: there are little sahibs, country-bred sahibs, hardly better than Eurasians, globe-trotting sahibs, whom a child can deceive, and who let you come into their presence with shod feet. And then remember the other side—that the babu has often been to England. The "Europe-returned," as they proudly call themselves, are usually of the inferior native races, and are of small account even among them. Yet they have been received in London or Oxford or Cambridge as equals—sometimes, on the strength of bold and undetected claims to social importance in India, almost as superiors. They have lost all respect for the European as a master, and acquired no affection for him as a friend. Every young Hindu who returns from England is a fresh stumbling-block to government in the interests of the Indian people.

For the babu does not govern for the people, whom he despises from the height of his intelligence, and whom it is his inherited instinct to fleece, but for himself, his relatives, and his class. To him mainly—helped by British pedantry—India owes the impenetrable buffer of files and dockets and returns which interposes itself between the white ruler and the brown millions of the ruled. The first impulse of the native who gets an appointment is to get some of the swarm of brothers and cousins who live in the same house with him to fatten under his shadow. He cares nothing for efficient work—why should he?—but he cares very much for his family. Instead of making less work, he strives always to make more. He sits a lifetime in the office and knows its working as do few of his fleeting European superiors. Everything—in the public offices, the army, the railway offices, it is all the same—must be copied out in triplicate, in quadruplicate, in quintuplicate. If a new and energetic European attempts to cut away the hamper, "We cannot do this," he murmurs, "under rule 12345, section 67890." The Briton sighs, but life, he thinks, is not long enough to try to move the limpet babu. But the babu, when he likes, can easily make out a case for the addition of sub-sections 67890 *a*, *b*, *c*. . . . . *z*—and there is more work for his nephews. "Your accounts have come up quite correct," wrote the leading clerk at Calcutta to the leading clerk in a provincial government; "do not let this occur again."

So the white man in the district sits at his desk writing papers which babus will docket and nobody will read; and, outside, his underlings oppress the poor.

XXXVIII

THE LAND OF IRONIES

INDIA is amazing and stupefying at the first glance, and amazing and stupefying it remains to the last. The long panorama ends as it began with the dazed murmur, " A new world."

The habit of travel extinguishes wonder, and begets a tranquil if curious acceptance of new surroundings. The professional traveller takes it as part of his daily life that he should wake up among habits, climate, growths, languages, and people which he never saw before. He knew they existed, and they are not much different from what he had pictured them.

But India disquiets the most sodden traveller. That it is vast and complex is nothing; but with its vastness and complexity it yet remains utterly alien to everything else. You have no foothold whence to advance upon a closer comprehension. Shut by its mountains into a corner of the earth, it has ever pursued its own mysterious ends; the breeds of men who broke through the passes it absorbed and quietly assimilated to itself. Stranger breeds of men have come over the sea; India has taken no heed of them. India is India, and ignores the world.

The Land of Ironies

Other countries have a measure of consistency:
they are either wholly civilised or wholly barbarous,
affect splendour or accept squalor. India sees stateli-
ness in the filthiest faded silk so it be shot with pearls;
and a trained mechanician burns a man alive to pro-
pitiate a defective steam-engine. Other countries hold
a degree of privacy essential to self-respect; India has
deliberately, by caste-brotherhood, cut privacy out of
its existence. Other countries aim at doing; India's
idol is inaction. Islam influenced other lands of the
East; India influenced Islam. The learning and the
letters of the West were sluiced into India in one
sudden stream; after a moment's astonishment India
accepted them, and studied them with prodigious facility, but without a spark of interest or an effort towards appreciation. To the West, the ordinary native of India is almost inhuman. The West can
admire the strength of his affections within his family,
and detest his cold-blooded malignity outside it; but
for the rest he appears now unearthly wise, now child-
ishly inane. The grave Brahman will unreel you
systems of metaphysics compared with which the
" Criticism of Pure Reason " is simple and concrete;
then he will depart and make his offering to a three-
headed goddess smeared with grease and red paint.
The very ryot seems an incarnation of the spirit of
husbandry, a part of nature, a primeval Pan—and he
will carelessly beggar his family for three generations
because it is the custom to waste money on funeral

feasts. Two students attend a college : one becomes senior wrangler, and the other is hanged for assassinating a policeman.

Into this maze of contradictions, to rule this blend of good and evil, steps Britain. And not content with ruling him—which is easy, for he accepts any master that comes—we have set ourselves to raise him, as we put it. Which means to uncreate him, to disestablish what has grown together from the birth of time, and to create him anew in the image of men whom he considers mad. This is surely the most audacious, the most heroic, the most lunatic enterprise to which a nation ever set its hand.

How, now, have we succeeded? Let it be said first that we have deserved success. If any enterprise in the world's history has deserved success, it is the British empire in India. Our connection with the country began as most legitimate and mutually beneficent commerce. It developed into conquest— not through any lust of dominion, but almost accidentally, and certainly against our will; it was the inevitable consequence of the weakness and dissensions of the Indian races themselves. Having acquired the empire, we have administered it with a single-minded devotion to the interests of its own people which has never had a parallel. We make India pay its own way, but beyond that Britain gets not a penny from it for any public purpose. We have imposed duties against our own products; in a hundred ways we refuse to facilitate the business of our own countrymen.

It is sometimes said that India offers desirable careers for our superfluous youth. This may be true spiritually. A nation like ours does well to offer adventures to its sons. Yet even spiritually we get nothing indispensable from India: the empire has half-a-dozen spheres where hardships and dangers can be had on terms as favourable as any that India offers. Materially, it is enough to say that every officer in our service, except less than a thousand civil servants, is heavily underpaid. If any nation ever deserved the reward of good work done for its own sake, it is Britain in India.

And on this comes in the hideous, if most inevitable, irony that the reward of our work is largely failure, and the thanks for our unselfishness mainly unpopularity. You might almost imagine there was a curse on British India, which ever turns good endeavours into bad results. The great gifts which we are supposed to have given India are justice and internal peace—and each has turned to her distress. The one is driving her peasantry off the land, the other is preventing an effete race from the renovation brought in by alien conquerors.

When we say we have given justice, we only mean that we have offered it—tried to force it upon peoples which dislike and refuse it. What we have really given is a handful of incorruptible judges, whose experience enables them to strike a rough balance between scales piled up with perjury on either side. Often and often a litigant comes to the European judge and says, " You were wrong to give that case against me, Sahib. The other side were all lying, and we—well, of course, we lied too; but the truth was such and such, and we were right. But of course you could not tell which was lying most, and we knew you did your best to decide rightly, only you were wrong." The litigant believes absolutely in the honesty of the sahib, and accepts it as part of his inexplicable idiosyncrasy; he does not seek to emulate it. As for the great mass of native judges, subordinate and supreme, who do the greater part of the ordinary business of justice, some are incorruptible : there were incorruptibles in India before we came. But the mass of them, as of the other native officials, are just as they ever were, and, with the whole country leagued to screen them, it is impossible that they shall be otherwise.

The difference under our rule is not so much that justice is done as that the law is enforced. The rich man benefits under this, for a Rajah's government would seldom let a rich man get out of a lawsuit with a full pocket; but the poor man suffers in the same proportion. In the old days the poor debtor was protected by the rapacity of judges and Government. The usurer dared not go before the Rajah for leave to attach the peasant's stock and crops and land. " Aha," his Majesty would say, " you must have been making money, my friend. We must look into this." But in a British court the sacred contract must be upheld, and the ryot is ruined.

The irony of peace is as bitter. Peace is sometimes a blessing, no doubt; but then so sometimes is war. War was the salt that kept India from decay. It caused horrible suffering, presumably, though in India not perhaps much more than peace; at least it conspired with famine and pestilence to keep the population down. All three have been greatly mitigated under our rule, and now a prodigiously increasing multitude is a dead weight on the general prosperity of native India and a night-mare to her foreseeing statesmen. But that is not the only, nor the direst, curse of peace. India is effete. It strikes you as very, very old—burned out, sapless, tired. Its peoples, for the most part, are small, languid, effeminate. Its policies, arts, industries, social systems stagnate, and the artificial shackles of caste bind down their native feebleness to a completer sterility. Now the old wars periodically refreshed this effeteness with strains of more vigorous blood. Most of the greatest names of Indian history, the wisest policies, the bravest armies, the noblest art, belong to races of new-comers. It seems that the soil and climate of India need but three or four generations to sap the vitality of the most powerful breed.

Now that Britain keeps the peace in the plains and

guards the passes of the hills, there will come in no invaders to renew the energies of the weakened stocks. With each generation of firm and just rule the ill effects will percolate deeper and deeper. Failing some new process of quickening, the weary races of India must inevitably dwine and die of sheer good government.

Whence is the new life to come ? From us ? The gulf between Briton and native yawns no less deep to-day—perhaps deeper—than when the first Englishmen set up their factory at Surat. Our very virtues have increased the gap that was in any case inevitable between temperaments so opposite as Britain's and India's. Justice India can do without; for peace she does not thank us. This, too, will grow worse and worse with time, instead of better. The men who knew the sufferings of intestine war are long since dead; their grandsons, not knowing wherefrom we have delivered them, are naturally not grateful for deliverance. Even the best educated natives are very ignorant of Indian history ; they simply do not know from what we have saved them. Even if they did, things would be little better ; for, although it is a silly fiction that no native of India can be grateful, political and national gratitude is a watery feeling at the best.

What else have we to count on for the regeneration of India ? Christianity ? It has made few converts and little enough improvement in the few ;

is it not too exotic a religion to thrive in Indian soil ?
Actual fusion of blood has done as little. It is usual
to sneer at the Eurasian as combining the vices of
both parents, but this appears to be a slander. In
the days when generals married begums Eurasians
counted many men of ability and character; that you
hear of few now is more likely due to the fact that
the modern breed is almost necessarily of a low type
on both sides. As it is, Eurasians fill a place most
creditably which nobody else could fill. Industrially,
as overseers, foremen, railway-guards, and the like,
they are an almost indispensable link between white
and native. But to expect them to form a link in
any deeper sense, even though a Viceroy expresses
the hope, is over-sanguine. It may be unjust, but
there remains a prejudice against them among white
and native alike.

And after all, what link could bind together such
opposites ? Language and education and assimilation
of manners are powerless to bridge so radical a contradiction. What close intercourse can you hope for,
when you may not even speak of your native friend's
wife ? Native men are antipathetic to European
women; native women must not be so much as seen
by European men. A clever and agreeable Brahman
told me that he would not let even his own brother
see his wife. I do know one white man who did
once see his native friend's wife. " This is my
study," said he; " that "—as a swathed figure shuf-

fled silently and rapidly across the room from door to door—"is my wife; that is the presentation clock from my pupils at the college." And he was an exceptionally broad-minded man. Those who know and like the natives best tell you that you can never speak with the best-known and best-liked of them for any time without a constraint on both sides which forbids intimacy. "Of all Orientals," says the one Englishman who has come nearest to knowing them,[1] "the most antipathetical companion to an Englishman is, I believe, an East Indian. . . . Even the experiment of associating with them is almost too hard to bear. . . . I am convinced that the natives of India cannot respect a European who mixes with them familiarly." Nature seems to have raised an unscalable barrier between West and East. It has lattices for mutual liking, for mutual respect; but true community of mind it shuts off inexorably.

Every loophole of optimism seems closed—except one. When all is said and done, we have only been in India a little over a hundred years—in many parts of it hardly fifty. To immemorial India that is like half an hour; and when we first went to India we were, after all, not very much less corrupt—whether there or at home—than India is to-day. To move the East is a matter of centuries; and yet it moves. Often it seems that to mean the right thing only ends in doing the wrong one. We have made, and

[1] Sir Richard Burton.

are making, abundant mistakes: in administration and education we seem to be running further and further off the right lines. But in the East it is especially fatal to say " Too late " too soon. We have done much good material work; everywhere we have made two blades of grass grow where there was but one. We have been honest and we have done our best. Whatever we have done or left undone, we have imported into public affairs a new morality. It may not yet have been widely imitated, but that is rather a reason for hope than despair. No morality worth having was ever adopted from the Sinai of a conqueror. What there is in native India of public spirit, of unswerving public integrity, of unsparing devotion to public duty, we may set down to our credit ; and we may say that if it grows slowly it is the likelier to live long. It is far too early to despair of India yet. It is not only the land of ironies, it is also the land of patience.

www.ingramcontent.com/pod-product-compliance
Lightning Source LLC
Chambersburg PA
CBHW051116120726

47905CB00005B/1305